# Dogs Don't Lie

## Books by Clea Simon

The Theda Krakow Series
*Mew Is for Murder*
*Cattery Row*
*Cries and Whiskers*
*Probable Claws*

The Pru Marlowe Pet Noir Series
*Dogs Don't Lie*

The Dulcie Schwartz Series
*Shades of Grey*
*Grey Matters*

Nonfiction
*Mad House:*
*Growing Up in the Shadow of Mentally Ill Siblings*

*Fatherless Women:*
*How We Change After We Lose Our Dads*

*The Feline Mystique:*
*On the Mysterious Connection Between Women and Cats*

# Dogs Don't Lie

A Pru Marlowe Pet Noir

## Clea Simon

Poisoned Pen Press

Poisoned Pen Press
6962 E. First Ave., Ste. 103
Scottsdale, AZ 85251
www.poisonedpenpress.com
info@poisonedpenpress.com

Printed in the United States of America

*For Jon*

# Acknowledgments

As always, many thanks to my readers: Brett Milano, Naomi Yang, Karen Schlosberg, Vicki Croke, Lisa Susser, and Chris Mesarch, my lovely agent Colleen Mohyde, and the indefatigable and wonderful Jon S. Garelick. Many thanks as well to everyone who helped me with the details of animal behavior, particularly Duxbury animal control officer Eddy Ramos and Vicki (again), as well as all the wonderful Cat Writers Association members. For general moral support, Ann Porter, Sophie Garelick, Frank Garelick, and Lisa Jones deserve bountiful pets and treats. My mother, Iris Simon, never got to read this, but cheered me on regardless. I'd like to thank her here, one more time: Thanks, Mom, for everything.

# Chapter One

The problem with murder is that it's messy. Not just the blood, the viscera, and what have you, but the boundaries. And when you're trying to save a life—provide an alibi—for someone you know is innocent, well, the guilt tends to splash back onto you. Especially when there's money involved.

That's the problem I was facing on a perfectly fine September morning, when I'd rather have been back in bed...drinking coffee on the porch...Cleaning litter boxes. Anything rather than trying to explain why I had my hands on the bloody collar of a panicked pit bull named Lily, and why neither of us was responsible for the corpse at our feet.

It had started four months ago when Lily's person, the mangled corpse formerly known as Charles, had first called me for a consult. As a rule, I don't like to work with pit bulls. It's not the breed, it's the people. Which, come to think of it, is usually the problem. But Lily was special. Lean and tightly muscled, with a short, soft coat of creamy white and the kind of brown eyes you could lose yourself in, Lily was a youngster who had been through too much for her years. She was safe now, but the memories showed, and that's where, in theory, I came in. I was going to help her get over those memories. Not forget them, I'm not a miracle worker. Just move on, reclaim what was left of her doggy life. Leave the past to be scooped up by some other poor slob.

People, they're trouble. But animals? When it comes to fur and four legs, I'm a softie. That's why I'm a behaviorist, or almost, because at some point way too long ago, I wanted to know how our fellow creatures thought, and why. If I could make a living translating that for other humans, well, I thought I'd be doing honest work. That's all different now, but this is my job, and I'm good at it. Most of the time, of course, the so-called owners don't want to understand what's going on with the animals that share their lives. They just want the behavior changed. Not that they're willing to change their own.

Which didn't explain what I was doing here in the sun-drenched living room with a bloody dog, a cop, and Charles. I had a hard time looking at Charles, what was left of him. Before something tore his throat open, leaving him to bleed out on his own refinished white oak floor, he'd been better than most. Tall, skinny guy, more brains than brawn, he'd had some heart, coming along for Lily when she'd needed him, and she'd had enough good animal sense to know it. All things considered, she'd been doing okay, too. Some nervous tics, fear issues ingrained on her from her less-than-ideal puppyhood. We were making progress. A little less frantic barking, a lot less cringing.

It didn't matter. Standing there, trying not to show the strain of holding back forty pounds of pure muscle, I knew how it would come down. The gore that had soaked into Charles' faded MIT sweatshirt would make everyone jump, and the pieces would fall like dominoes. An autopsy would list cause of death as heart failure, brought about by a combination of shock and blood loss. Forensics would show canine saliva in the jagged wounds that kept drawing my eye. If I were Lily's guardian, I could probably press for DNA that would show the shell-shocked animal had nothing to do with the raw tears in Charles' neck. But I wasn't, and Lily would be dead by then anyway, euthanized as a precaution. Click, click, click.

"Lily—" I'd slipped up. On her license, the three-year-old white bitch—I use that word in the technical sense—was listed as Tetris, after the game. An ugly name, but one of Charles' little computer-nerd jokes. "I mean, Tetris is not a vicious animal."

"And you are?" The young cop who'd gotten the call was in a bad mood. Tossing your breakfast burrito at a crime scene will do that to you.

"Marlowe. Pru Marlowe." Usually my first name gets me a slow once over and a smile, the kind I didn't mind missing. "I'm the behaviorist." A blank look, blue eyes flat as slate in his unlined face. "Like a trainer. I'd been working with Charles, with this dog, for a few months."

"Really." I'm good with animals, but I couldn't read this young buck. "And do you train dogs to attack?"

Half hour later, the young cop had all my info, and I didn't like it. Anyone in town could have told him who I was. It was more the way he asked his questions. Tall and impassive, he had the cocky look of a high school stud who had kept both the muscles and the attitude, wondering out loud why I'd come back to this nowhere burg and why I seemed to be siding with the panicked beast still screaming herself hoarse in her crate.

I'd given him what I could, but there was a lot I couldn't say. Not and stay a free woman. And pup that he was, that young cop sensed it. This was, I realized, the perfect crime. A murder disguised to look like an animal attack; poor Lily made the fall-dog for someone else's misdeeds. And by stepping in to protest her innocence, I'd only made them interested in me. I mean, I had Charles' key, and here I was saying I had come in to find him like this, all the while protesting that, no, the dog didn't do it. I couldn't explain that I knew Lily well enough to know she'd never willingly kill again. That she still had nightmares about some of the darker scenes in her past. That she was, at the moment we were speaking, telling me that she had nothing to do with Charles' death. To do that, I would have to explain that although I was a few credits short of my certification as a behaviorist, I was a natural animal psychic. No, this young cop, all pissed off after he'd puked his guts out in front of me, would not go for that.

Best I could do was buy some time. The folks at animal control knew me, knew my record anyway, and I'd been back in town long enough to help them out of some jams. Summer people's pets, a nuisance in season and abandoned in autumn. The occasional hoarder. Small towns tend to get the crazies. Yes, I had some credit there. Still, if I didn't act fast, Lily would be as dead as the man who had bought her four months earlier for a hundred bucks from a busted-up gambler who'd needed cash fast. In any other hands, Lily would have been dead already. She wasn't a fighter, not at heart. I needed her to be safe. I needed her to calm down, so I could figure out what had happened. Otherwise, she'd take the rap, and a murderer would go free.

◇◇◇

"Dogs." Wallis hissed out the word, as close to a curse as she comes. "They lie."

Wallis is a thirteen-year-old tabby with whom I share my rundown old house. As a cat, and the matriarch of our little household, she holds rather firm opinions. No loud noises. No cursing, and definitely no dogs.

"Lily isn't lying." I was home, trying to sort out my thoughts. Wallis, sprawled across the big farm table that served as my all-purpose food and workspace, wasn't helping. "She isn't that bright."

I was pandering to Wallis and she knew it, rolling back over to tuck her feet under her snowy white breast, all proud of herself with that satisfied smile. I needed a little space, a little quiet, to work things out. But what I'd said was also the truth. Lily, like most dogs, was too straightforward to lie. And although the creamy bitch didn't have a mean bone in her muscular body, I knew she was also too inbred to plan a sentence before she spoke it. *"Let go,"* she'd yelped as I'd held her, leaning back against her constant forward thrust. *"No! No! Let go!"* She wanted to run to Charles, and I could see him as she did. Could see Charles' face, his soft pale hands reaching out to adjust her collar or to rub the sensitive spot at the base of her ears, as they had in better times. That's what he was to her, all smiles and pets; a series of images that was already fading. *"Let go! Let go! Let go!"* But I couldn't. She'd only have dashed back to her person, and her attempts to revive him would have looked like further attacks to the young cop. More to the point, they'd have messed up the crime scene even more. *"Let go!"* I'd wait until she calmed down and see if I could get any sense out of her.

"Dogs." Wallis sniffed and closed her eyes. Cats can be like three-year-olds, making you disappear when they're finished with you. The twitch of an ear gave her away. "Dogs have *fleas.*"

I didn't argue. I could have. While I do have this odd gift, the ability to hear what animals are "saying," I can't usually converse with them in a human sense. It's more like I eavesdrop, pick up the images or, sometimes, the meanings behind the growls and snorts. With Wallis, for some reason, the communication goes both ways. I think it's because we've lived together for so long—seven years come November. She thinks it's because she's a cat. But as I boiled the water for another round of joe, I realized more was brewing than coffee. I'd brought the white dog over to the town pound, as I'd told that young cop I would. And even as I left her, I'd found myself second guessing my suddenly law-abiding move. I don't like the pound. Under the jurisdiction of the police station right next door, it feels too much like a jail, all cages and rules. We have a shelter, a decent one, two towns over and less than an hour away. As a taxpayer in the same county, I probably had the right to bring an animal there, too. Unlike the pound, the shelter has a full-time vet, a real staff. Everything a traumatized animal needs. Instead, I'd toed the line, and now I was regretting it.

Partly, it was that cop. I'm not shy, far from it. But since I'd come back to my hometown I'd been laying low. And the way that young cop had looked at me made me think of small rooms with bright lights and too many questions to answer.

Partly, it was shock. Let's be honest, even for me the morning had been tough. I'd felt for Lily; the poor girl didn't have many resources to start with, and after whatever she had seen, she had just about lost it. I hadn't been at my best, either. When

I'd brought the poor beast in, still shaking, I'd seen the looks. I'd thought they were for Lily. Blondes always get the attention, and the only professional in the bunch—the sheriff's animal control officer-slash-drinking buddy—was off chasing a raccoon or something. I'd refused to hand her over to the wide-eyed staring deputy. You could tell he had sweaty hands. Instead, I'd walked her back to the isolation cages myself. Locked her in with a pet and a promise. Left a bit of my heart behind me when I stood up. That's when I caught that they were staring at me: a deputy from the cop shop next door, some dude on the desk, a file clerk. I know I'm easy on the eyes, even with my long black hair tied back and my work clothes muting what have been described as dangerous curves. Still, it had been a rough morning, any way you cut it, so it had to be the blood. I was covered in it, and without the distraction of a forty-pound case of nerves, I could feel how it stiffened the legs of my jeans and made my work shirt stick to my chest like it was silk rather than denim. I'd pulled at the sticky cloth to detach it from my body and caught the deputy's gasp. Real weirdo. That's when I realized I needed a change. Barring that, a bath and some more coffee would have to do.

Poor Lily. She'd been a wreck when Charles had bought her back in May, underweight and shaky. Afraid of her own shadow, literally, or of anything else that moved suddenly or made a noise. He'd seen her outside a bar, he'd told me that first day. We were sitting on the floor, me trying to avoid eye contact with the terrified pooch until she could deal with it. He'd been walking back from a meeting, something with investors, when he'd seen the skinny thing tied to a parking meter. She was whining, shivering in the chill of an early spring evening. We're not that high up, but we get a country cool out here in the Berkshires. Too much fresh air. Whatever, he'd felt for her.

"Maybe it's 'cause she's white." I could hear his voice. "She just stood out. It was dark, and there she was."

I'd had to shush him. He tended to get worked up, and Lily didn't need that. Not then, not now. Maybe that's why he'd lingered, feeding her the remains of a good steak dinner until her owner came out of that bar. Three sheets to the wind, he still could spot a sucker, and Lily went home with Charles that night. A C-note was nothing to him. It meant life for Lily. Until now.

"Nuff." Wallis' dismissive sniff pulled me out of my thoughts, and I poured the water over the grounds. "Head case."

"I'll assume you mean the dog." I don't like taking that tone with Wallis. We live too close, even in this rambling wreck of a house. But some things are personal, and she rolled over on her tiger-striped back to look up at me. She didn't need to say more. Noon, and I was back in my bathrobe. It had been all I could do to strip out of those clothes and shower. All I could do to throw them in the old washing machine. Even my bra had blood on it, and peeling the stiff, tacky fabric off my skin had reminded me of how I'd held Lily's wet muzzle against my body, first to attach her lead and then simply to offer the comfort of my body. Had reminded me of Charles, what was left of him. Disposable wardrobes only go with disposable incomes, however, and I'd turned my back on that life months ago. "It was pretty bad, Wallis."

"You turning soft?" The cat flipped one ear toward me.

I took a big hit of coffee. The bitter heat helped me focus. "He was my best paying client."

"Not that he knew it." We were on familiar turf here. It was true, I'd had a few gigs since coming back to Beauville, but nothing major. There was an aging bichon I walked each day for his equally aging human; once around the block did it. An aquarium at the local Chinese place. They could've gotten a high school student, but I must have seemed more trustworthy. Occasional cat sitting for the summer people, the ones who bought up the pricey condos in the new development. To the regulars around here the idea of cat care tended toward leaving a bowl of dry food and hoping kitty would still be around when you returned. Even my occasional "pet therapy" clients would disappear once the foliage fell. Not much to live on. I didn't have a mortgage, but I did like to eat. Besides, even with the house coming to me free and clear, I had property taxes to pay, including some overdue notes that my mother had let slide in those last years. So, yeah, I'd pegged Charles as a newcomer and had charged him city rates. What of it? I'd been city trained.

"And your last check was?" Wallis reached out to grab my hand as she questioned me. To an outsider it must have looked cute. The kitty and the coffee cup. But I felt the claws under the velvet.

"Two months ago." I put the mug down and stared out the window. My view was as pretty as the one from the new development, but in the first flash of autumn color I saw winter coming. Heating bills. "Shit." What with one thing and another, I'd forgotten my already casual bookkeeping. Charles' account was long overdue. I'd been meaning to ask him for a check this morning....

"Well, don't worry about me." Wallis sat up and flicked her tail. "There's a new colony of mice in the mud room wall, and I'm sure the squirrels will be moving into the attic for the winter."

"Cut it, Wallis." The stout tabby might hunt for pleasure, but I knew she expected her Fancy Feast fresh and on time. "Look, I'll try to find out what's up."

She shot me a glance. I downed what was left of my coffee. "The guy had money, Wallis. Someone's got to inherit—and that means taking over the bills, too."

"You just want to check on that...*dog*." Her voice could have fixed the polar ice caps.

I shrugged and stood up. Time to get dressed again. Time to get back into the fray. "What of it? She's connected to the account. And animals are property in this state."

She jumped off the table and left the room without another word.

# Chapter Two

"What's with you, anyway, Pru? You used to be such a nice gal."
Albert was all right, as far as town officials go. But I was at the
pound to see Lily, not discuss my personal life. "You get your
heart broken or something?"

"It was you, Al." Clean and freshly caffeinated, I'd figured I'd
start here, move onto the cops next. Wallis might have nailed
me in terms of sentiment, but there's no arguing with bills. "I
never got over you."

Albert snorted. Fat, bearded, and dressed in flannel from
Labor Day to July 4, he'd been a few years ahead of me in school.
Unlike me, he'd never left. Story was, he'd been a cop himself for
a few years, until the booze started to tell. He must have drunk
with the right people, though, and rather than let him go, they'd
moved him next door into the shelter job when old Sheldon had
died. Sheldon had been an old-school dog catcher. Albert had
taken a week of training and knew words like zoonotics, but
basically he sold licenses, trapped the occasional questionable
raccoon, and housed found animals. Anything more serious was
passed on to the county shelter. Or to me, since I came back. As
I've said, animal control owes me some favors.

"No, really. You took off out of here like a bat from hell.
Then, what, fifteen years later you come back? Don't tell me it
was just to nurse your mother."

I didn't, it wasn't. Though I now live in the house she left me,
the same house I used to sneak out of as a teenager. "I'm here

about Lily." Basic principle of training: no response often gets the best results. This time, it got me a blank look. "The bitch I brought in this morning?"

He started to snigger, and I stared him down.

"I don't have any record of a Lily," his voice had gone sulky. I was standing in front of his desk. He was sitting behind it, and he wasn't going through any paperwork.

"Tetris, I mean." I turned away and tried to focus. Something was nibbling at the corners of my consciousness, distracting me. "Her license says Tetris." That's when I saw Frank, Albert's masked ferret, curled upon the guest chair beside the desk.

*Under the bark, under the bark…grubs grubs grubs.* The little bandit was dreaming. No wonder I was preoccupied. A wave of sensation hit me: a rich, dark scent. Mulch.

"Take your pet to work day?" *Tree mold, tree mold. There!* Frank was a little obsessive. It's a weasel thing. I couldn't help smiling as I watched those tiny black claws twitch. He was certainly preferable to Albert. Cleaner, too.

*Get it get it get it. Sweet!*

"Perk of the job." It wasn't, but I turned my smile his way anyway. I needed info. He reached to pet the ferret, trying for nonchalant. *Asshole.* "Ow!"

"I think you woke him." I couldn't be sure if the ferret had appropriated human invective or if that had been a comment on Albert's hygiene, but I made a note not to shake his hand. "Better put some antibiotic on that."

Albert whipped his nipped finger out of his mouth, drying it on today's flannel. This week's anyway. Another reason to avoid contact. "It'll be fine. Ferrets are like that."

I nodded; the lie wasn't worth the energy. "Tetris?"

"Yeah? The killer dog? What do you want with that animal anyway?"

"Nothing, just thought I'd peek at whatever license info is on file." Now it was my turn to play it cool. Albert was essentially harmless, but he wasn't above a little blackmail.

"That's confidential, Pru." His eyes left me feeling greasy. "Government property."

"I only want to see what he wrote down." I kicked at the linoleum like a schoolgirl.

"Yeah?"

For a moment, I thought I'd overplayed. But in for a penny, in for a pound. At this pound, anyway. "I was the dog's trainer, Albert. I assume there's going to be an investigation." I lowered my eyes and my voice to match. "I only want to get ahead of it. I mean, it's just me now."

"I don't think anyone could blame you for what happened, Pru." Bingo. He was up and looking through the file cabinet behind his desk. "I mean, Chuck was the one who adopted that mutt."

"I don't think she's a mutt, actually." The ferret's vivid dreams must have slowed my reflexes; I was getting images of shiny things. A piece of foil, a sparkling stone. Something decayed. Very distracting. "*Chuck*? You knew him?"

"Yeah, sure." Albert gave up on the cabinet and squatted on the floor to paw through his desk drawers. From what I could see, the files inside were more of a mess than the ones in the cabinet. But after only a few seconds he pulled a manila folder out, giving a grunt of satisfaction as he sank back into his chair. He didn't see Frank as the slinky beast slipped into the drawer. Nor did he hand the file over. "Chuck wasn't a bad guy." He lay the folder over his crotch and smiled. "For a yuppie carpetbagger, anyway. I used to see him down at Happy's. He liked to toss a few back, and he didn't mind rubbing elbows with the locals. Rubbing more than that, if you know what I mean."

"Oh?" I slid into the guest chair, swinging it around to face Albert. "Anyone in particular?"

"You didn't know?" Now it was Albert's turn to grin. Not a good look. "He was a friendly guy, our Chuck. I guess money's a big turn on."

"Hey, I worked for the guy. That's it." I didn't know why I was protesting. Small towns are the same everywhere. Still, I could use the information. I glanced down at the folder. Back up at Albert. Stopped just short of batting my lashes. "Doesn't mean I didn't wonder."

"Sorry, Pru. You were too long in the tooth for him, anyway." He leaned in until I could smell his breath. "Word was, he'd gotten pretty serious with Delia Cochrane."

"Word?" Albert's people skills were as reliable as his hygiene. I'd never seen another human in Charles' house. He'd never mentioned a significant other, either.

"Okay, I saw them together. She'd come meet him at Happy's. But, you know, she and Chris Moore go way back. So, I didn't know. You know."

"Yeah." I didn't, but I'd sort it out. Delia Cochrane had been a few years behind me at Beauville High. I thought of dirty blond hair, awkward elbows, and braces, but people change. She'd be in her late twenties by now. Maybe thirty. Old enough to drink, anyway, and Happy's was the bar where Charles had found Lily. "I get you." I leaned forward, onto the desk, and tried not to inhale. "The license info?"

He forced his mouth shut. "Oh, yeah, it was all in order. Got to be, with a pit bull, or whatever that monster is."

I dropped my voice lower and tried to tone out the ferret. He'd found something tasty. "You have any info on next of kin?" I forced myself to focus on Albert. "Who gets the animal, maybe?"

"Who gets it? I think that bitch has got two quick shots and an incinerator in her future." The way he said "bitch" made me think he meant more than the dog. I ignored it. "Uh, legally? Chuck's mom, probably. She was listed on his contact forms. Pretty sad, huh?"

I looked at the fat, slovenly Albert and tried to piece it together. "Why do you say that?" I had to focus, but the smell of chewing gum was overpowering. Frank had found the mother lode.

"Guy was thirty-three. His closest contact was his mother?"

"Least he had one, Al." My age. Funny, I'd pegged him for younger. "And, hey, you should keep an eye on your pet. Gum's not a proper treat for ferrets." I nodded toward the desk drawer and, with a glance at me, Albert pulled it open. Frank jumped out, holding a small ball of wadded foil. *Rat!* I had to bite my tongue to keep from responding and forced my attention back to Albert. I could tell I'd confused him. Best to get back on track. "It's the sugar, Albert. It's not good for them. Now, tell me, do you have her number?"

"You swing that way, Pru? I can tell you, Delia's not telling any tales." He made air quotes, so I'd get the pun, such as it was.

"The mother, Al. I want to talk to her about the dog."

"Christ, Pru." He pushed his chair back, a pained expression on his pale round face. "Her son's just been killed. I don't know if she's even been notified yet."

"So, do you have it?" He blanched. "Her number, Albert."

"No, I don't know. She's someplace in Raynbourne, I think." He shoved the folder under his desk blotter. "Why don't you ask the cops?"

"Yeah, maybe I will." So Charles hadn't been a city boy. Not originally, anyway. I stood up. "The keys, Albert?"

"Huh?"

I walked over to the metal door beside the file cabinet. "I assume you keep this locked, Al. What with your concern for the public safety."

"You sure you want to go in there?" I fixed him with a look. "Okay, your call." He opened the first door, and we passed through a room lined with cages. The only occupant, an exhausted tabby, dreamed of a softer bed. The next door, which led to the isolation area, was either soundproof or Lily had barked herself out. Through its small, wired window I could see the white dog pacing in the farthest cage. Albert followed my gaze. "We're just holding her till we get clearance, then…" He pointed his forefinger and lowered his thumb like a trigger.

"They do it by injection now, Albert." I kept my voice calm but my mind was racing. Clearance? I'd assumed there'd be an investigation. Charles' house being a crime scene and all.

"Either way, that dog's a menace."

"She's had her shots, so she's not a public health risk." I needed to talk to the mother, maybe the girlfriend, definitely to Lily. "Maybe I can dig up her records. I was working with her."

"Great job you did." He unlocked the door. "Call me when it's time to lock up. Or I'll listen for the screams."

◇◇◇

The reek nearly floored me. As it was, it took all my will power not to bolt. Instead, I backed up against the door, my hand on the knob as a promise that I could, and tried to keep my breathing shallow, through my mouth.

At first, I couldn't see, the stench was so strong. Warm and sweet, like barbecue sauce gone bad, with something metallic—shredded foil?—in the mix. Something darker, too. Sweat and shit and…

"Oh, God." I gagged. I couldn't do this. Then I turned around, my vision cleared and I knew. That smell wasn't real. Not now anyway. Not here. I turned and found myself staring into the lost, dark eyes of Lily. This was the poor beast's personal hell I was experiencing, just as she had since that morning. I'd walked right into it.

"Lily, it's me. Pru. Can you focus on me, sweetie?" I kept my voice low and moved slowly toward the cage. It took all my energy to block out the scent memory, while focusing on the dog. "Can you do that for me?"

She turned to face me, her broad flat muzzle now clean and white. I wondered briefly how that had happened. She'd been hosed down, I'd bet, with no concern for the chill of autumn or the force of the water on her skin.

"What did they do to you, Lily? Can you tell me?" That wasn't what I wanted to know. But she was barely here. I needed to ground her, bring her back, for both our sakes. "Honey?"

I held my hand out, palm up and lower than her heavy head. This dog had been hit so often in her youth that her first inclination was to shy away. We'd gotten past that, but that had been another day. I cursed my lack of foresight. Dog biscuits are a trainer's basic tool. Instead, I slid my hand closer. I wanted to pet her, but I couldn't tell how she'd react. I needed to reintroduce myself first. She sniffed and looked up. She wasn't seeing me. Not really.

"Lily?" I opened up, cautiously, but it was no good. All I was getting was horror, a silent scream of scent. All bad.

I sat there for a while, my back up against the cinderblock, singing tunelessly. Something about "Lily being a good girl." I don't think she heard me. The white dog was as close to catatonic as I'd ever seen an animal. Time was my only ally. She'd gotten used to me once. Learned to trust me, even begun to trust the world again. Anyway, I had nowhere else to be.

"Lily, Lily, Lily girl." A knock startled me out of my reverie. Albert was peering through the little window. I waved. If he'd been hoping to see some carnage—or some girl-girl bestiality— he was out of luck. He moved away.

*He's the only one.*

"What?" The interruption had shaken something out of Lily. I turned toward her, fast, and immediately regretted it. Blood, blood. More blood. I'd startled her.

"What did you mean, Lily? Are you talking about Charles?" I tried to visualize her former owner. I didn't know what name she used for the smart, skinny man. He'd always been with us during our training sessions. That had been the point.

*Takes care of me.* With that, she'd taken the two steps to the other side of her cage and began rubbing her face on the bars, a low whine starting deep in her throat.

"Lily, honey, don't do that." I'd seen nervous behaviors like this before. An animal could rub its face raw in no time. "Lily?"

*Take me home.* Damn, I'd have to get over to the shelter. See if I could get some drugs for her. I needed Lily alert and remembering, but if she made herself sick she wouldn't be useful to either of us. I stood up. Albert was nowhere near the window. Could I sneak her out?

Then it hit me. Our training regimen. Charles had always been the one to put her in her crate and to take her out. It was a way to establish him up as the alpha in the household. So whatever had happened, someone else had to have been in the room. Someone else had opened that crate to let her out. To set her up. After Charles was already dead.

"Lily, you hang in there." This wasn't proof exactly, and nobody else would buy it. But it was good to have confirmation. "I'll get you out."

I pulled on the door and found it locked. Damn that Albert. Not until I'd pounded on it for a good three minutes did he finally show up, grinning.

"Thought you two were getting cozy in there."

I pulled a smile on. I might need him down the line. "You never know." That would have been my exit line, but I was caught up short by a sudden blast of empathy.

*Confusion and deep sadness.* I turned around, surprised. *A longing for home. Confusion, grief.* Frank was standing on his hindlegs, his lithe body elongated, his masked face staring. *Lily really needs you, Pru.*

I caught myself before I answered out loud. Albert was looking at me, funny. I'd wanted to leave him on edge. A little afraid. "Nice pet you got there." I hoped Frank didn't mind. "Take care of him."

I winked at the ferret. "And quit staring at my ass."

# Chapter Three

The vet wasn't in when I called from the car. The shelter line was busy when I stopped for groceries. By the time I got home, he'd left for the day.

"Small towns." I was pacing. Wallis was watching me, bemused, from her seat on one of my mother's placemats.

"We can go back to the city any day, babe." She eyed the bag I'd dropped on the counter. "What did you get?"

"Chicken. For me." She didn't blink. "Bones, Wallis."

"I'm not a *kitten*." She turned her back on me.

"You used to like Fancy Feast."

I saw her shift. I'd made my point. "That was when I was starving. And you were…uncooperative."

I stacked the cans in the cabinet, knowing I'd never open them. "I didn't know, Wallis. I mean, it's *cat* food."

She shifted again, flipping her ears back to catch my words. "You weren't listening. You were so busy with your training and your life."

I caught the peevishness sneaking into her tone. "Wallis, at least back then, I had a life."

"As I recall, you were the one who wanted to get out of town." The round tabby turned sideways on the flowered mat and started washing her hind foot. "I'm at home anywhere."

"Wallis." I could hear the anger creeping into my voice, but she didn't look up. Those toes were going to be awfully clean. "You know why we left."

More silence. Nobody can ignore you like your cat. I grabbed a head of garlic and began peeling.

"I couldn't handle it anymore." I might as well have been speaking to myself. She started biting her hind claws, trimming them down to size. "The cacophony, the constant noise."

She glanced up at me, holding that white bootie up to dry. "The voices, you mean. You claim you want to hear us, to understand us. And then when you do, you freak out." She went back to the foot. "What's that about, do you think?" As I heard her, I got the distinct feeling of fur in my mouth. "And could you not put so much nasty garlic in that?"

"It's *my* dinner." Another look. I slumped into a chair. "One thigh, Wallis. That's it. And could you not do that while we're talking?"

She shot me a look, but at least she paused.

"Look, I freaked. Okay? You know that."

She sat up to face me. I had her full attention now. "I'd been talking to you for years, you know. Sometimes, I swear you heard me."

I nodded. I'd gotten messages from her. We all do from our cats. "It was the other animals, mostly." Mostly true. "And, okay, once I started hearing you for real—in full sentences, well, I lost it."

"You *thought* you'd lost it." She blinked slowly for emphasis.

"Well, there's no precedent."

"Oh, please." She turned away and made to jump off the table

"Wait a minute, Wallis. I need some advice."

She hit the floor with a thud, but she didn't walk away.

"Lily's still not making sense." I felt, rather than heard, her smirk. "Seriously, I want to get her some tranquilizers. But Albert's ferret—"

"*What?*" I'd overstepped. Animals don't belong to people.

"His name is Frank. Anyway, he seemed to be listening. He thought Lily was confused, that she'd seen something and couldn't make sense of it."

"She's listening to rats now." She lashed her tail.

"Wallis, come on." Swipe, swipe. "He's a ferret. They're related to polecats." Swipe. "I could use your help now."

"Well." Tabbies are vain. It's the stripes. "Now that you admit it."

"Do you think a ferret could be picking up something I wasn't?"

She collapsed on the floor and studied me. Those green-gold eyes had seen a lot. "What are you asking, Pru?"

"I don't know exactly." I didn't. "I want to understand why this happened—and who did it."

She rolled on her back. In previous years, I'd have thought nothing of petting her fluffy white belly. That was before I knew her so well. "You still want to get that dog off."

I nodded. She stretched. "*Cherchez la femme.*" Wallis likes to think of herself as sophisticated.

"Delia? The girlfriend?" Wallis reached out to grab the leg of my chair. "Yeah, I need to speak with her. But first, I think, the mother."

One green eye looked up at me. "You are a cold one, aren't you?" There was a note of admiration in her voice. "If you'd ever had children of your own...."

"Wallis, you've been neutered."

"*Spayed*, please. And I had a life before, you know."

There was no use arguing with Wallis. I didn't know how many of her stories were true, I just knew she had them. "Charles' mother might be important. She's the one who controls Lily's fate now."

"*Dogs.*" Another stretch. "Dogs and rats."

"Ferrets, Wallis. Frank is a ferret." But she was already asleep.

I could have followed her lead, crashing out on the lumpy sofa in the next room. There was too much going on, however, and if the last few months had taught me anything it was that I had to take care of myself. That meant food, that meant time. And not pouring myself a water glass of Maker's Mark whenever things got rough. What I'd said to Wallis was true. I'd fled the city in a panic, with only a cat carrier and a suitcase, convinced that I was going mad. My mother was already in her last months by then, and her illness gave me cover. I crashed in her old house, and before long I was spending my days by her bedside at the hospice. Some people thought I was a saint. Others saw me as the prodigal daughter. After all, I hadn't visited much since I'd left, too happy to be out of this one-horse town and on to a city that didn't believe in last call. Wallis and I knew the truth. Sitting in that antiseptic environment was the only peace I had. No strange voices, no sharp scents or sounds more vivid than those we poor humans face. Just breathing and the occasional hushed interruption from the hospice staff. By the time she died, I was at peace, as much as I could be with my changed world.

When the chicken was ready, I put on some music. Baroque violin, low and soft, and brought the food out to the table. True to my word, I'd kept one thigh separate: no garlic, no salt, and when Wallis hopped back onto the table to begin licking at its crisped skin, we shared a companionable silence. From the table, I could see out over my mother's land. Two acres, tumbling down to a brook. Soon autumn would be making the hills beyond into something like a postcard. If I were a little closer to the mountain, I'd have realtors falling all over themselves trying to give me cash for the old place. Times like this, I wasn't sure what I would do if they called.

"The ferret might be wrong, you know." Wallis' voice intruded on the plaintive strings. "Especially this time of year."

I knew what she meant. Whenever I went outside, I caught it: the hustle, the rush. Everyone a little on edge. "You think he was tuning in to something else?"

She hesitated, and I glanced over. With one paw she had the chicken piece pinned. All I got was a low growl as she pulled the flesh from the bone.

"*Bird.*" I didn't think I was supposed to hear that. She licked her chops. "You said the ferret said that the dog was confused. Well, maybe. And there may be other reasons for that. This is a crazy time. Busy. Autumn coming up and all. He could be wrong, too." She ran a foreleg over her face, wiping grease from her whiskers. "We're not all psychic."

"But he could be right." I gestured with the drumstick. "He could have been getting something I didn't." I was still learning about the limitations of animal communication. While Wallis and I had open lines, it seemed there were other animals I couldn't read at all, or not correctly. "Besides, I don't have anything else to go on."

"Sometimes I don't think you've the sense of a kitten." She paused while combing a paw over her ear and looked up at me. "You got a scent image, right?" I nodded, and she went on washing. She could read my memory. "Well, that's how dogs think, isn't it?"

"You may have a point." I didn't want to go there. Didn't want to feel that hot, sweet flood of pain.

"Course I do." Face clean, she jumped from the table, leaving me to finish alone. "Not the sense of a kitten sometimes. Not at all."

# Chapter Four

I'd had the rest of the afternoon to think things over. I'm no bleeding heart, but Lily was more than a paycheck to me, and there were still too many loose ends to let any of them go. When I'd walked in Wednesday morning, Lily had been barking like mad and running free. Right away, even before I'd seen Charles, I'd known something was wrong. For starters, Lily should have been in her crate. That's where she goes each night. Where she spends the greater part of the day, and that's where she should have been that morning, waiting for our weekly session.

Don't get on me. I said crate, not cage. It might look small to you, but to her it looks like security. We're talking a hard-luck bitch here. A girl who's seen too much of open space in the form of cold dirt yards. Too much of "freedom" in the sense of fend for yourself when the scraps are thrown. And if those scars around her neck and ears were any indication, she'd valued the privacy, too. Nice to be able to sleep without worrying who might be coming for you.

So someone had let her out, and it wasn't just for morning walkies. I might've been thrown by the sight of Charles, what was left of him, throat torn open. But at some level, I'd registered what was going on and now, going back over it, I was sure. There had been no leash in sight. Not by the body, not on the floor. Charles knew the rules. He'd not open the crate without the leash in hand. Routine, that was key. He was a programmer. He knew about rules.

So someone else had been in the house. Someone had seen the muscular white dog in her crate and popped the latch, maybe hoping she'd do the job for him. Hey, it wasn't that much of a leap. You see that jaw, you hear the stories.

Poor little bitch. Despite the reputation her breed has, something happened with her. The blood hadn't run true. Lily wouldn't fight. Couldn't, in some primal way, maybe, and that meant she wasn't even a good "bait dog" to train the others. It was no wonder that her prior owner wanted to get rid of her. The miracle was how she survived at all.

It wasn't that she was useless. Far from it. Lily should have been a farm dog, living some place where she could run around till she was wiped. Do some work. Build up whatever shreds of self esteem she had left in that thick canine skull. Did you know pit bulls were farm dogs once? Yeah, strong and tireless. Traits the so-called sportsmen recognized and put to their own uses, decades before the gangstas and their ilk. Lily could've been a throwback. A dog to follow you out to the herds, help you with the cattle. Earn a decent living and a good night's sleep.

Not that she'd have changed places, not in a minute. Lily was smitten. Charles wanted a house dog, she was there, lapping it up. There's no accounting for taste, and the computer geek wasn't half bad. Until yesterday, I'd thought he'd come from the city, like so many of them, and seen only the big old houses. The mountains in the distance. The quiet nights. Knowing that he'd grown up around here—Raynbourne was only about a half hour away—made me respect him more. He knew what this area was like, and he'd come back anyway. And not to one of those new developments, either. Maybe they were too close to his old home. Maybe they couldn't offer what this place did, with its wraparound porch and a view down to the river. Still, he'd put in the effort.

I had no idea what the house had looked like before, though I bet it hadn't been good. Nobody who has stayed here has the money to fix anything up. He must have gutted it—the room where I'd found him was open clear through from the front porch to the big picture window in back. That was his workplace. His play space, too. He'd had the money to wire the place up to his specifications, make it the headquarters of GeekBrain West, or whatever he called himself. He'd hired locally, I'd heard. And he'd been good to Lily. Much as I dislike people, I had to give him that.

I thought of the timid white dog as I'd left her. Shell shocked and wired, tucked into a cage at the back of the town pound where her voice would go hoarse before her master came for her. I'd made myself retire early and slept badly for my pains. Maybe Wallis was right. Maybe I should have paid more attention to the images pouring from Lily's horrified mind, but I didn't want to face them. Having them come to me during sleep was worse, however, and I woke near dawn wet and shaking. There was no point in trying to get back to sleep. Why chase what I didn't want? And although the growing light was making interesting designs on the peeling paint of my bedroom ceiling, I deeply suspected my time could be better spent.

"Directory assistance?" I lay on top of the covers, watching the ceiling slowly start to glow. Somewhere a cricket sang for a last chance at love. "Raynbourne?"

"No, don't connect me." Much to my surprise, there was a Harris listed in Raynbourne, and only one. With my luck, it was unrelated, but calling pre-dawn wasn't the way to introduce myself. I went back to the shadows. Either one was growing, or there was something alive up there.

Thud! I jerked my feet back with a gasp. It was Wallis. "I cannot believe you're going to call that woman."

"Eavesdropping isn't a very nice habit, Wallis." I tucked my feet under the covers, trying for nonchalant.

"Please." She settled by my feet and began her toilette.

"Must you lick your ass right on my duvet?" After my nightmares I was in no mood.

"Must you jump at shadows?"

I opened my mouth—then shut it. I still wasn't sure how far our psychic connection went. "I didn't hear you come in. You startled me."

She continued her tongue bath. "*Someone* got up on the wrong side of the bed this morning."

She was right. "It's those images, Wallis. They're pretty rough." I didn't know how the overwhelming scent of blood would translate to a feline. To me, and to Lily, it had been a horror.

"Then why keep at it?" She'd moved onto her thigh now. She didn't have to finish the sentence.

"Because Lily's a dog? Is that it?" Angry was better than frightened.

Wallis held out her foot, toes spread apart the better to get into the spaces between. "Because you don't know what you're getting yourself into, Pru." She paused, glanced up at me. "Think of it this way. Someone already rescued her once. Look where that got him."

I was up and showered before I thought of a comeback. Even then, I didn't know if it would play. Wallis had her own set of rules, and they were tougher than mine.

By the time I had my first hit of coffee, I was ready for the fight. She'd been sunning herself along one of the kitchen windows when I came in. The sun highlighted the guard hairs on her back, and I longed to dig my finger into her thick, lush fur as I'd used to do. This was a different world now. We were playing by different rules. Instead, I got the skillet out, making enough noise so I knew she was awake before I addressed her.

"Why did you say that about Lily, about rescuing her?" She shifted on the sill, ignoring me. "Wallis?"

One ear twitched as I cracked the eggs. The other followed as I opened the refrigerator for the butter, and I turned away to hide my smile. Some things don't change. Swiping my finger along the bar, I held it out for Wallis to sniff. Her nose was damp, her tongue rough. She hadn't said a word, but the offering had been accepted.

"Look, Pru, you trust me, don't you?" She looked up at me, licking her chops. I nodded. "So take my word on this. You don't know what you're getting into."

I walked back to the counter, surreptitiously wiping my hand on my jeans. "Wallis, you know. Better than anyone. I don't want to know what I know." This was ancient history. "But I do, okay? And since I do…" I lopped off a sizable chunk of butter and dropped it into the pan. I'm not the do-gooder type, and she knew it.

Wallis stretched, the question implied in the arch of her back. I sliced off another pat for her.

"I have to, Wallis. She can't speak up for herself." I held the butter out to her: a blatant bribe.

"Most of us can't. We manage." She turned back toward the window, and I dropped the pat in her dish. She had a point, and I knew it. It would be so easy to just let this go.

I turned the gas up and watched the butter skate around the pan, my thoughts just as frantic and hot. "But I can hear her. I can't turn that off." The butter sizzled. "And I know what happened."

"You *think* you know." Wallis jumped off the sill and went to examine her dish. The butter had softened a bit, and she licked it. "Humans. You think you understand everything."

"I understand *some* things." We were on familiar ground now, and I turned my attention back to the skillet as I poured in the eggs. "Someone wants that dog to take the fall. She was set up."

"And you weren't?" Wallis had made quick work of the butter and was now washing her face.

I paused, spatula in hand, and thought of the day before. The young cop with his questions. "What do you mean by that?"

Whiskers clean, she walked back to the window. A moment's hesitation, a quiver, and she was on the sill again, staring out the window.

I shoveled the eggs onto a plate and joined her by the window. Together we looked out on my front yard of scrub bushes and old trees. "Wallis?"

Unlike the view from our New York apartment, the birds here were smaller and faster. With the window open on the warm autumn morning, I could smell the woods and hear the twitter and rustle of life. From Wallis, I caught an image, a flash of what was holding her interest. A small brown wren hopped on what had once been a lawn.

"Wallis, I know that if I push too hard, the cops will like me for it. I'm not a fool." A twitch of the right ear was her only comment. "But why do you say 'set up'?"

She kept staring. Somewhere up in one of the trees a blue jay cawed. The wren paid no mind.

"Some animals are prey, Pru. That's just the way it is." She was on her haunches now, staring at the wren. Whiskers forward. "And some walk into trouble, eyes open."

"Are you saying Lily's a natural victim?" I didn't think animals felt empathy, but this was harsh. I was glad for the screen that kept Wallis from pouncing.

"Forget the dog, for once." Out loud, Wallis began chattering softly with excitement, her soft, sharp mews mimicking the bird sounds. "It was the man who was killed. Quite savagely, if your reaction is any indication. Or don't you remember?"

"I remember." The morning scene was suddenly clouded, the scent of death strong in my mouth. I put down the plate, no longer hungry for fried eggs. Outside, something flew by—a hawk, a cloud, a shadow—and the wren was gone.

# Chapter Five

Most of the eggs went into Wallis' dish. She'd given me food for thought. I wasn't particularly worried. I mean, I didn't know anyone here well enough for him to want me dead. Still, something nasty was out there, and it wasn't Lily. I tried to think what kind of weapon would leave a gaping wound so similar to a dog bite and recoiled from the idea that any creature would chose to do that to another. Any *human*, which ruled out food or pure animal fear, and reinforced my new policy of isolationism. Too much had gotten into my head. I just wanted to be left alone.

Still, I had some kind of professional obligation, didn't I? At least on the animal-trainer level, the one that people knew about. The shelter didn't open till nine, but I had the vet's private number. By eight, I'd gotten him on the line.

"Tranqs, Pru? I don't think I can." Doc Sharp was a good enough guy, but I was sticking with the basics as I explained Lily's behavior and my concerns. Even on a Thursday morning, I could hear frenzied barking behind him.

"Or Prozac. I could do the dosing, doc. I'll swing by." I had that bichon to walk. The little neutered male would be ready to pop. But after.

"It's not the time, Pru." I waited. "Or the money." But before I could jump in, before I could offer to cover the costs for some doggie pharmaceuticals, Sharp was explaining. "Blood tests, Pru. The county's going to want to know what was up with that animal. To see if it was hopped up on some fighting drug or infected somehow. I don't want to skew the mix."

I opened my mouth to protest. That's my nature. Like I've said, I'm not a people person. I had a good argument ready, too. Something about needless suffering. Maybe Sharp was better with humans than animals. At any rate, he kept talking.

"It's not a question of cruelty, Pru. It's a legal issue. This isn't some stray. You're asking me to treat an animal that may have killed its owner. That animal now either belongs to the owner's heir—or to the state. So there's nothing you or I can do at this point. Not until a judge weighs in."

I felt like I'd been punched. He must have heard the sharp exhalation of breath. "I'm sorry, Pru. I really am. However, if you're searching for lost causes to take care of, I've got a Persian here who could use your services. He keeps biting his own fur off."

"Fascinating, doc." It was probably fleas or some skin irritation nobody had caught yet. Odds were, the owner was using perfumed shampoo on the poor beast. But I caught myself. Sharp meant well. And he paid. "I'll be by later to take a look."

◇◇◇

Ignoring the expression on Wallis' face, I took the phone out to the back porch and keyed in the number from that morning.

"Harris residence."

I didn't think anyone in Raynbourne had staff, but it had been a while. "Mrs. Harris?"

"Oh, lord, no. This is Sal. Her neighbor."

Of course, small town etiquette. Slipping back into the training of my youth, I took a seat on the sprung sofa my mother had dragged out here and introduced myself as a friend of Charles'. Trying to sound more relaxed than I was, I expressed my condolences and settled in for a chat. What I wanted was to find out about Charles' will, specifically who now had possession of Lily. What I found myself promising was a casserole. I don't do cakes. After twenty minutes at least I had directions—and a reason to come by.

The bichon held his water till I got there, although his owner was near to bursting. After the dog and I took a quick turn around the block, Tracy Horlick cornered me in her foyer, dragging me into the house with a clawlike hand. I expected a tongue lashing. Once you hire out your services, some people will only see you as a servant. I'd forgotten the small-town grapevine.

"Sally says you found him. That you had to pull that dog off him." Her pale grey eyes glittered through the smoke of her ever-present cigarette. "That it had eaten most of his face."

"Sally doesn't know what she's talking about, Mrs. Horlick." The real memory had sprung back into my mind, and I busied myself with the bichon's collar. "It—he—wasn't like that." I swallowed. Hard.

"That poor Delia Cochrane must be completely beside herself." For some reason, this made the old biddy grin. "He was this close to proposing, I heard. Though I don't know if there was any love lost there. I've heard she could smell money—"

It was too much. I turned toward the door before I tossed my toast on her grimy linoleum.

"Oh, you poor thing!" I felt her hand clamp back on mine, cool and dry like a bird's claw, and I fought the urge to slap it away. "I didn't know."

In confusion, I turned back to her. Hadn't she been trying to pump me for information?

"You must have been sweet on him yourself." The smile on her face could have cut glass. "And you just back from the big city and looking to settle down."

I rinsed the sour taste from my mouth with a cup of bad gas station coffee. I needed to keep moving, and I'd told Sharp I'd come by. Whatever hopes I'd had of wangling some meds out of him—for Lily, though I could have used them too by then—died as I checked in. The barn-like shelter was as busy as usual, the barking and howling of abandoned summer pets always a sad September constant. But the doc in charge was nowhere in sight.

"He's out doing a rescue," said Pammy, the shelter's full-time vet tech. Twenty-something going on fifteen, she had her fair hair up in a pigtail that bobbed as she led me back to the cage area. As cheery as her singsong voice, the room still reminded me of a hospital with its high concrete walls painted mint green and white. A hospital with cages along each wall and a row of plastic seats down the middle. At least it didn't smell.

Pammy brought me down the line, and I found myself stiffening. Sounds of confusion, one pained cry—"*Rolly? Rolly?*" Pretty much par for the course. Clean as it might seem to us humans, the shelter would be a welter of strange scents to these inmates. Not any place an animal would chose to be. "He said you'd want to see this one." With a nod of her head, she motioned toward a large black Persian. As I looked past her into the cage, I couldn't help noticing how her pale locks set off the cat's glossy midnight coat. This was a gorgeous beast. But even before I noticed the bald spot behind his ear, I heard the low whining cry. When he turned, I saw it. Bald and bloody, this was pain personified. Any animal who would do this to himself was suffering. Unlatching the cage, I reached in for the unhappy cat.

"You checked for fleas? Ear infection?" Except for the bald spot, with its angry, raw center, the cat seemed in good health. Solid, clean. No mats that I could feel or see. "Mast cell tumor?"

Pammy nodded and popped her gum. Those possibilities—even the tumor—should have been eliminated by a basic physical, but sometimes the basics get overlooked. "Couldn't he just be bored?" With one finger, she began to play with a loose strand of her own hair.

"Maybe." I used my thumb to open the cat's mouth. His teeth looked fine, sharp and white. Even his gums were good. I wondered about Pammy's, but not that much. "Who brought him in?"

"One of the Ridge folks." I nodded, grateful that despite my fifteen-year absence nobody spoke of me with that tone. "Pissed off that he doesn't look good, I figure."

"At least they didn't abandon him." The Ridge meant money, the new money that was pouring in despite the economy. And rich folks, I'd learned, were no nicer to their animals than poor ones. I turned the cat over. Even for a Persian, he was unusually docile. "Dr. Sharp give him anything?"

She shook her head. "He wanted you to see him first." She sat down with a thump, and I wondered how to get rid of her. This cat wasn't talking, and I needed to find out why.

"Pammy, I'm wondering if this cat might relax more if we were left alone." Subtlety wasn't my strong point.

"Looks pretty relaxed to me." Nor hers, either. She looked settled in, too, sitting on her hands and swinging her legs back and forth under the plastic seat. Talk about compulsive behavior. "Hey, Doc Sharp says you were asking about that killer dog?"

"Charles Harris' pit bull." I sighed. She wasn't going away.

"I wanted to ask you about that."

"Yes, it was horrible." Why wait for the inevitable?

"Nah, it wasn't that." She popped her gum. "I mean, you've been to college. You were trained right?" I grunted something that might have sounded like assent. "So why do it?"

I looked up from examining the cat's eyes. "Why do what?" If she thought I was going to justify studying animal behavior to her, she could think again. The field didn't need her.

"Pit bulls." She kicked her heels. "I mean, why even bother? They're illegal in most places anyway."

I shrugged. Thought about explaining, but the truth was I wasn't sure anymore. Lily was a victim, sure. But there were too many elements piled up against her.

Pammy didn't wait for me to answer. "Besides, I think they're really ugly, you know? With those flat wide faces and those nasty teeth." She popped her gum again.

"Pammy, do you mind? I'm trying to work." I'm not an all-purpose psychic. I can't make humans read my thoughts. I'd learned a thing a two from Wallis, though, and I fixed my stare on the young tech until she gave a little whimper—"jeez, you're friendly!"—and left the room.

"So what is it, kitty? What's going on with you?" Left alone at last, I put the troubled Persian down on the concrete floor and sat beside him. "Why are you doing this to yourself?"

In response, the cat started to wash. Licking the black pads of his left paw, he reached back to the bare spot and started rubbing. I got the sensation of prickling, a combination of itch and the annoyance at an itch, nothing more.

"Is that bothering you? It probably is." Sharp had put some kind of ointment on it, an antibiotic with something to soothe the irritation of a scab, I guessed. A restraining collar would have fallen just at the wrong spot and he had to do something, but any self-respecting feline would have had the ointment off seconds after the vet left. What I was reaching for was something deeper. Why had that one spot behind the cat's ear been worn raw to start with? "Can you tell me?"

When I first realized I was psychic—"sensitive" as they say in the few books on the subject—the connection had come in a flood. I'd get images, wild and scattered, that packed the emotional wallop of a train wreck. Pain, fear, lust, rage. Everything we humans have appropriated for ourselves, only more so, unfiltered by society or language. It was too much. I'd been coming off a fever, anyway. A bad flu made worse by cigarettes and coffee, too much time at work and too little time asleep. This just threw me over the edge, so, yeah, I'd spent some time in a quiet room. By the time I'd gotten out, I'd quit the cigarettes. I still couldn't quite block the signals, but I was learning to manage. Being away from the city helped. Strangely, so did talking to Wallis. I mean, maybe I was mad, but she accepted it and we'd moved on.

"So, kitty, talk to me." I didn't like anything about this gift. You think your mind is your own, until somebody else's trauma starts pouring in. But it did have its uses—especially since I'd never gone back for that last round of exams. Not finishing bothered me because I'd spent too much time and money to be a glorified trainer. Still if I paid attention, this could be useful.

Warmth, the smell of a person. That itch, that terrible itch was it. What wasn't I getting? "Kitty?" Sometimes physical contact makes the connection stronger, and I reached forward to place my hand on the sleek black back.

"*No!*" Wrong move. I got a wave of aversion. Not fear, but something strong. He pulled away. "*Not you!*"

I sat back, startled. Did this cat see me as an individual, recognize me as Wallis did? "Kitty?" It felt disrespectful, but I didn't have a name.

Nothing. That feeling of an itch, the warmth of a hand. The Persian had turned in on himself again, and I was at a loss.

"Pammy? *Pammy?*" I was being punished by the vet tech now. She pretended not to hear me after I'd come out of the cage room. I wanted to check in, but this was ridiculous. "Okay, I'm going." I don't play those games.

"Wait, don't you want to talk to Doc Sharp?" She turned away from the shelf she'd been restocking. I tried to imagine her face covered by tawny fur. I didn't want my dislike to show.

"No point." I wanted to talk to Wallis, but I remembered my classes, too. If the cat wouldn't tell me what I needed, I could do my research old school. "I need to get some background. Find out what's going on in that cat's home life." That sounded normal enough, didn't it? "You have the owner's address?"

Maybe it sounded normal, but according to the young vet tech I was still in the dog house. "I'll have to look it up." She snapped her gum and turned away. "I should be able to get it to you by the end of the day."

"Thanks so much." I headed toward the door. Some things it doesn't pay to be too sensitive about.

It wasn't until I was halfway home that something Wallis said resurfaced. Words about not understanding. It's funny, that way. Since this all started—this hearing animals and everything—I hadn't really questioned what was coming through to me. What I understood and what not. I mean, someone slams into you, you don't think about the subtlety of his touch. In some ways, I was still recoiling from that blow.

But that's not what I'd set out to understand when I first decided to work with animals. I'd spent hours in classrooms, then, learning about the biological basis for behaviors. Memorizing how certain chemicals came out of the brain a certain way, and what they meant. Why all of us—humans, too—do what we do. I'd done my practicum in one of the city's biggest shelters, witnessing the kinds of trauma no human would survive. The one lesson in all that? Animals feel. They're just as sensitive as we are, maybe more.

The next part was something I'd forgotten. How they react to those feelings. Not just the behavior, but the way they interpret their experience—the way they see their world: That was their own, and very different from the way we humans live. Sure, I'd been feeling what they felt, seeing—or smelling or hearing—what they sensed. But I'd been thinking about it like a human.

Sometimes I'm as dumb as Pammy. I hesitated for a moment and pulled over onto the shoulder of the road to make a U-turn. Only then did I notice the blinking light on my cell telling me I had a message.

"Ms. Marlowe?" I couldn't place the voice. "This is Officer Creighton." The young buck from the crime scene. "I'd like you to come in to answer a few questions. Please call me at your convenience."

My convenience would be sometime in the next century, but since I had the phone open, I scrolled back. He'd already called three times. He was a cop, and I didn't need him pissed at me, and so I hit "call."

Creighton answered right away, the number obviously his private extension. Whatever hopes I had of distracting him, he was all business.

"Ms. Marlowe, I need you to come in." His voice sounded older than he'd looked. Tired. And that set off alarms. Tired cops want to close cases quickly.

"How about Monday? This week has just been an awful shock." I wanted space and I wasn't above feminine wiles.

"How about today? I'll be here at least until six." Pity when wiles don't work. I was saved by his mention of the time.

"And is it three already? Oh, gosh, I can't." That was probably overdoing it, but in for a penny. "I'm going over to Mrs. Harris' and I said I'd bring something."

Checkmate. But he didn't like it. "Tomorrow morning, then, Ms. Marlowe. I'll be waiting."

Lies have a way of tripping you up. Back in the city, I'd have been able to buy something to bring. Beef stroganoff, "homemade" meat loaf. A complete Thai feast, and at any hour of the night, as well. Out here, well, we're not exactly the sticks. Only the closest gourmet food store was over in Beckett, and midweek there was no guarantee when it would close. Nothing for it, then, but to shop and cook. Murder was making me domestic.

Chopping onions leaves you free to think. Both the black Persian and Lily were trying to tell me something, only I wasn't getting it. Standing in the big, open kitchen that was my house's best feature, I opened the ground beef and stood there waiting, hoping the scent would lure Wallis from whatever hiding place she'd found. I could use the consult, though in our current relationship I no longer felt I had the right to ask after her whereabouts—or even to keep her inside, despite my concerns for her safety, and the birds'. Now, in true cat fashion, she'd absented herself when I most could have used her company. As I scraped the onions into a casserole, listening to them sizzle in the hot oil, I tried to remember how I'd used to think, back before Wallis started talking to me. Or rather, before I started hearing her. Before —

"What horrid concoction is that?" As if on cue, Wallis appeared in the doorway, stifling a yawn.

"Napping, were we?" I heard the waspish note in my voice. I'd been about to put something together, and her tone didn't improve my mood.

"Working." She sat and began to wash her face. "Some of us have lives, you know."

I didn't bother responding. Instead, as I stirred the beef into the casserole, I tried to recall what had been on the tip of my consciousness. Something about thoughts, about connections.

"Speaking of which, shouldn't you be getting out more?" Wallis' voice entered my head like a cold draft. I spun around to face her.

"Are you reading my mind now?" She kept washing. "Wallis, would you answer me?"

"Not on a general basis." She seemed focused on one ear. "Too dull, really."

"Wallis, don't be such a cat." She looked up at that, meeting my eyes with her cool green ones. "I mean, don't get all legalistic on me." Nothing. "Please."

"I know what you mean." She finished her bath. "Don't get your panties all in a bunch. Yes, I can listen in, when I want to. How do you think we're conversing anyway? How do you hear all those other voices?"

I hadn't thought about it, but she had a point. "I just do, that's all." That flood, that curse of consciousness. "But since we live together, you could try to respect my privacy."

"I thought you wanted my help." She jumped up on the counter and watched as I cooked. In previous times, I might have shooed her off. Now it would seem rude. Instead, I scooped out a hunk of meat and held it out to her on my wooden spoon.

She sniffed and turned away. "Too many onions." Still, she seemed pleased to have been offered, and settled into her sphinx pose while I worked. "You're starting at the wrong end."

"The onions?" I was humoring her. It worked. She smiled, as only cats can.

"Humans! So linear." She tucked her paws beneath her. I knew a lecture was coming and opened a can of tomatoes while she gathered her thoughts.

"My thoughts are perfectly gathered, thank you very much."

I broke the tomatoes into the meat. "Sorry, I was waiting." I tried to keep my mind blank.

"To start with, I still don't understand why you care so much about a dog. Especially a dog like that."

"A pit bull?"

"An animal too dumb to survive on its own." Before I could protest, she continued. "Animals get killed, and that Charles may have been your best client, but that simply illustrates his inability to get along on his own." I'd thought she was talking about Lily, but I guess to her, the dog and its owner were one and the same. "But I understand. For whatever reason, you do care. That's obvious. For some reason, your so-called advanced intelligence needs to understand what happened. And you're still clearly confused about your gift. So why not approach the killing from the other end?"

I looked at her, confused. Surely she wouldn't need me to voice the question in my mind?

"*Cui bono.*" I must have been staring. " 'Who benefits,' isn't that the number one question of any crime investigation? Watch it with the cumin. It smells like fireweed from here."

She was right, I'd been shaking the spice in without thinking. Ah well, I stirred it in. I didn't have to eat this casserole, only bring it. "Where did you learn that?"

"Did you think I was asleep all those nights when you were watching *Law and Order*?"

I burst out laughing. The idea of my cat learning to investigate crime from a TV show, it was all too much.

She stood up, clearly offended. "Well, if you don't want my help." Tiger-striped haunches quivering, she prepared to jump down.

"Oh, Wallis, I'm sorry." Dropping the wooden spoon, I scooped the tabby into my arms and held her close. It had been a while since I'd had any warm body against my own. I'd forgotten how good it could feel.

"If you'd get out more, maybe that wouldn't be the case." I twisted back to peer into those clear green eyes. "After all, I may be spayed, but I have had other lives."

I put her down on the floor and she sashayed out of the room, purring.

◇◇◇

"*Cui bono*." Wallis likes to think she's sophisticated, but some-times she's right. If I wanted to understand what happened, I'd do well to figure out why. Or in this case, who. And the question did add a little more savor to the evening's entertainment. Being stuck in a house of mourning is a tad too grim, even for me. Charles' mother's place turned out to be a neat little bungalow right on the edge of Raynbourne, another old mill town further down the river. Nothing fancy, but someone had cared to find and nurture flowers that would bloom in New England's rocky soil, even in September. Too bad the careful landscaping couldn't hide the gloom inside.

"Good evening. I'm Pru, Pru Marlowe." I held up the Dutch oven as some kind of proof. "This is Mrs. Harris' place, isn't it?" The little white-haired thing who'd opened the door nodded and I stepped in, over a mat depicting posies. To my right, a cheery plaque declared "Time Spent in the Garden is Never Wasted." The crowd in front of me looked like they could use some fresh air. This was going to be a long evening.

"Hot plate. Coming through." It wasn't, not anymore, but as soon as I stepped into that living room, I knew I needed to keep moving. Outside, autumn had already put a slight nip in the air. In here, it had it be over eighty; the steam quotient ratcheted up by a house full of mourners who murmured and buzzed like so many flies. "Coming through."

My voice at normal volume sounded harsh, but it got their attention and with minimal bumping, I was able to make my way through to a kitchen already full of aluminum foil, baked goods, and something that smelled of burnt cheese.

"A casserole?" A tall redhead with a face ten years too old for her brassy hair reached to take my Corningware. She was wear-ing an olive pantsuit that brought out the green in her dye job. At least in here, people were talking like the living. "Meat pie?"

"Chili, sort of." I relinquished my offering. Something about her was familiar, but it took a minute. She looked like all my mother's friends had, twenty years ago. The voice, however, that was more recent. "Are you Sal?"

The redhead smiled. "You're the dog trainer, right? Isn't this sweet of you."

"Well, considering." I'm not good at these kinds of situations, and the time warp—everything but her face—didn't help. Not to mention that I'd been working with the dog accused of killing the man being mourned. Maybe that's why Sal was looking at me funny. "I did want to show my respect."

She nodded and bit her lip—peach frost—and I let her lead me through the crowd to a large and highly polished dining room table.

"Let's see now. Would you get that trivet for me?" I swung around until I saw a decorative tile printed with three garden hoes, all wearing Santa hats. With a grateful sigh, Sal put my dish down. "Seems like we have enough food."

"I wanted to do something." It sounded lame, even to me, but I'd hit the right note. Sal smiled at me and took my hand.

"You're a good girl." I waited, but she didn't let go. "Have you met Nora?"

I shook my head no.

"Come with me, then." She pulled and for a moment I couldn't move. It wasn't just the crowd, it was the mood. I'm not sensitive to people, not like I am to animals. But there was something palpable in this room, something bad. A man had been killed. Maybe I'd been spending too much time around animals, recently. They know to leave the dead alone.

"Nora." She led me over to an overstuffed recliner cradling an understuffed woman. Nora Harris had probably been small to start with, but tragedy had flattened her further. "Nora?" The tiny woman played with the oversized buttons of her bulky knit cardigan. If I'd lost a son, I'd tune out the world, too. "Nora."

Sal reached for the small veined hand, pulling it gently away from the wooden button. At the same time, she propelled me closer. "This is—" She paused. Of course. She wouldn't want to bring up the subject of the dog.

"Pru, Pru Marlowe." I crouched down and took the old lady's hand. It was as cold as I'd feared. But whether it was the touch or the sound of my name, something sparked a light in those deep-set eyes.

"Pru, yes." Her hand tightened on mine. "Welcome to my home. Charles talked about you."

"He was a good man." Hey, he'd saved a dog. Got her in more trouble in the long run, but at least he'd tried. "I was working with him pretty closely for the last few months."

"Yes, yes. He was—"" The spark was gone; those blue-gray eyes fixed on something I couldn't see. Her mouth set in frustration. I wasn't going to get anything out of this woman. I doubted she could tell me her phone number. Meanwhile, the buzz was getting louder, and my thighs were sore from crouching.

"Are you all right, Mrs. Harris?" The crowd parted, and the buzzing died away as a new voice came through. Warm, soft, and strong. "Do you think you could eat something now?"

My interview was coming to an end. Before my legs gave out, I had to try. "Mrs. Harris, can you tell me about the dog? Do you have any plans for Charles' dog?"

The warm voice was right beside me now. "I don't think we need to think about that right now." I caught a whiff of perfume. Expensive and not too obvious. "Won't you try a sandwich?"

The blue grey eyes looked up, alive again. The gnarled hands reached up for the proffered china plate.

"Actually, I'm afraid we do have to." I leaned in as the old lady took a bite so small it wouldn't have fed a mouse. God, I hated being the heavy. "Charles'—the animal is in the town pound now, and I'd like permission to treat her."

I was pulled to my feet by the woman next to me. She might talk softly, but she was a strong one. "I do not think this is the time or the place." I turned and found myself staring into the kind of blue eyes you only read about. Turquoise, almost, and set into a face better suited to poolside Hollywood than a Berkshire wake.

"But—" Beauty has its advantages. My tongue was tied.

"I don't mind." The small, grey voice broke our staring contest. "Really. The police talked to me about the dog."

Goldilocks didn't relax her grip on my elbow by much, but I managed to turn back to the woman in the chair. "And would you be willing to relinquish control?"

"Of course." But she wasn't finished. I held my breath. "He told me they should do a test first." She blinked, lost in the middle distance again, but something brought her back. "For the public good. A rabies test. After that."

"Rabies? But her tags." I tried to visualize Lily's collar. Thick black leather and a couple of tags: one big round one with her name and address. Some charm or other, and the state ID, blue metal, with the date of her vaccination and the vet's license number. I remembered the slight jingle as she'd shake herself after a roll in the grass. "There should have been a rabies tag on her collar."

"I don't know. Maybe it fell off. They said they had to do a test."

I thought as fast as I could, and I kept my voice soft. "If you'll give me permission to look for the dog's papers, Mrs. Harris, that won't be necessary."

"No, no. I think they're right." I was losing her. "It's for the public good."

"You heard her." Goldilocks was pulling me back up. "After the test."

I tore my arm away. "Do you know how they do the test?" Blue grey eyes blinked up at me. "They don't have to test the whole dog. They just send the head to the lab."

"Oh, my." That had been my last shot, and it had been as effective as a body blow to the old lady. Any hope that I might have had of rousing the latent animal lover in her was lost as the blonde turned me around and pushed me through the crowd. It parted easily this time, nobody wanting to get in the way of the lioness and the jackal she was kicking out of the jungle.

"Pru Marlowe, I can't believe you said that to her." My escort was talking, as well as she could through gritted teeth. "What were you thinking? That animal is a menace, and bringing it up to Charles' mom—"

"Wait a minute." Those eyes had me fooled, but something about that voice was familiar. "How do you know my name?"

We'd reached the front door by then, and she'd let go of my arm. An older man with a beard like underbrush was coming in. I grabbed the door before she could close it. It was the eyes: they must be contacts.

"It's true what they say. You leave town, and suddenly you forget where you're from." She was slouching now, leaning against the door frame in a way that made me think of gym class, of lockers. "And all you care about is that horrible, stupid dog. The dog that killed my fiancé."

"Delia. Delia Cochrane." Everything clicked into place. "Look at you. All grown up."

I stepped back as the door slammed shut.

I'm not, as I've said, good with people. But I am not usually a total hardass. If I'd seen any sign of grief, I probably would have come up with a better closing line. At least I like to think so. As I walked back to my car, a couple of thoughts kept rattling around my mind. Charles had never mentioned Delia. More important, he'd never brought her in for any of our training sessions. To a behaviorist, that meant he didn't consider her part of the family. She wasn't someone who had to learn how to handle Lily, someone Lily should get to know. So that talk about a "fiancé" sounded fishy. And now that I'd seen her again, I did remember her other beau, Chris Moore, the one Albert had mentioned. People move on, and people change, sure. But I recalled the skinny cheerleader and the lanky basketball center as an item since puberty. Had she traded in true love for a better lifestyle? Had someone made a point of getting in her way?

That's what was churning around my brain as I turned onto the state highway. That, and the fact that I'd probably never see my casserole dish again.

# Chapter Six

Lucky for me, I'm lousy at proportions. I'd bought too much meat and was frying up the rest of it when Wallis sauntered into the kitchen. The angle of her tail was smug, but I knew she wanted to know. I dashed on the Tabasco and waited.

She sniffed the air, winced at the spice, and sat.

Ignoring her stare, I stirred the ground beef, enjoying the greasy-hot aroma. It had been a while since I'd had an all-meat meal. While I'm carnivorous by nature, a burger and beer gal, I'd found myself going off red meat in recent months. Something about hearing animals makes them less appealing on the plate. Not that that had ever stopped Wallis.

"You know you want to tell me," she said finally, as I scooped up a spoonful of my makeshift meal. "You like the girl for it?"

If I'd been greedier, I'd have choked. As it was, I only gagged a little. By the time I'd chased the hot meat with some water from the faucet, Wallis was looking quite pleased with herself, sitting sphinx-like on the counter. "So do you?"

"I wish you wouldn't do that." No point in taking a harder tone with a cat.

"Why not? It's what you do."

"Excuse me? I'm slow today." Sarcasm is mainly lost on animals, but Wallis had spooked me. Nobody over the age of eight wants her mind read.

"That's it. You read our minds, as you call it." Wallis shuffled a bit, rearranging her furry bulk on the counter. "You eavesdrop."

I mulled that over, uncomfortably aware that even as I did Wallis was listening in. It was true, that's more or less what I do: eavesdrop on animals' most private thoughts. The fact that I never wanted to probably didn't count for much. As I scraped up the last of the browned beef, I weighed the implications.

"I don't choose to hear what I do." I kept coming back to this. "And I don't think they know I do."

She shrugged. Cats can. "And that matters, why?"

My cat was beginning to sound like me, and another thought struck home. How long had Wallis been privy to my thoughts? I looked over, but she had turned her back toward me. Just like a cat.

"I don't mean to sound insulting, you know." Her answer rang loud in my head. "But you do learn to block it out. Most kittens can by the time they're weaned."

"Great, I'm as helpless as a newborn kitten." She turned at that, and the appraisal in her eyes made me laugh out loud.

"So, do you think the blonde did it?"

Back to that again. I scrubbed at the skillet and thought it over. "She says they were engaged. If they went through with it, she would have had a lot more—and had some security, too." If, that is, she were telling the truth.

"And if she really wanted to." Wallis finished my thought. "Maybe they were breaking up. Maybe he had another woman."

I spun, angry now, and shook a wet sponge at her. "Would you cut that out? It's unnerving." I searched for a word that would hit home with her. "Rude. But you're right, I've got to see if I can find out what the deal was with them."

"Or not." The flecks of soapy foam had landed too near Wallis for her to remain settled. She jumped to the floor. "Maybe it's time to just let sleeping dogs lie."

Lily. How could I have forgotten? Without Nora Harris' intervention, she'd be euthanized for a rabies test. "The dog is running out of time."

"And you can stop that?"

The tabby had a point. I didn't want to get more involved in this. Not anymore than I already was. I'd tried to talk to the vet, to Charles' mother. Tomorrow, I was due in the cop shop, and as it was I'd be peddling fast to explain my initial certainty that Lily hadn't done it. After that, maybe it was time to let nature—or the law—take its course. I sensed a purr starting up in Wallis' throat.

But I'd also heard the panic in Lily's voice. The combination of terror and overwhelming loss. And I had run when she had tried to show me what she'd seen, when I'd glimpsed the horror she was living with. No. I put the skillet back on the flame to dry. I couldn't walk away.

"*Cherchez la femme?*" Wallis was still staring at me. I turned to watch droplets of water sizzle and die.

"Or something." Wallis may consider herself cosmopolitan. I didn't feel any more worldly than any other small-town girl. And as I felt her purr grow stronger, a strange idea struck me. If I was going against my cat's advice, why was she purring? Had she been manipulating me all along?

"Wallis, about this mind reading thing…" I turned from the oven, but she was gone.

*Cherchez la femme.*

The theory was good, but before I started following anyone else's tail, I needed to save Lily's. I had a feeling my morning appointment with Officer Creighton was not going to be easy or brief. If I wanted anything like an edge, I needed more information. Plus, if I was going to save Lily's skin, I needed her papers. Hard proof that she'd been vaccinated would be the best way for her to avoid a summary execution. Which is why that evening, after making my other rounds and waiting for the late summer sun to finally douse itself in the hills, I was back at Charles'. Crouched under an old lilac, listening to the birds and contemplating a break in.

The lilac wasn't cover exactly, its old trunk too gnarly and bare. However, its deep shadow did shield me partially from the road. If anyone saw me, well, I was resting. I hadn't been back long enough for Joe Neighbor to know I was no nature lover. Breaking in was the obvious choice. No way could I just waltz into the house while Creighton or any of his colleagues were around. They'd like me for the crime, if they couldn't frame Lily. The birds, well, they were my lookouts.

Like I've said, I don't talk to the animals. With the exception of Wallis, they don't seem to talk to me in any personal way and that's fine. Birds especially. There's a reason we humans have the expression "bird brain." But even a non-psychic could pick up the contented good-night cooings of the mourning doves, the last-chance call-outs of that macho mockingbird, everybody getting ready to nest down for the night. I just hear it differently. Hear the intent, if that makes sense. So if anything, even the neighborhood tom, had come around, you'd hear squawks. I'd be getting panicked little shrieks. *Flee! Flee! Flee! What? What? What?* I wasn't, but I wanted to make sure. I shifted on the hard roots of the lilac. Ten minutes more, and if everything remained quiet, I'd go in.

I didn't mind being alone. Gotten used to it certainly, but something in Wallis' comments had hit home. There'd been men back in the city. More than a few. Men liked me, and I liked them, at least for a while. But I'm a loner by nature. Sitting here, uncomfortable as it was, gave me a chance to think. Wallis' jab combined with the night noises set my thoughts on Stevie, the most recent of the bunch. A jazz pianist, Stevie had hands like caged doves, all fluttery to watch but more powerful than you'd think. That had been a while ago. For an artist, Stevie had been surprisingly concrete, and I hadn't been able to explain my "gift" once it had come. Nor to anyone else, for that matter. Plus, he had the most annoying schnauzer that kept yelling obscenities at me. So that had been it. I'd become one of those women who lives alone and talks to her cat. I figured I had a good six months before I started eying the gas station attendant with impure thoughts. And I had my nights free to sit in the bushes outside the house of a former clients. It could be worse.

◇◇◇

The last of the chittering died away, and all I got were vague images of warmth and down. It was time. Quietly as I could, and stiff from the roots, I rose and approached the house. Funny, it looked bigger at night, the windows like eyes, staring down.

Somewhere back in the bushes, I heard a rustle. I froze, and thought of the switchblade in my pocket. A flash of something fat, white, and juicy made me relax. An opossum was hoping for grubs, and I was being ridiculous. Shaking my head to clear it, I walked around to the big front porch. As tempted as I was to break in, to see if my knife would slide me in the back verandah, I had no need to actually test Charles' locks. He'd given me a key when he'd hired me. The fact that he'd always been home when I showed up didn't change that.

I paused. He'd always been home. He worked there, with a wired-up office that housed more equipment than the rest of the Berkshires put together. Was there an alarm system I didn't know about? Something that would start wailing or—worse—click in silently as soon I opened the door? The local cops didn't worry me. They hadn't even sealed the front door, and the yellow crime scene tape was easy enough to duck under. But Charles was big city. He might be wired into the state. My hand hesitated, holding the key. I was already halfway to the porch. Could I expect sirens?

Charles had expected me yesterday morning, too. Whatever alarm system he'd installed hadn't been activated then. After all, someone else had gotten inside his house, as well.

I unlocked the door and waited. No electronic wail. No sound on the street, either, though what the response rate would be in our sleepy burg was anyone's guess. With a shrug, I made my way in. To the left was Charles' open-space living and work room. I remembered the pooling of blood, and turned away. In front of me, a flight of stairs led to the second floor. To the right was a kitchen-dining area done in the height of '50s fashion, a stark contrast to the ultra-modern work area. Not a cook then. I wondered briefly how he'd found our meager take-out facilities, took a deep breath, headed up the stairs.

To the right, over the kitchen, I found two bedrooms. One held dusty furniture and a load of boxes, probably not touched since moving day. In the other, a tousled blue comforter and two misshapen pillows reminded me of the gentle man who had once slept here. Charles wasn't my type, never had been. But nobody deserves to be left to die, bloody. Not in his own house. I let myself pause for a moment, remembering Charles, and then moved on. Past the master bath, I hit gold. Two more rooms combined into one made a home office fit for a rising entrepreneur. Unlike the spare downstairs, this one had file cabinets. A table top of white and silver, screens big enough for a movie theater with a speaker system to match, faced another picture window, a smaller version of the one downstairs. The moonlight was way too weak to see the view, though I could guess which mountain lay outside. Inside, the vista was stunning.

Not being a complete yokel, I knew enough not to handle the keyboard. A small brush and—yes—the screen came alive. Using a pencil I hit "return," eager to move beyond the screensaver. I was rewarded with a corporate logo—a glowing green brain—and a request for a password. So he didn't have an automatic logon, not even in his home office. I'd have been more curious, but just then something clicked in. A low whirr from deep down in the house—air conditioner? dehumidifier?—spooked me to step back from the desk, and then I heard it.

A voice, the hint of a voice. Soft as that machine whirring, but coming from somewhere much closer. A whisper. And that was it.

I lowered my flashlight to floor level and began to crawl, peeking under the table. Under the baseboard heating. The place was ridiculously clean, especially for a bachelor. With this much equipment, maybe that was necessary. Or maybe someone had gotten here before me.

That thought woke me up to why I was really here. Motive—or some threatening letters—would have been great. But Lily's papers, they were key. Using that same pencil, I hooked the desk drawers open. I was betting on the right hand side, where we keep our personal stuff. If I was wrong, I'd hit the file cabinets. The man was neat, too neat for my taste, but I relaxed a bit.

Anyone who would alphabetize his warranties might actually have done the kind of complete clean up I was witnessing. It wasn't just warranties, either. After a folder on his refrigerator—a Kenmore—I found it: *Tetris/Papers*.

But just then the whirring stopped. In its place, a deep silence that spooked me more. And so I stood up and brushed some nonexistent dust from my knees, just to make myself feel better. I tucked the folder inside my jacket and was making my way out of the office when I heard it again. That voice, that hint of a voice. So soft it had to be nearby.

My footsteps sounded loud on the hardwood floor, and I fought the urge to run. I was upstairs already. Clearly trespassing. Better to act cool and keep my head. If there was someone here, so be it.

There—what was that? A little voice, young and vulnerable, and I was struck by a new thought. I was sensitive to animals. Could I also be hearing ghosts? A year ago, this would have all seemed impossible, and I'm no sucker for supernatural mumbo jumbo. Knowing what I now knew, it was all I could do to step out into the hall.

The voice was getting louder. I was closer. I could feel the sweat on my back and hear every squeak my sneakers made. I was almost at the stairwell.

"*Mama?*"

What? I envisioned an infantile ghost, the spirit of some child locked in a closet here a hundred years ago.

"*Mama?*" A baby, hidden in the wall, centuries past. I already had what I'd come for. I quickened my pace and was almost down the stairs, when it hit me.

"*Mama?*" Not only was I being a wimp, I was missing out on a great source of information. What was out there that could really hurt me, I mean, anymore? And besides, there was something sweet about that voice. "*Mama! Help…*"

I took a deep breath and went back up the stairs, reminding myself with each step that I was the badass in the room. That voice sounded—

A scratch, a scramble. Back in that top hallway stood a tall, vented linen cabinet. I saw no lock, and at my touch, the latch popped open with a click. Just then the humming started up again, and as much as I'd like to think that was coincidence, I found myself breathing faster. I opened the door and looked inside. Instead of towels, something glowed, small and green. Components. The whole damned place was probably wired. Was that what I had heard? But there was something else in that closet. Something alive.

*"Mama."* Down on the bottom, pressed into the back, a tiny orange kitten was huddled, eyes shut tight. I'm not a softy, far from it. But this would've made steel melt. *"Mama."*

"And how did you get here?" I squatted, the better to consider the kitten, and heard my knees crack. So much for country living. Then I heard it, for sure. The soft "snick" of a door closing. Someone else had come into the house; someone else with a key.

"Come on, kitten." I scooped the fuzzy bundle up as the downstairs lights switched on. "We're outta here."

# Chapter Seven

He'd kept me waiting. I'd known he would. Tom had taught me that. A homicide detective, Tom had given me my knife during the six months we'd been together. Got it off some street punk, he said. Switchblades aren't legal, but he liked me having it. He had told me a lot about police procedure, as well as showing me the gritty underside of the city I'd come to consider home. In retrospect, he'd enjoyed the underbelly too much, which was why Stevie, with the hands, had seemed such a breath of fresh air.

But I loved my knife, and information is always useful, no matter what the source. And if I'd learned a bit more about the cops than an honest woman should, well, I'd paid for my education in kind. Now I had the advantage of some inside knowledge. The unwritten rules of the game. Officer Creighton, the blue-eyed wonder, was keeping me in the fancy new waiting room of Beauville's fancy new police headquarters in order to up my anxiety level. A neat trick, but not one I wanted to play. I'd considered dropping in on Albert on the way. The folder I'd found did indeed have Lily's complete veterinary history—at least since Charles had adopted her. The vaccine certificate couldn't get Lily off, but they could save her from a grisly test, and the two offices shared the same building. But as I'd walked up to the awkwardly geometric pile of bricks—the material chosen to fit with our quaint New England image, even if the architecture didn't—I realized that its sudden appearance might lead to a longer conversation. I needed to handle the cop first. Besides, Albert wasn't known as an early riser.

Jim Creighton—the duty roster ID'd him as "James"—was an unknown. I'm pretty good with faces, especially one like that, with a chin from a movie poster and eyes like mountain ice. He was either younger than me or from one of the other small towns that huddle down into the Berkshire foothills like so many scared possums. I was betting on the former. He seemed to take his job seriously. If he were any good and not from our town, he'd have fled to the city by now. That had its plusses and minuses. As far as I knew, he didn't know me, didn't know my history, but he'd have sources. People who could tell him more about me than I'd like. And while he seemed to have more enthusiasm than experience, there was something about him that worried me. A dogged edge, something Tom had had, too. Specifically, I didn't know what he thought about me defending Lily, but I bet he thought it odd. Most humans would, and Creighton seemed like the kind of cop who would trust that instinct and follow up on it. In retrospect, I'd let too much show for my comfort. I'd have to see what I could do to rejigger that first impression.

I paused before the double glass doors that led into the cop shop, remembering to smile just in case anyone was looking out. From here on in, presentation mattered. Creighton had taken against me. Add in that I'd spent the evening before breaking into the murder victim's house and possibly, just possibly, been seen by another invader, a dark shadow I had slipped by on my way out a back window, and I knew I wanted to appear as cool as a cucumber, no matter how long he left me to simmer. And so I fixed my smile and pushed the door open, entering through a glass foyer that felt like an air lock. The receptionist, an old timer with dead eyes, took my name and nodded me to a seat. I picked up an outdated *People* and caught up on the latest Angelina Jolie news. Some things about waiting areas never changed. I couldn't find anything about her pets, though.

Sitting in the large, open room, I wondered what she would have made of the scene at my house, last night, when I'd come home, kitten in tow. Wallis had been horrified. As soon as I'd entered the house, I could feel the tension, and when I switched the light on I got a full view of a furious tabby, complete with arched back and puffed-up tail.

"And what is *that?*" The fur was just for show. She was no more threatened by the tiny kitten than she'd be by a moth, and that thought made me keep the kitten in my hand.

"It's a kitten, Wallis." Sometimes the direct approach is best. "She's—" I stopped. I didn't want to say "witness." I didn't know what the tiny catling understood. "A guest."

The kitten must have gotten something. She blinked up at me, blue eyes big in that orange tabby face. *"Mama?"*

"Christ." Wallis turned tail and walked away before I could tell her about the folder. I knew she was heading for my favorite chair, and not to curl up for a nap. We were in for a rocky night.

Wallis had gotten me up before dawn, and I was paying for it. The walk with the bichon had kept me from going back to sleep, and I'd barely managed not to bite off the head of his stupid owner. Still, I'd made an effort before coming downtown, and, as I sat there waiting, I knew I looked good. September still hadn't made up its mind, flirting with summer before leaving him for fall. I'd opted for a sweater. Seasonal, and just the right amount of cling to distract the most inquisitive sort. In this case, I was innocent. Well, if you didn't count the break-in last night. But I wasn't stupid—and I had a tricky role to play. I wanted Creighton and his colleagues thinking, looking beyond Lily for a human perpetrator. At the same time, I had to keep any of them from liking me for the crime. As I sat there, Angelina's lips puffing up at me, I thought about how easy it would be to just let so-called nature take its course. Maybe Lily was one of life's victims. There were plenty of them around these days. But something in me just didn't like that. Maybe it was the thought that somebody had killed my best client, and I still had no idea why.

With the magazine selection limited, I had no choice but to move onto the crime report after *People*. Beauville is still a small town, but between the summer people and the newcomers over by Raynbourne, at least our tax base was growing. As a result, along with this fancy new building, came the trappings of some place bigger. The crime report—a weekly newsletter—is part of that. For that matter, so were most of the crimes. Vandalism was a big one, along with petty theft, and as I read I saw hard evidence of the tension between the townies and the newcomers. A "decorative mailbox," whatever that meant, had gone missing. A picture window had been smashed, and someone had sprayed graffiti on the high school gym. When times get hard, people get stupid. Drive out the summer people—and who else would have a mailbox shaped like a cow?—and the jobs would go, too, right down the state highway toward Tanglewood and Becket.

It wasn't until I was on my second read, wondering about the "threatening gesture" someone had made on a bicycle, that I realized the obvious. Charles' death wasn't in here. I checked the date. This issue had been printed up this morning, time enough to report a killer dog attack, or whatever they were calling it. Which either meant that his death had already been ruled an accident, or that someone didn't want everyone talking about it.

Too late for that. I thought of my visit with the bichon. This morning, I'd only gotten a nasty look from that nosy Tracy Horlick when I'd come for the dog. That was fine, as long as she kept paying. But if she wasn't getting info from me, I knew she'd be digging it up somewhere: the beauty shop or the mini-mart where she bought her off-brand smokes. Small towns have their own grapevines, and sometimes I wondered if people also picked up news telepathically, like I did from their pets. The bichon had only been focused on his own concerns during our walk, specifically the scent left by an intact German shepherd male who'd been out a bit before us. From the images in the bichon's mind, as well as the alarmist chatter of the squirrels, I knew the shepherd was eight years his junior, in his prime, and twice the bichon's size to boot. Worried that the little dog was dreaming of a fight, I'd kept him on his leash. I didn't say anything as we made our rounds, though. His excitement made him move faster, and we all have a right to dream.

Maybe that explained the smile on my face when Creighton finally appeared in the open doorway and motioned for me to follow him down a short hallway. Something about him made me flash on a past experience, a summons to a similar room back when I'd been a kid, and I felt my smile evaporate. That hadn't been for anything half so serious, just beer and boredom, and the police station had looked like one then: the linoleum and fluorescent lights making even a wild teen appear jaded. The lighting was better now, no doubt. But that casual gesture—a hand hooked, a certain look—brought it all back. If I'd been a jungle animal, I'd have chewed my own leg off to get out of here. As it was, I felt my teeth clench as I tried for a neutral expression.

"You look happy." I didn't believe him, but his voice let me know that even my attempt wasn't a good thing as he led me into a small office more than filled by a desk, a file cabinet, and the smell of burnt coffee. Pushing his unbuttoned cuffs up on thick forearms, he took a seat behind the desk and pointed to a flimsy chair, all plywood and tubing, for me. I had a flash thought that it would be easy to kick out from under someone. The smile got stiffer, but I nodded as if he'd offered me a gracious invitation and sat down.

"Why shouldn't I be happy? It's a lovely morning." The scent drew me to a stained mug on his desk. I forced my eyes away. I'd had my morning dose. If his game was not to offer, I'd be damned if I'd ask.

"You want some coffee?" He'd seen me, but I tried to turn it around.

"Thank you, yes." I worked at keeping it natural. Leaned back in the flimsy chair and crossed my legs. "Black's fine."

Without comment, he left the room. But before I could read any of the papers on his desk he was back, a Beauville Chamber of Commerce mug slopping over with joe that smelled as rancid as the room. I accepted it with a smile, as gracious as a duchess, and waited for him to begin. And waited. That was another of Tom's tricks. Silence. Hold it long enough and most people start to talk. If that was this guy's idea, he'd ruined it with the coffee. It might taste like the pot it had been burned in, but simply cradling the hot china made me as mellow as Wallis in the sun. I pretended to take a sip and smiled some more, trying to remember just which flower had that same shade of blue. Finally he broke.

"Charles Harris." He pulled a folder out of one of the desk drawers and opened it. "You were his dog trainer?"

"In effect, yes. I'm not yet certified, but I've trained as an animal behaviorist, and so, yes, I was working with Charles and his dog." Watch it, I warned myself. Keep it short and factual.

"And you were the first on the scene Wednesday morning." I nodded. He knew all this. "Why don't you walk me through the events of that morning."

I tried to resist the urge to sigh. This was all in the report, already typed up in that folder on his desk. I didn't know if he thought I'd change my story. Despite the sweater, I didn't think he'd choose my company. So I kept it sweet and brief: Weekly routine. Doorbell, lock, greeting. My slight confusion at Lily's barking—I wasn't going to say her panic—and then the shock of seeing Charles, his throat torn open, in his own living room.

The young cop was silent through all this, and despite myself I found my thoughts going back to that room, to that morning. Something had been very off. The crate being open, that was part of it. The dead body on the floor, for sure. And something else.

"Did you get a sense of anyone else in the house?"

I looked up, startled, unaware that I'd spoken out loud. But any fears I had about Creighton's clairvoyance faded as he continued with what sounded like routine questions.

"Was Charles in the habit of having guests over during your lessons?"

"No." My mind jumped back to the night before. Someone else had a set of keys, but there was no way I could tell this cop that. Not without explaining why I'd been there in the first place. Meanwhile, he was watching me. Waiting. "We had our sessions alone."

He raised his eyebrows, waiting for me to continue. With a small sigh, I complied. "We were working on trust issues." Before Creighton could say anything, I filled in the blanks. "The dog had been badly abused before Charles rescued her. It's important to establish a strong bond between the owner and animal before anything else. We were working on that." Too late, I realized that what I'd said could sound bad for Lily. "She was working on trusting other people, but she loved Charles. She owed him her life."

Creighton remained silent, but his face said it all. He thought I was anthropomorphizing, crediting Lily with gratitude I thought she should feel. Now I wish I had pushed the socializing, introduced some other people into her training. Gotten another witness to her devotion. Unless…

"Was Charles' girlfriend saying she was there Tuesday night?" It was conceivable. It was also the kind of question I'd hoped would throw the cop off guard.

"Ms. Marlowe, I'm asking the questions here." He wasn't playing. "Did you hear anything when you arrived that morning?"

I kicked at the desk. "No, just the barking. That wasn't usual."

He raised his eyebrows.

"The dog wasn't a barker." I left it at that. Any more and I'd get us both in trouble. But Creighton kept watching me, waiting for me to spill. I looked around the office. Behind the desk, a poster touted steps to fire safety. I hadn't known that as I ran panicked from a blazing house, I should close the door behind me. I tried to focus on that. This silence thing was getting out of hand.

"Ms. Marlowe, there's clearly something on your mind."

Great, now everyone was a mind reader. "Look, Jim—it is Jim, isn't it? Why don't you just call me Pru. I mean, we were probably in school together, right? Beauville High?" I was stalling, and he knew it.

"All right, Pru." He smiled. A nice smile. "Go Beavers. Now, let's get back to that morning. You came in like you usually do.

You didn't hear anything out of the ordinary, except for the dog barking. But something was different."

"You mean, besides the dead body of my client?" He blinked once. I looked up at the poster again. "There was something."

He waited. He was good at this, and that made it harder for me to organize my own thoughts.

"Someone had opened the dog's crate. That wasn't normal. Usually, Charles and I open it together."

"Isn't it likely that Charles opened it himself? And that the dog attacked him?"

How could I explain myself? "No, he wouldn't have. Most mornings, yes. He comes to the crate with the leash in his hand. Lily—Tetris—knows she's going for her walk. But on Wednesdays, our day, he comes to the crate with me. And Lily knows she's having her lesson."

"Why do you keep calling the dog Lily?"

Damn it, I'd slipped up. "It just seemed to fit her. Tetris is a silly name anyway."

"Did you feel like the dog would have been better off with you? That *Lily* really belonged to you?"

I didn't like the way he said that, the emphasis he'd put on her name. "No." With animals you must be firm and direct. "Lily was Charles' dog. He'd saved her life."

"Ironic, isn't it?" He was watching me, waiting for a reaction. "And I hear you want to save hers?"

"Look, Lily—Tetris—whatever you want to call her, was devoted to Charles." I was going on bluster now, with no evidence I could share and a nagging thought distracting me. Something had gotten to Charles and dug in; someone had struck him multiple times to do that kind of damage. "Have you even had anyone look at the wounds?"

"The county coroner is doing a thorough autopsy." Great, our county coroner is a retired GP. "And the dog had blood all over its snout when I got there. But maybe not when *you* got there."

This is why I hate people. They're always searching for something. Always pushing. Not content to merely be. I hadn't wanted to get involved in this. I'd wanted to help Lily find some peace. To pay my bills. To be left alone. That's all. But it was beginning to look like Wallis was right. I was going to have to get more involved, before I could get out. So even though my first response was to shut down, to stare down this young pup, I knew I had to start talking—and fast.

A thought struck me. "If I'd been involved, wouldn't I have had more blood on me?"

"Not if you commanded the dog to attack."

"What? No!" I started to stand—to storm out—but he waved me back down.

"A hypothetical. Please. Sit."

I did as I was told. "It wouldn't work anyway. She doesn't—" I paused. "Not anymore. That's probably why Charles was able to get her so cheaply." One eyebrow went up at that, so I gave the cop Lily's history: Happy's, the gambler, the rescue. The hundred-dollar dog. Only as I was talking, I remembered what Albert had said. Charles hung out in that bar. He'd met Delia Cochrane there. So had he really been just passing by? Had the meeting been by chance? Maybe I should have paid more attention to the man and less to the dog.

"Ms. Marlowe, are you good at what you do?"

"Pru." I didn't know why we were back on formal terms, but I didn't like it. "Yes, I am."

"So, if you're so certain that the dog would not have attacked its owner on its own accord, who, pray tell, would you suspect?"

I had to remember to close my mouth. It was that little rhetorical flourish that got me. He was only repeating what Albert had said, but it all had more weight when it came from a cop. Besides, I'd finally worked out what else had been bothering me. Whoever had let Lily out of her crate must have already killed Charles. It must have been too late for her to protect her master. But she was still a guard dog. If someone had freed her, why hadn't she gone for him?

◇◇◇

This was the question rumbling around my head as Creighton made some more noises and finally waved me to go. I needed to get over to the pound. I had Lily's rabies vaccination certificate, which should serve as a stay of execution, but she was still a dog in limbo, and she had her breed's reputation going against her. It's funny, really, how public perception changes. Used to be, pit bulls were models of loyalty. Remember Petey, the smiling pup on the Little Rascals? Yeah, he was a pit. They're powerful dogs, sure, but that muscle, that determination can go both ways. I know as well as anyone that none of us are born bad. And no matter what this cop thought, Lily wasn't half as tough as she appeared. For that reason alone, I wasn't looking forward to taking in her bloody memories. Still, there were too many questions jangling around in my head, and she was the only one who could answer them.

I was so preoccupied by my own thoughts that I almost didn't hear the young cop coming up behind me.

"Allow me." He pushed the door to the lobby open and I jumped, getting another sharp glance for my effort. Great, I was really reassuring this cop. "Stay in touch." His voice was more than half growl. As I walked toward the main glass doors, trying not to run, I heard him warm it up at least ten degrees.

"Delia? Delia Cochrane? Would you come this way, please? I'm so sorry for your loss." I turned back to see Delia, her head bowed. She shuffled toward the offices, sniffling. Right behind her, a protective arm supporting her willowy waist, was the onetime basketball champ of Beauville High, Chris Moore.

# Chapter Eight

I watched them go in, but not before noting how Creighton's voice modulated down from a bark to a caress. Something soft for the grieving girlfriend. Hearing him talk, all the bluff attitude gone, was enough to underline the difference between us, at least in the eyes of that brash young cop. Delia was to be coddled. I, and here I pulled myself up to my full five-eight, was not. Never mind that I was the one who had actually seen the ragged mess that had been the victim. I was older, tougher. An outsider, not to mention a brunette, and I was on the short list of suspects, if I could get the buff cop to look for a human at all.

It was a conundrum of the first order, and as I stepped outside, I tried to figure out my next step. Being outside the Beauville cop shop helped. Even standing in the parking lot, I could breathe again. And if I could breathe, I could think. Of course I was a suspect. The fact that I'd found Charles was reason for that, and my added cool around the corpse had probably damned me further. Yeah, there was something about that cop I didn't like. Something in all the muscle and the attitude that set my teeth on edge. Still, there weren't many people who I did like. For all I knew, he might just be doing his job

What was up with Delia? The tears had clearly bought her preferential treatment: was that why they'd been pumped out? I'd seen her at Charles' mother's house, dry eyed and calm, only the night before. Grief is a funny thing, I knew that. So is anger.

But she was going to get a pass while I was not. That, along with the tears, made me want to suspect Delia. Still, what had she done, beside be pretty and a few years younger than me? Not a crime, not yet, and I couldn't see how she would stand to benefit with Charles out of the picture.

There was the Chris Moore angle, but I just didn't know enough. Now that I'd seen him, I remembered Moore better. As a high school basketball star, he'd been a teenage giraffe, towering above our classmates. In the intervening years, he'd filled out, or at least grown into his oversize ears, and he'd let his sandy buzz cut grow out just enough so as not to resemble a new recruit. Even back in his gawky days, he'd been what some women considered cute, with a heavy jaw and a nose like an afterthought. Now those same women would probably go nuts. To me, he looked like a block of wood. But that meant solid, and some women liked that. Perhaps Delia had been keeping him all along or perhaps he'd just stepped up now, seeing a chance to play white knight and maybe move back into his former role. Come to think of it, the high school heartthrob had more motive than the bereaved girlfriend.

I thought about Happy's, where supposedly everybody spent the evening. I hadn't been there since the bad old days. Well, Wallis had said I should get out more. Maybe tonight I'd make a start.

In the meantime, I had business. I got the rabies certificate from my car and turned back toward the official building, pausing to look at the morning light on its glass front. I told myself I was shifting gears. The truth was, I was scared. What Lily had shown me, that one hit of sense memory, was as close as I wanted to come to hell. Still I was her only ally now that Charles was gone. If I didn't help her through this, nobody would. Besides, I realized as I took one last deep breath of the cool morning air, Charles deserved justice, too.

"Hey, Albert." The fat man started as I walked in, a thin patina of grease making his opened lips particularly red. Seeing a sprinkle of sugar on his plaid shirt, I made a mental note: the man liked his donuts. "Found this in my client files."

I waved the certificate, with its distinctive state seal, in the air. The key was nonchalance. Albert reached for it, but I stepped back. I'd worked too hard to get it. Besides, his hands were covered with sugar. "Let me run off a copy for you."

Albert was too lazy to stop me as I stepped behind the front desk and flipped on the Xerox. While it warmed up, I browsed the guest area. "No Frank today?"

"What are you talking about, Pru?"

"Your ferret. He's not here?" I reached for the visitors log and signed myself in—it was time I started obeying the rules—and coincidentally browsed through the other names in the oversized black ledger.

"Oh, Bandit." He laughed, and I cursed silently. I kept forgetting that humans and animals have different names for themselves. "It's funny you should call him Frank."

"Funnier than calling a masked ferret 'Bandit.'" I kept my voice low as the copier whirred. I wasn't here to fight with the fat man. I was here for Lily.

I flipped back a page, but didn't see any names I recognized. Summer people, maybe, or new residents. I was about to close the ledger when a scrawled signature caught my eye: Delia Cochrane. On a mission of mercy?

I turned to Albert, about to ask, and then thought better of it. Lily herself could tell me who had come and gone, showing me the faces of any human who had visited her pen. Albert was too fond of games. Instead, I fixed what I hoped was an amused expression on my face and dropped a copy of the certificate on his desk. "Guess that takes care of one question." Before he could raise any others, I walked over to the back door. "Wanna let me in?"

Albert grunted. I didn't ask him to repeat himself, and just when I was getting sick of waiting, he pushed himself out of his chair and came to my aid.

"You gonna give that dog its last rites?" He unlocked the door to the kennel area and made a show of holding it open for me. "Or were you hoping for a confession?"

"Just checking in on her." I squeezed past Albert's belly. But his comment made me wonder. Maybe Delia hadn't visited out of kindness. Maybe there was some tangible evidence, something I had missed—and that Officer Creighton was too chicken to seek out—on the dog herself. I was sorry Albert hadn't brought the nimble ferret into the office today. A predator, but small enough to live by his wits, he could have contributed some keen observations.

The idea of other witnesses intrigued me. The first room of the kennel was quiet. The sleepy tabby was gone. Home, I hoped. In her place was a sleek tiger queen, nursing three blind kittens. As we walked by, I tried to send my thoughts out to her. I pictured Delia and fought down the temptation to see her as a lioness, all tawny and strong. Maybe the nursing mother had seen her, but all I got were waves of warm contentment. It had been cold in the park. It was warm and dry in here.

"Cute kitty." I stalled, looking into her cage, and tried again. I thought of Lily, focusing on her panic and grief, rather than those wide-set jaws. All I got was a steady hum, the lullaby of a purr. Those bright eyes were closing, the soothing rise and fall lulling both her kittens and herself to sleep. She was tired, I got that. Taking care of kittens is exhausting work. I leaned, in putting my hand on the bars of her cage and then jumped back. As I'd touched the thin bars, I'd caught a clap of sound, as loud and hurtful as a slap in the face. It came from the bars, but no, these weren't moving. What I was getting was memory, the faint sound of my hand on her enclosure triggering memory of other bars, slamming shut. A trap, the humane kind, but for a nursing mother a reason to panic. Hours she'd been in there, or so it had seemed as she'd paced and fretted. She'd heard her kittens calling and torn by doubt she had called back. "Stay still! Stay still!" Her paw pads were torn by the time the trap was opened, the pebbly leather of her nose worn from trying to wedge a way out. But the hands that reached in were wide and gentle beneath their thick gloves. As soon as she smelled them, she'd relaxed. She'd sensed kindness. Warmth.

The rest of the memory flooded through me. Whoever had done the trapping had the sense to look for the kittens—and to place them with their mother before transporting her to the pound, bringing the family in before the autumn night grew cold. The pound had seemed welcoming to the young mother. It had been a while since she'd slept on a pillow. Longer still since she'd eaten kibble, but it was coming back. Velvet lids settled over those yellow eyes. The kittens kneaded, and she purred.

I was stepping back, quietly as I could, when the alarm startled me. "Car! Car!" I had to stop myself from whirling around. What was going on? Then my eyes caught the mother cat's yellow ones. I'd thought she'd been dozing, but if she had, she was awake now. Still, what I'd heard made no sense. Was she seeing me as a danger? Albert?

"You coming?" Albert was at the far door, the one that locked Lily in isolation. He was jangling his keys, impatient and bored. I turned back toward the cat. Her eyes were already closing. The threat had passed. As an animal out on the street, she couldn't be too careful, especially with young ones.

"Yeah, I'm coming." I looked back, but only got the slow sounds of sleep.

Albert skipped the funny stuff, stepping well back after he unlocked the second door. He needn't have bothered. Lily was sleeping, curled up in the corner of her enclosure. I relaxed a little. I'd been braced for a flood of memory, the scent of blood and fear. What got me instead was the real stench.

"Hasn't anyone been walking her?" I looked in at Lily. The corner she'd huddled in seemed relatively clean. The rest of the cage was a mess, the torn paper not concealing the feces. The sharp reek of urine making my eyes water. She still wore the muzzle I'd put on her, at Albert's request. Even with her big jaws held shut, she'd tried to keep herself clean.

"When Joe's here, we get her into the run. But he's not been in today."

I didn't try to hide what I was thinking. Every animal deserved a clean enclosure, and a dog like this needed exercise, a lot of it. I stormed back into the kennel area, grabbing one of three leashes off the wall.

"You're not taking that dog out, Pru."

I stared Albert down. After all, I had a long leather strap in my hand, with metal fittings at the end.

"Okay, it's on your head."

I opened the latch on Lily's cage. "Come on, girl. Time for walkies." Whatever peace she'd acquired in sleep vanished as her head came up, too quick. Startled. "Come on."

I didn't want to flinch, not in front of Albert. I only hoped he couldn't tell I was grinding my teeth. Lily climbed to her feet and shook the sleep from her body. And as soon as she'd lifted her head, the memories had come flooding back. Something sweet, something acrid. The incredible tug of love. *"Let go! Let go! Let go!"*

"Poor girl, come here." I steeled myself against it. I had to. There was too much pain. I could hear Albert's muttered curses as I opened my arms and took the big dog into my embrace. There was a lot of dog to Lily, and most of her muscle, all tensed up. I held her close, reaching around to pull her to me, despite her yells. Did she still think she could rescue her master? Did she still want to run to him? Her head leaning up against my shoulder, still shivering, rattled with the pain. The longing.

Longing? Damn, I missed that ferret now. Frank might look ratty, but that small hunter had more wit about him than most of the people in this town. I'd have to come up with an excuse for Albert, a reason to get Frank back in here—or me back at Albert's house. I grimaced at the thought. For now, I needed time alone with Lily. Time to find out what she saw, maybe even *who* she saw.

"We're going out, Albert." I clipped the leash to her collar and grabbed my bag. Her poor, cropped tail gave a brief wag and I felt my throat closing up. This wasn't a bad dog. Far from it. "So you can clean up in here."

He watched us go, a strange smile on his greasy face. "They're still going to kill that dog, you know," he called after us as I pushed open the back fire door. "They just won't need its head."

Ignoring Albert, we stepped into the sunshine. The dog run, such as it was, was a small, enclosed yard. A few clumps of grass survived in the hard dirt, but otherwise the only relieving feature was a small concrete basin, half birdbath, half trough. Lily turned toward that, and I gently pulled her away. If she was going to have any kind of a life, or be of any use to me, she needed clean water and fresh air, and I knew where to take her.

Beauville, like many towns here in the hills, was built along a river. At one point, it had powered mills. Wood, textiles. I'd zoned out of too much of my school days to remember. Nowadays the waterway's prime economic value was as a tourist attraction. We didn't have any covered bridges. But we did have hiking trails aplenty, now that the city people had discovered us, and access to the river was well marked from what passed for Beauville's downtown. In spring, we got the kayakers, running the snow-fueled rapids. In summer, sometimes it was deep enough for a canoe. In fall, leaf peepers took their overpriced picnics down to its banks, blissfully unaware that its waters were probably too acidic for anything but the occasional deformed catfish.

Didn't matter. It wasn't fish or fowl I was after today, and I picked up our pace as we threaded through the edge of town to the thin strip of woods that runs along the river. I didn't know if the average person on the street would recognize Lily, but I didn't want to take the chance. From what Tracy Horlick had said, it sounded like the town had weighed in, and found Lily guilty. I thought otherwise, but I needed time to get to the truth. The river path might just give me the leverage to find it. Pre-foliage season we'd probably have the trail along the bank to ourselves, and both Lily and I needed the space to breathe.

As soon as we got off the paved sidewalks I knew I'd made the right move. Pit bulls need to run—several miles a day if possible—and Lily craved air as much as exercise. She looked up at me, those huge eyes soft and grateful. I didn't even need to see them, though. In the shelter, I'd felt her panic, now frozen with exhaustion into a kind of loop. Charles' face, his hands, his voice, but all muted, as if the pain were too great to let them in. Now I sensed a loosening. A hint of relaxation and normalcy. A bird broke from the underbrush, and Lily turned. Some small animal, readying for winter, scurried through the leaves and dived into the perpetual blanket of mulch that kept the earth moist and fragrant. Out in the water, improbably and much to my surprise, something broke the surface, grabbed a skimming insect and dived down. The world was alive, and Lily was opening to it.

It isn't often that I enjoy this power, this so-called gift. I want my privacy. I'd prefer to have my mind be my own. Right now, feeling what she felt, hearing and smelling the richness of nature around me was a beautiful thing. Or would be, if people didn't intrude. I let out more leash. What with one thing and another, I didn't dare let Lily off her lead. But she felt the slack and, with a moment's hesitation, took it. Running up the bank to sniff at—yes—a rabbit hole. Toward the gnarled base of an ancient beech: I got a mental image, flipping by at lightning speed, of the thirteen other dogs who had visited this spot. We jogged for a while along the dirt path, for the sheer joy of stretching our legs. Half hour later, when we came to the picnic grounds, deserted on this cool day, I felt sweaty, but refreshed. I pulled a folding dish out of my bag and used my water bottle to fill it, saving some of the water for myself. We both drank. We both gazed down at the river as it eddied around the rocks. We were at peace together. Somewhere, a mockingbird sang. With a deep breath, I readied my questions.

"Lily?" I spoke out loud, as I had during our training sessions. With most animals, it seems I can hear their thoughts, but I'm never sure how far it goes the other way. Maybe they're just better at blocking out what they don't want to hear. Maybe I'll learn that, too, in time. "Lily, girl, can we talk a bit?"

She looked up at me. Her cropped tail thwacked against the dirt in acknowledgment. She knew my voice, knew the tone meant something good at any rate. I lowered myself off the picnic table's built-in bench to sit in the dirt beside her and wondered how to proceed.

"This is going to be hard." I put my hand on the back of her head, partly to ease communication but largely to comfort her. Her heavy tail—what there was of it—slapped the ground again, two, three times.

"Can you tell me about Charles?" Blankness. She was watching the water. Looking for that bubble to appear again. Trying to get a scent under the rich leaf mulch, and I realized once again how much I didn't know. Did Lily have a name for her person? Could she understand my question at all? I tried to conjure up my former client's face. He was tall and skinny, rather than slim. Every inch a geek, but a sweet one. I tried to build a mental image. Charles standing in the living room. Charles as he would appear from Lily's crate. His curly hair, a little too long, backlit by the sun coming in through the big back window. I imagined his jeans, worn at the knee. The MIT sweatshirt—and suddenly I remembered it as I'd last seen it, black and sticky with blood. Lily started, and I grabbed her collar, whispering to her to calm us both down.

"I'm sorry, girl. I'm sorry."

But my blunder had done the trick. Memories came flooding out now, the hungry fish forgotten. Charles. His hands, again, on her collar. Gentle. Then his voice, loud. Was he yelling in anger or fear? What were his words? But the memories were coming too fast for me to examine. Charles' hands raised, fingers spread. Bloody. Charles on the floor. That smell, that smell—sweet and acrid and hypnotically strong. A feeling like longing, like desperation, like despair. Hope draining away. Charles, Charles, Charles.

I couldn't take it. I pulled my hand from the dog's back and stood up. I walked away, stumbling. I felt sick, woozy. Sweaty again, even as the afternoon turned raw. No wonder Lily had blocked this out, let an eternal present take over. This was too much, too strong. I leaned forward, hands on knees, to breathe, and as I did, a thought took me. Where was Lily during all this? Why hadn't she defended her person?

"Lily?" She wasn't responding. Frozen there, shivering now, her open eyes staring into space. I returned back to her and prepared myself for the shock. "Where were you, Lily? Where were you when all this happened?"

Nothing, and so I gingerly reached over. Her back was shaking, the short fur along her neck on edge, like a cat's. I repeated my question and leaned over, placing my face against her warm body.

The rush of images continued, joined now by her silent cry: *Let go! Let go! Let go!* But something was different. I closed my eyes, breathing in the warm dog scent, rich and musty, trying not to let that sweet death stench overwhelm me. What was it?

Then I saw, through Lily's eyes. She had focused entirely on Charles. Had watched him yell, had watched him pushed back. Had watched him fall, had watched him bleed. But some of the scent—some element of that horrible sweet stench—had been there from the start. Before the fall, before the blood. And the scene that played through Lily's mind, like some infernal tape loop—was drenched in longing. A yearning for—what? I focused in, but all I could see was framed through bars. Lily had been in her crate, helpless to stop tragedy. Helpless as she lost the only home she knew.

# Chapter Nine

"And so that's your big breakthrough? The dog's homesick?"

I'd woken Wallis on my return. I hadn't meant to, but she's a light sleeper for a cat, and I'd figured I might as well get her feedback. I should have expected her to be pissed off as she stretched to her full length along the back of my sofa.

I shrugged. "I guess not. I did get confirmation that she was crated when it happened."

"Wonderful guard dog he had there." She jumped down to the seat and began kneading. I realized I had only about five minutes before she resumed her nap, so I didn't try to explain the intensity of what I'd felt. The horrible, sad ache. Lily whining, a low despairing sound. *Home, home, home*, she'd cried. It didn't matter. I couldn't give that to her, not anymore.

Wallis must have picked up on some of that. "By the way, that infant you brought home?" She glanced up at me to make sure she had my attention again. "I think she's retarded."

The kitten. I'd get to her later. "She's very young, Wallis. I'm sorry to dump her on you like that. And, well, Wallis, I'm wondering if you can help me here?" A blatant appeal to her vanity, but she cocked an ear, so I continued. "Lily doesn't think like you or I do." I was laying it on thick. "I mean, I don't seem to be able to ask her questions. She doesn't seem to understand that I want to see who was there. Who killed Charles." I swallowed, hard. Maybe I didn't want to see that either.

"You don't. You've got *some* sense." Wallis was still kneading, but at least she was looking at me.

"You're right. But I need to find out. I mean, pit bulls have a lot of hound in them, right? So what she's smelling must mean something."

"Blood smells the same to all of us." Wallis had turned back to her pillow. I was losing her.

"But there was something else. Something sweet." I tried to conjure up the memory as I'd experienced it, second hand. Lily's strongest recollections were scent: the strong metallic and, yes, vaguely cloying smell of blood. Something else, too. Rich and fruity, almost flowery. Sweet.

"What is this 'sweet' you're talking about?" The pillow properly prepared, Wallis lay down.

I could've kicked myself. Cats don't taste sweet. I fumbled for a translation. "Tasty, good. Not savory, though. More like fresh fruit or candy. Like Petromalt?"

I got a quick hit of revulsion.

"But you like Petromalt."

"No, I find it…interesting." I heard her voice fading. "The texture…."

"Wallis, do you have any idea what Lily could have meant?"

"She's a dog, for Christ's sake. She could have been smelling her own waste." She must have felt my exasperation, because she roused herself for one more thought. "What you said: flowers, food. Maybe something dead." Then she was out.

It's no use trying to force a cat to communicate. Even when you can talk to them, you can't compel them to pay attention. And so I went in search of the tiny orange kitten I'd brought home the night before. Wallis had a point. I'd set the kitten up with her own food and water dishes, knowing how fastidious Wallis can be, and shown her the litterbox. But then I'd collapsed into my own bed. No wonder my elderly tabby was miffed.

"Where is—" Nope, no point in asking. Even if Wallis were awake, she had made her point. I needed to leave her alone for a bit, so I went in search of the kitten.

"Kitty? Kitty cat?" It had been so long since I called out to a feline as if it were just an animal, but I wasn't sure how else to connect. I'd gotten her weak cry last night, but I didn't know if she could hear me. "Kitty?"

As I climbed the stairs, I felt a vague stirring. Something was up there. "Kitty?"

Nothing on the bed, but thinking of last night, I opened the closet. Something was in there, something afraid. "Kitty?"

I sensed rather than felt the response. A shuffling, a crouching down as if the small creature could make herself smaller. My old house doesn't have a light in the closet, but that hint of movement was enough. I pulled out the basket where I throw my dirty laundry. Underneath a worn T-shirt, I saw two blue eyes.

"*I didn't! I didn't!*" She backed away from me, too small or too scared to even hiss. "*I didn't do anything wrong!*"

"Nobody's saying you did, kitty." I said the words out loud, trying to keep my voice and thought soft, my curiosity in check. "You're safe here, kitty." I held out a finger for her to sniff, then gently scooped the frightened cat out of the basket. At least she hadn't used it for a litterbox.

"*I didn't do anything wrong!*"

I had to smile. "No, kitty, you were very good. Now how about some food. And then we'll check out that litterbox again, see if you might want to use it." I trusted Wallis not to bully the poor animal, but I couldn't count on how scary my big tabby might seem to this little one. Nor, come to think of it, how young this kitten might be. I'd seen her dig into a can of wet food last night, so I knew she was weaned. She'd have been box trained by her mother, probably.

I opened a new can for her and watched her eat. Wallis would give me hell for that, I knew. For years, before she and I began talking, I'd kept her on a strict diet of one can a day, and she'd been an adult, too. Well, my plus-size tabby was asleep, and I had a kitten to console. When I carried her over to the mud room, she got right in, and did her business. One worry taken care of.

"There you go." I had questions, but the best way to get answers would be to put her small mind at ease. "I can see that you're a good girl."

The kitten looked up at me. I could've sworn she was puzzled by my response. "*I didn't do anything wrong!*" There was something else going on here that I wasn't getting. "*I didn't.*"

"What is it, kitten?" I picked her up with one hand. Quite a change from Wallis. But she turned from me. "Do you have a name, little girl?"

"*I didn't do anything.*" With that final iteration, she turned around twice, tucked her nose in her tail and fell asleep in my lap. Leaving me to wonder if this small animal had been taken from its mother too soon or been otherwise traumatized. And also, incidentally, how I could extract myself without disturbing her.

I needn't have worried overmuch. The kitten barely stirred when I lifted her onto the sofa and left her to get myself dressed. Happy's. I'd been in once or twice since my return, checking out my options along with the bourbon. There hadn't been many, as I recalled, and I'd ended up drinking in silence, finally settling on a bottle at home. Wallis made her feelings known about that, but since she had a thing for catnip we'd found our way to a truce.

The bar looked a lot smaller than it had when I was growing up. It had been there forever, stuck on the end of our main street like a punctuation point. As a kid, I'd not paid it much mind. Maybe my dad had gone in there. He'd left before I'd become too clear on his habits. My mother pretended it didn't exist, walking by its brick front with her nose up so high I always expected her to trip. There was parking in back; even in Beauville, downtown can get crowded. But she never parked there, preferring instead to walk a block down, even when it was raining.

Happy's wasn't the only place in town that sold booze. You could even get a highball at the diner. But no place else was strictly for drinking. Or, if the rumors were to be believed, drinking and cards. Most nights after Happy locked the front door, he left the back open, people said. All-night games for big money drew out-of-towners long before we had the jogging paths.

I should have hated the place. I vaguely recalled my parents fighting about it. Once, some dishes had been thrown, and I don't think it was the booze or the women that had started it.

But by the time I was in high school, the little bar had the allure of the forbidden. Nothing showed through its one dark window, and the sounds when the heavy door pushed open called to me. Laughter, the tinny noise of a jukebox. Smoke. A dozen times I'd gone in, the summer after I graduated. I don't think my fake ID fooled anyone. Half the town knew my mother; the other half had known my dad, more closely than I liked. Maybe it was that everyone knew I was leaving. Going away to college and the big city. Maybe they felt that earned me entry. That's when I'd discovered how small the old bar really was: six tables, maybe seven. A dark wooden bar scored and notched from years of fights and burning butts; a row of booths along the back wall. I'd had one or two adventures in that parking lot, too, that summer. Nothing to write home about, but enough to take some of the mystique off the place. I'd left town with no regrets.

Coming up on it now, it looked almost homey. That same heavy door, the varnish worn off in spots, still separated the quiet street from the revelers within. The same neon sign still beckoned. The cloud of smoke that greeted me could have been the same as well, for all I could tell. State law says "no smoking," but nobody ever minded it at Happy's. So maybe it was the cold, clean air that came in with me, or the fact that I let out some of the accumulated cloud, that explained why the looks I got weren't the friendliest.

"PBR." There was plenty of space at the bar. The bartender wasn't someone I recognized, and I knew the original Happy had been gone for years. Emphysema, I'd heard. The current bartender was just an employee and looked none too happy with the low-key crowd. I thought about feeding the jukebox, but wanted to get a feel for the crowd first.

"Hey, gorgeous." Not original, but I turned anyway. I didn't mind what I saw. Tall, angular, with dark hair falling into his face and a smile just off enough to be natural, he slid onto the stool next to me as if he owned it. Up close, he looked white as porcelain, his beard showing blue in the dim light.

"Do I know you?" Friendliness is not one of my natural attributes, and the grin seemed just a little too easy to me. But the barkeep brought him a lowball glass of something amber, and I figured he came with the territory.

"Mack." He held out a hand big enough for a lumberjack. Always a good sign. "Mack Danton."

I raised my bottle in a salute. That was me going part of the way. "Pru Marlowe."

"I knew that." He withdrew his mitt without seeming to mind and took a healthy swallow of his whiskey. I saw a muscle move alongside his jaw and turned away. "I've been meaning to look you up."

I bit my tongue on that, thinking of my cop friend's trick. My face must have shown something, though, because the big guy's smile grew even wider. "I'm a friend of Chuck's. Was, I guess. And, well, I heard…." The wattage faltered and despite my best instincts, I took pity.

"Yeah, I found him. I was working with his dog." Something about this guy was getting to me, maybe it was the smile. I caught myself before I started explaining more.

"Rough." He sounded as if he'd heard me anyway and drank some more, the muscle moving up and down again along the side of his face. "He and I went way back. We were working together, some, on his new project."

Funny, this guy looked nothing like Charles. Chuck, as he called him. If he worked with systems, I'd have guessed they were wood and water based, maybe outdoors or with animals. Or, considering that white-blue pallor, stuck in here, dealing cards.

"I didn't know Charles had a partner." I didn't know what Charles did exactly, but there was no reason to let this guy know that.

He nodded. "Yeah, we were getting ready to launch, too." I couldn't tell what was making him sad, the death of his partner or the delay in a product. I told myself that it was for Lily that I needed to know more.

"And that product was—what exactly?" I leaned in. The bartender gave me a look that said he'd seen this move before.

So had Mack. He laughed, that big smile springing back into place. "Proprietary software, Ms. Marlowe. If I told you, I'd have to kill you."

The bartender turned to him. I did, too, as his face went blank. "I'm sorry." He sank his face into his hand. "Old joke, but it's not funny anymore, is it?"

"Hey, it's okay." I heard my own voice grow soft. "It's still so new."

"Tell me about it." He looked up at the bottles across the bar and raised his glass. The bartender refilled it from a bottle of Jim Beam. "I guess I'm still in shock. But you. I'm surprised you're still walking."

"Why do you think I'm in here?" Two drinks later, we were back on familiar territory. Barroom flirting, trading tragedies, and I was enjoying myself. But I wasn't here for fun, and the good-looking stranger saw me looking around.

"Meeting someone?" His voice was cool, though its hint of jealousy warmed me.

"Just curious." I turned back to face the bar. The mirror behind the bottles was webbed with age, but it still gave me a pretty fair take on the room. It wasn't as large as it had loomed in my dreams, back when I was a bored teen. Still, Happy's had the essentials. Low lights shaded with red glass made the folks at the tables seem a little rosier, a little healthier than they might otherwise. Here at the bar, the light was more golden—or that could have been the beer—and a little brighter. I looked past Mack at a worn blue sweater. Something about the wearer was familiar.

A cough brought me back. "Curious?"

"Okay, I'll 'fess up." I put as much charm as I could into my smile, hoping to mask the lie. "I feel a little odd about what happened. With Charles and all. I was hoping to run into some of his people. Maybe his girlfriend, or someone."

I left the name blank, just in case he might name someone other than Delia. It wasn't likely, but then motives for murder don't grow on trees. If I was hoping for gossip, though, I was out of luck.

"You found me." He leaned in. "I don't think you should feel strange. You couldn't have known that dog would turn on him, could you? What I heard was that he got it from a dogfighting ring."

"Really?" I knew as much from Lily herself. I hadn't realized that was common knowledge. "Did Charles tell you that?"

"He said he got the dog off some gambler he knew. I don't know if he lost a bet or what." I raised my eyebrows at that. "Nobody I know," said Mack, backpedalling.

"Hey, the dog wasn't the one who ripped his throat out."

Mack blanched. I'd gone too far. I reached over and put my hand on his forearm. He was wearing a denim work shirt, its texture pleasingly rough to my touch.

"I'm sorry."

He stared down at the bar. "I just can't get my mind around it, you know?"

We sat in a companionable silence. Someone finally got the jukebox going. Vintage soul. Smoky and full of possibility. I'd met my jazz pianist in a bar like this, but that was in a bigger city and a very different time.

"You going to the funeral?" Mack's question broke into my thoughts.

"I don't know." I turned to face him. Even in the bar light, his eyes looked blue. "I honestly hadn't thought about it." I swallowed. "Truth is, I don't know when it is."

"Sunday." He named one of Beauville's three churches and gave me a time. "It's not much of a date, but I could pick you up."

"Thanks, but—" I fished around for an excuse. "I've got a dog-walking gig. Rain or shine, with no days off for holidays." It wasn't true. The bichon's owner took charge of him on weekends. She said she needed the exercise. In truth, I think she just wanted to avoid my higher weekend rates.

Mack nodded. "Well, if you want to talk to anyone, come." He shrugged. "You'll probably see Delia there."

"Delia, yeah, that's her name." A stray thought struck me. "Why is the funeral in Beauville? His mother lives over in Raynbourne, and you'd think she'd want him buried over by her?"

"Beats me." Mack signaled to the bartender that he wanted to settle up. "You can ask Delia. She's been helping the old lady out. That's how she met Chuck, I think."

I thought of Charles' mother. She hadn't seemed feeble, not more than the death of a child could explain. "Delia is her housekeeper, or some kind of aide?"

Mack stood up, pulling out his wallet and enough bills to cover both our drinks. "I don't know what the deal was, but it worked out all right for her, didn't it?" He flashed that smile again. It faded quickly. "For a while, anyway. So hey, I'll see you around?"

"Sunday, definitely." We both got up. I waited, to see if Mack would follow up with an offer—a ride, or a nightcap somewhere private. But Mack was talking to the bartender, and I remembered those late night games. I had had other activities in mind, but a lady likes to be asked, and instead I made my way over to the door.

How had Charles—excuse me, "Chuck"—gotten involved with someone like Mack? For that matter, what exactly was Charles' project and how close was it to completion? I was mulling these questions over when the front door opened, letting in a stream of light and unexpectedly cold air. Together, they made patterns in the smoke, illuminating the dark back booths, and I saw Chris Moore, sitting alone, as he looked up expectantly—and not at me. I followed his gaze as Delia Cochrane stepped inside, the street lamp making her golden hair glow like an angel's.

"Be right back." I heard the bartender excuse himself and start toward the newcomer as she stepped by me, toward Chris' booth. I started toward them and stopped. I didn't know what I was going to say. This was a small town, and these were people who knew each other. Who had shared a great grief. Still, something was off here. There were connections I wasn't seeing. I paused by the jukebox. Smokey had given way to something newer, a young singer faking passion to a disco beat. What was I going to ask Delia? Who was I to intrude?

I looked over at Chris' table. He'd not noticed me; he only had eyes for Delia. She had bent over him as she came nearer, saying something close in his ear that made him smile as she slid into the seat opposite his. I had no place here. But as I stood watching, listening to the dance beat, I realized I could smell her perfume. Lightly floral with a note of something else, too, more sophisticated than I'd expect, coming from our little town. The fresh air from the door and the smoke all around was swallowing it up, but I could just catch it. A hint of spice. Something sweet.

# Chapter Ten

The morning of the funeral dawned cool and clear, the kind of Indian summer day we in New England pray for. It's also the kind of day we usually overdress for, and by nine, I had already shed one layer of fleece.

Funny, I never used to be a morning person. Bars aren't as much fun when the light is new and strong. But since I got out of the hospital, I've been sleeping less, waking earlier, and craving that early morning air. The sleeping part is odd. When I checked myself in, their diagnosis was "exhaustion." True, I hadn't slept for something like three days by then. It wasn't fatigue that was doing for me. Albert had it partially right. I had changed, but that had happened before the aides in white coats. The doctors were there to help me. In fact, I'd called them. Not that it had done any good.

No, I don't know what caused it. Maybe I never would. I'd been working myself sick, so maybe diagnosing exhaustion wasn't that far off. I was still in school, so close to getting my certification that I could taste it. And between biochemistry and my practicum, the internship that behaviorists have to do to learn the realities of the gig, I was up all hours. That wasn't new to me, and I kind of liked it. I was getting ready to kick Stevie out of my life. Those wild hands had strayed once too often. It was time for Pru to focus on Pru.

And then I'd gotten sick. Really sick. Lie in bed and listen to the clock tick sick.

Now, when you're living with someone, getting the flu can be kind of fun. Your boyfriend, husband, whatever, is there to fetch for you. To bring you aspirin and juice; to call the doctor if your temperature spikes once too often.

When you're living with an animal, you don't expect this kind of care. Sure, I'd heard the stories of dogs that fetched the phone for injured humans. Of cats that curled up and purred over surgery incisions. I'd even believed a few of them. Domestic animals know which hand has the thumbs to open the cans, after all. And so when Wallis started licking my temples and then the insides of my wrists, I wasn't freaked. I'd been sweating, during those good hours when my fever would break and I could sleep. My skin was probably salty as hell. And when she kept coming back, leaving me only to eat or use the litterbox, I attributed it to some vague maternal residue.

But then she started talking to me. Telling me, specifically, that I had to "get over" myself, drink some water, and consider bathing, then I knew I was sick. The funny thing was, the lecture worked. Sympathy is nice, but I never took it too seriously. Having someone yell at me, tell me, basically, that I was going to die and it would be my own fault if I didn't do something, that I believed. And so I got up and stuck my head under the kitchen tap, drinking like the parched thing I was. Wallis was sitting on the counter by the time I looked up.

"And perhaps you'd like to follow that with some food?" Her voice fit her neat tabby style. Very sure of itself, a little smug.

"I'm hallucinating." I said the words aloud, partly to make sure my voice sounded different from hers. It did. But the water had helped, and I grabbed a loaf of bread from the fridge, eating one stale slice while two others toasted and chasing it with juice straight from the carton. "I'll be better once I eat and drink." I didn't say those words aloud, but the answer came loud and clear.

"If you're really better, you might consider drinking that in such a way that half of it doesn't spill over your face." I choked out a mouthful and looked over to see Wallis staring up at me.

"And you really might consider a shower, as well, before going back to sleep."

I think I dropped the container. It was mostly empty anyway, but the noise—or maybe it was the look in my eye—made Wallis take off. I did shower then, letting water beat down on me until my fingertips were wrinkled and the chills had started to come back. But I didn't go back to bed after that. Instead, I dressed as quickly as I could, aware all the while of Wallis' eyes, watching me, and hailed a cab. I don't remember what I said to the admitting clerk, but as a student, my health insurance was good. They gave me something, and I slept until my flu was gone.

The voices had never stopped. They had, in fact, gotten worse on my return. Not only did Wallis talk to me, I found myself overhearing every animal I came in contact with. Everything, constantly, and before you start thinking cute Dr. Doolittle thoughts, try to imagine what that's like. In a city, you're not just surrounded by pets—inbred Yorkies consumed with petty jealousies and neurotic housecats—but by all the wildlife we like to pretend doesn't exist. Rats. Skunks. Pigeons. There had been a pigeon nest right by my bedroom window, and for years I'd been blissfully unaware of its existence. My first night back, they woke me at dawn with such inanities that I would have sicced Wallis on them, if I could.

But by then, we were barely speaking. She had reacted badly when I'd taken off, and in all fairness, I hadn't thought to call a cat-sitter or even refill her bowl of dry food. She'd survived my three days on the ward, but my lack of gratitude was not to be easily forgiven. She made that clear. And when I started throwing things in boxes, unable to cope, she had fixed me with a steely gaze and read me the riot act.

"You are not going to run away from this. This is a gift, Pru, and if you can't accept it, you're less of a human than I'd judged you."

"I'm not—" I remember stopping myself. Was I really talking back to my cat? And the hospital had released me?

"Yes, you are. Do you have any idea what you are doing, or even where you are going?"

That had stopped me. She was right, I hadn't made any plans. I was simply going to run. And so I lay back on the bed, drained by my sickness and the events of the last week. And I found myself petting a familiar warm back as I thought.

"Beauville." I announced finally, sitting upright.

"Excuse me?" Wallis stopped purring.

"My mother's place. She's always asking." That was true, though I had no desire to share the rambling house with anyone, particularly a sickly septuagenarian and her aide.

Wallis stared without commenting.

"It'll just be for a while. A week or two. Just until I figure out what to do next." *Until I figure out how to make this stop*, I promised myself. If Wallis was listening, she didn't say anything.

A few weeks had turned into a month, and my insomniac self was welcomed by the aide, who took advantage of a few nights off. When my mother went to rehab, I gave the aide notice. I could see what was happening. Sure enough, my mother never came home, moving directly to hospice, and by spring, the house was mine. But I'd never really started sleeping again, and now I was stuck with country hours in a country town, staring out at a damned perfect day.

"You're wearing that? How imaginative." Wallis settled her front paws over each other, as if afraid they'd be soiled by her dripping sarcasm.

"Look, it's black, okay?" Time was, most of my wardrobe was this color. Back in the city, black was my fail-safe: good for the clubs and reasonable for work. In my few months here, I'd begun adding color to my wardrobe. Not because of any change in my basic outlook: if anything my illness, my "change" as I'd come to think of it, followed by the long drain of my mother's final illness had made me more dour. Nor because of any protective coloration. Although I'd come to realize that Beauville was, like any small town, a tightly knit community, I'd chosen it because of the sparseness of its population. I didn't *want* people around me. If the few who tried to get close got scared, so much the better.

But while I'd never been flush, I was now closer to flat broke than ever. My student loans had, reasonably, disappeared when I dropped my classes in midterm without explanation or excuse, and my weeks of inaction following my hospitalization drained what little savings I had. I'd dumped or given away most of my possessions, taking only what I could fit in my battered Toyota. And even though I'd given up everything but good coffee, life out here in the boonies hadn't been as cheap as I'd hoped, and the back taxes on my mom's house took everything she had left, too. So these days I bought what I could afford, picking up fleece and flannel as it became available and as the nights became raw. These days, I wore a lot of orange, hunters' seconds, I assumed. Not appropriate for a funeral.

The outfit I'd pulled out that morning was one of my old stalwarts. A long-sleeved black jersey, which fell to my knees, black tights, and my biker boots. As I looked down at my feet, I sensed Wallis' disgust.

"What?" She'd turned her head away, as if unwilling to act as witness. "They're boots. It's chilly out, okay?" She tucked her own soft paws under in a silent protest, and I considered my options. Sneakers, snow boots. A pair of black pumps that I'd hung onto because of the way they lengthened my legs. "I'm not wasting the heels on this. If there's any mud, it would ruin the suede." The tabby turned and jumped from the bed with no further comment.

As I walked into the packed church, I had to admire the soundness of Wallis' fashion sense. I'd been thinking of graveyards and grassy knolls, but the clump of my boots caused every face to turn toward me as I walked through the tall doors. The white clapboard outside opened onto a light interior, the high windows letting sun beam down on the white walls and pale wood of the pews. This was a classic New England church, a design that sent tourists into spasms.

"Too bad I don't do quaint," I muttered under my breath, and looked for an opening that I could slip into. Up front, I could see Delia's golden hair. She was leaning over a shorter, grey head—Charles' mom, Nora, I figured. I remembered what Mack had said about Delia helping her out and determined to keep an eye on her. After the service, I'd try to get her alone. I had to find out why she'd been to the pound. If she had an honest interest in Lily, I'd eat Alpo. Speaking of mouth watering, Mack himself sat a few seats away, his dark hair unruly despite a heroic amount of product.

I slipped into a pew about halfway up, muttering something that I hoped sounded sympathetic to the wiry couple who squeezed in to make room for me, and went back to work examining the chief mourners. Maybe because of our encounter at Happy's, I found myself staring at Mack, at the curls that just wouldn't stay down. Delia's sleek golden coif would have made a perfect counterpoint, I couldn't help noticing. But, hey, she seemed to have made her choice. Between them, Chris Moore, his back as straight as a poker, separated them as completely as a brick wall. About as flexible, too: the former athlete's eyes were fixed straight ahead. A coffin, draped in a white cloth, held the place of honor at the front of the church, an oversized framed photo of Charles on an easel nearby.

I was staring at the portrait when I heard a familiar voice mutter my name. Startled, I jerked back. Albert, his customary flannel covered by a dark blue pullover, was blinking down at me expectantly. The wiry couple to my left had already moved down the few remaining inches.

"Sorry." I shifted over, and waited for Albert to squeeze in beside me.

"Didn't know you'd be here." He kept his voice low, but the crowd was quieting down. The minister had appeared at the podium. "I was gonna call you."

The woman in front of us, with steel-colored hair and a face to match, turned to give him a pointed look. I followed with one of my own, and he gave a sheepish shrug. "It's just, I found something."

"What?" Impatience made me careless of volume and earned me a loud, reproving *"shush."*

"Tell you later." Albert mouthed the words, and I slumped down in the pew. This kind of suspense I didn't need. Nor did I need Albert's thigh pressed quite so close against mine. Up close he smelled like warm bologna.

Still, anxiety and growing fury kept me awake as the service started. The minister, a nice-enough looking man with a birthmark to rival Gorbachev's, didn't sound like he'd known Charles, but then after a while funerals all tend to sound alike. Commitment to his community, friends, family. Someone must have given him a tip sheet at least, because he mentioned kindness to animals. That brought a small cry from up front, and I saw Delia patting his mother's back. Lily wouldn't get any such consolation. Nor that kitten, either.

I was thinking about the kitten, about where it might have come from—and what it might have heard or seen—when a commotion in the back caused the dozers to wake and the more attentive to turn. Jim Creighton, alone, and dressed in civies had come in. He seemed younger in his blue suit, a recent haircut giving him the big-eared awkwardness of the boy he must have been not that long ago. But there was nothing boyish about the look he gave the crowd, who all quickly turned back toward the minister. Just how small a town was this? Was Jim the only cop on the case, or had he really been a friend of the deceased? I turned away before he could catch my eye, but I sensed that he was watching me throughout the short service.

As soon as the final prayer was over, I grabbed Albert's arm. "What is it?"

"Cool it, Pru." He pulled his hand back as if I had insulted him. "You don't have to get bent out of shape. I mean, he can't help it."

"Albert." I took a breathe. "Would you please tell me what you're talking about?"

"Miss?" I was blocking the exit from the pew, and so I followed Albert out to the aisle and then through those tall doors into the fresh air. The sun was high, the day wonderfully warm with just a hint of autumn cool in the light breeze. An apple of a day, crisp and fresh.

The portly pound keeper didn't seem to be enjoying the fine weather though. He hung his head and mumbled. "I can't help it. It's what he does."

"Who, Albert?" I was losing patience and had to remind myself of the rules of training. Calm voice. Steady persistence. "Tell me what you are talking about, please." For me, these played out in stilted diction. It's just easier with animals.

"Bandit. He likes things."

I nodded.

"Shiny things, most of the time. I don't know." Bit by bit, I got the story out of him. Albert claimed he was cleaning out his desk drawer. I suspected he was looking for that last bit of gum the ferret had found, or something even older and gamier. Whatever the initial goal, his search had turned up a small cache of personal items. A long, glittery earring. Albert called it diamond, but I'd bet rhinestones. The caps to a half dozen pens. The earpiece to a set of headphones, and something else. "One of those computer doodads," said Albert, outlining a shape about the size and width of his thumb in the air. "You know, that you carry around?"

"A keychain drive?"

He shrugged. "Anyway, I reckoned I should ask people. I don't remember you wearing earrings like that, but the computer thing, I thought."

"Yeah, thanks." I barely had to think about this one. "Yeah, I did lose a USB drive right off my keychain. I was wondering what happened to it." People keep info on those things, and information was just what I was lacking. It wasn't rocket science, but it might be a clue. "Did you happen to look at what's on it?"

"Nah, I reckoned it was private." Of course, I translated, he didn't understand how to use it.

I did. "Can I come by and pick it up later?" The crowd was milling around the sidewalk, overwhelmingly overdressed for the day.

"You're not going to the grave?" I shrugged. Even my light dress was sticking to my back now. "Well, I didn't plan on opening the office up today." He gazed off into space, and I played my last card.

"What about the animals? I could go over, feed and water them." Get that drive.

But Albert shook his head. "I had Jeremy come in. I think working today would be, I don't know, disrespectful." He was going fishing. Either that, or he'd start drinking early.

"I'll come by tomorrow then." I turned toward the street when a last thought struck me. "Hey, Albert." He turned back, a worried expression on his round face. "What about that earring? Any ideas whose it might be?"

Now it was his turn to shrug. "Who knows? It's too pretty for someone to wear to the pound." He paused as a rare thought made his face go blank. "Unless maybe someone is sweet on me." He looked up. "You think?"

I watched him walk off, biting the inside of my cheek to keep my response to myself. I had questions, but none that Albert could answer. Frank—Bandit—would know where he'd gotten the tiny drive. The earring, too, if that were important. Even if either object had been kicked around the floor before he'd found it, the little hunter's keen sense of smell could probably answer a lot of my questions for me. But how could I ask to interview a ferret? No, I'd just have to hope that Albert brought his covetous pet in again. Or that whatever was on that drive would make things clear.

True, the drive might have nothing to do with anything. I might boot it up to find the Mayor's tax records or an unfinished novel. Beauville could be a bit of a backwater, but the summer people—and their money—had brought us into the new century and such things were not unheard of, at least by folks with a little more on the ball than Albert.

The earring was another matter, one that might not count for anything but gossip. A long glittering dangler? That was evening wear. Someone had either not gone home before dropping by the animal control office, or had found a lost jewel and was carrying it around, probably planning on returning it. If it were evidence of some late-night tryst, that earring might have potential. But I had a feeling about that drive. Someone had broken into Charles' house looking for something the same night I had, and whatever he—or she—was seeking, it wasn't the folder with Lily's veterinary records. And the log at the pound had shown Delia there. She might be taking care of Charles' mom, but I didn't put her down as an animal lover. No, my money was on Delia, hunting for that drive. I looked around for her golden hair.

I needed to talk to her, see if she'd lose any of her cool. Sometimes, when working with certain animals, trainers try to get them off their guard. They'll pinch the ears of a dog until it retrieves. Shock a competitor till it takes an agility course faster and then faster still. It's not a technique I've ever liked, not even before my change. I'd rather not take advantage of anyone's vulnerability. But humans could look after themselves, and I had no sympathy for murderers. If Delia had lost a keychain drive—or an earring—she might be getting a little frantic. I'd use it, if I could.

The sun was high in the sky by now, and the crowd thinning out. "I'm sorry for your loss." I practiced the phrase as I drew up to Charles' mother, trying to ignore the insistent call of a wood thrush: *"I'm here! I'm here! I'm here!"*

"Pru, glad you made it." Mack came up behind me, putting his hand on the small of my back as if it were the most natural move in the world.

"I respected Charles." I stepped back. The man was a looker, but like most handsome men, he knew it. I thought of the earring. He'd be the kind of man who'd notice a trinket like that, left on a nightstand or tangled in a pillow. Women probably left their belongings at his place all the time, marking their territory.

"Are you going to the graveside?" His voice showed that he'd taken the hint, and raised it as a challenge.

"Why not?" It was a Sunday. If Albert wasn't going to cooperate, what else did I have to do? Besides, even if she was attending Charles' mother, I might manage to get a word alone with Delia.

"Great, we're all leaving." Mack turned away. "You can follow."

"Sensitive, isn't he?" I was talking to myself, another bad habit I'd picked up out here. At least with Wallis around, I didn't feel quite so desperate.

"I think he's hurting more than he lets on." I turned in surprise. Delia had come up behind me.

"Delia, I'm so sorry." I could feel the flush grow in my cheeks. If only I hadn't let that damned thrush distract me.

She waved my concern away. "It's just odd, you know? You expect someone to be there and then suddenly, he's not." I knew what she meant, but took the opportunity to check out her turquoise eyes anyway. There was some smudging of her makeup, but not much. "It's worse for Nora."

I nodded. "I can believe it. How's she doing?"

"A little more confused than usual, but she'll be okay. There's just been so much going on." Delia smiled, a small, sad smile. "She's been gardening like mad. I guess that's her outlet." As she spoke, she brushed back a stray hair and I noticed her perfect French-tipped nails. Whatever help she gave the old woman, it didn't involve digging in the dirt.

"Isn't it a little late in the season?"

Delia's smile grew until it reached her eyes. "You'd be surprised. I was. There's all kinds of transplanting and fertilizing, not to mention putting in bulbs. Our soil out here is tough, full of roots and rocks. But she loves it. Charles had been making plans to move her into his place, and she'd been working a lot there. But now, well, she won't be giving up her own garden. I guess she wants to whip it into shape."

I pictured the old woman, on her knees. I could see the satisfaction, for a certain type. Me, I preferred other recreational activities. Delia must have read my mind, because she looked behind me. I turned, too. Mack was standing over by the church door. From his posture, I'd bet he'd been up late, and I wondered if he'd had company. As we watched, he rubbed one large hand over his face and through those black curls.

"So, are you a friend of Mack's?" Her voice was soft, and I couldn't read it.

"We just met the other night at Happy's." Let her make of that what she would. Besides, I had questions for her. "Was he close to Charles?" From her expression, that wasn't the question she was expecting.

"I guess so." She shrugged her pretty shoulders, and I noticed that she'd removed the jacket. The September sun had gotten warm. Her skin was tan and smooth. "He looks like a mess, doesn't he? To be honest, I bet it's more about the money than out of friendship."

"That's pretty harsh."

She shrugged. Another realist.

"You mean, because of the launch?" I still didn't know what their product was, but I threw out the words like bait.

"The *launch*." She threw it right back as if it had a bitter taste. "I don't know—" But before she could finish her sentence, Chris was by her side.

"Del, everyone's waiting," he said, keeping his voice low. He turned toward me. "Do you mind?"

I didn't budge, and he stepped between us, wrapping one meaty paw around my wrist. I fought the urge to pull away. This might be concern, but it was misguided. I looked up into a face as stolid as a tree and met his gaze with everything I had. He didn't blink. We could both feel people staring at us, but he held on for another few seconds, making his point, before he released me with a nod and walked away. Delia followed.

I sighed and rubbed my arm. No way could I hitch a ride with that crowd. About twenty feet away, a uniformed driver was opening a door for Nora Harris. Jim Creighton was standing by her side, supporting her. Waiting for her assistant.

"I'm sorry." Delia turned back toward me, her voice low but clear. "I don't mean anything bad about Mack. It's just that he was the money man, you know? He had a lot invested in this."

I nodded. No, I didn't know. The birds were at top volume now, declaring themselves and their territory. It was getting hard to focus.

"Coming?" I blinked. Mack was beside me, car keys in hand. How much had he heard?

"I'll be there." But as we headed toward the parking lot, a cry spun me back around. Nora Harris had fainted. The chauffeur and Jim Creighton were laying her on the ground. Delia was racing to her side. "Oh my God." I surged toward them, but Mack grabbed my arm, holding me back.

"Let them be. She's had these spells before, and that cop can get an ambulance here faster than any of us, if she needs one."

I pulled away, annoyed at his presumption. But what he'd said made sense, and I only walked as far as the small crowd that had gathered, buzzing like a hive.

"Poor woman. The service, the shock." Most of the congregation was waiting and watching, it seemed. "And she's still driving?" "He was so young." "Such a sadness!"

"That wasn't grief." Through the hum of vague sympathy, one voice sounded clear. The speaker was the wiry man who had moved in to make room for me. I looked at him, but he was speaking to his wife. "That was shock. I heard what the cop was saying to her. He just told Mrs. Harris that her son was murdered."

# Chapter Eleven

I was dying to barge right in. Murder? I'd known that from the start, but how did the cops? And why tell her now, at the funeral? Perhaps more to the point, if they were now considering this a homicide, that meant a human was responsible—and Lily should be off the hook.

It wasn't graceful, but I confess I pushed the wiry man out of my way, determined to get to Creighton and find out more. Before I could go three steps, a strong pair of hands grabbed me from behind, nearly swinging me around.

"Whoa, there, little lady." It was Mack again, looking amused. "And where do you think you're going?"

"I just heard." I tried to pull away, but he was strong. "I've got to talk to that cop."

"You do?" He wasn't letting go. "Is that wise?"

He'd leaned in to ask that second question, and although his breath was warm on my ear, there was a note in his voice I didn't like. A hiss, almost, like he knew something I didn't want him to, and it acted on me like a slap, bringing me right back to earth. We were standing on the edge of the crowd and while most of the black-clad attendees were watching the opened limo, where the grieving mother now sat with her head bowed to her lap, a few stragglers had turned toward us. Animals know when to play dead, and I stood still, waiting for him to release me.

"Good girl." He noticed, and let me go. "Now, tell old Mack what you're up to."

I opened my mouth to speak and drew a blank. I couldn't exactly tell him about Lily, not and be believed. But I had to say something. "Look, that bombshell the cop just dropped? That's not news," I said, finally. "I knew that Charles wasn't killed by his dog, and I need to find out what that cop knows."

Mack looked like he was going to grab me again, so I kept on talking. "I'm more than a trainer," I said. "I'm a behaviorist, or almost. I didn't quite finish my training."

I was explaining more than I had to, a sure sign of panic. To stop my own blabbering, I closed my mouth and swallowed hard. "I worked with Charles, and I worked with his dog," I said, my voice back under control. "He rescued that dog that from a horrible fate, and the dog knew it."

Mack smiled, but I cut in before he could make a snide comment.

"I'm not anthropomorphizing, Mack. Some animals are loyal; that's their innate nature, and Lily—that is, Tetris—had that classic dog temperament. I don't know what happened that morning, but I can tell you one thing. I've worked with animals all my professional life, and that dog did not kill Charles."

"Well, maybe not by choice. And, yeah, I heard what you said the other night. But can't they be trained to attack?" He looked quizzical now, like he was actually thinking about what I'd said.

"Not their owners." And before he could take the next step that the young cop had, that maybe their *trainers* could issue the command, I stepped back, out of his reach. "Now, if you'll excuse me—"

"Not so fast." He didn't grab me, quite, but he did put his hand on my arm. I whirled and glared up at him. We call it establishing dominance.

"You are not my keeper." I kept my voice low, but something in my tone must have carried. Out of the corner of my eye, I saw Albert smirk. Great, more grist for the town gossip mill.

"Hey!" Mack threw both hands up in mock surrender, stepping back as he did so. "My bad, sorry." He was talking louder now; a couple standing a dozen feet away turned to stare. "I just thought we could talk about this, maybe over coffee later." That grin again, wide and easy. Sexy as hell, and he knew it. "After all," his voice dropped again, low and confidential, "it doesn't seem like you really want to go to the gravesite. And there's nobody left for you to question."

I whipped around again and kicked the dirt in frustration. Sure enough, the limo had left, taking with it Charles' mother, Delia, and, I assumed, Creighton. But lingering by the curb, his short cropped hair half a head above the small crowd, stood Chris Moore.

"Excuse me," I said, my tone having nothing polite about it, and made my way over to the tall former athlete. If I couldn't question Delia, I'd start on her once and future beau. "Chris! Chris Moore?" I had to push my way past several people to get to him and when I did, I reached out to get his attention, putting my hand on a bicep of granite. Maybe he hadn't meant to hurt me before. "It is Chris, right? I'm sorry if I was monopolizing Delia before. It's been ages." I smiled up at him, determined to win a second chance. Man, he was tall.

"That's okay." He was shaking his head, about to say he didn't know me, when suddenly a neuron fired and that heavy face lit up. For a jock, he had half a brain. In high school, I had a certain notoriety. "Pru Marlowe. It is still Marlowe, isn't it?"

"Yeah." My smile widened with relief, and I pulled him further from the crowd. "I just moved back a few months ago. I was working with Charles—Chuck—Harris?"

He smiled back, and I did my best to bat my eyelids. Whatever works. I needed information.

"Delia said something."

I was sure she had, but at least Chris had given me my in. "I remember you and Delia back in high school." His grin had faded, but I upped the wattage on mine. "Looks like you two are still friends."

"Yeah?" A wariness crept into his eyes and he pulled away, just a bit. I reached out to hold his other arm, hoping the contact would convey warmth or security. Damn, this was easier with animals.

"She's just been through so much." Falling back on my training, I lowered my voice and kept the tone even. "I would imagine she needs support now." It worked; he seemed to be calming.

"Yeah, well, not everyone sees it that way." He looked back to where a dozen stragglers were still milling by the curb, and by reflex, I did, too, in time to see someone turn away. We must have made an odd pairing, especially if they'd seen our face-off only a few minutes before. "People can be mean."

"Tell me about it." I heard the edge in my own voice and decided to use it. "I know how gossipy this town can be. Beauville as Peyton Place."

He smiled in recognition, despite the vintage of my reference. I guessed even jocks know TV. "Everyone here knows we *were* an item, and so now…"

He didn't have to finish the thought. I nodded in sympathy and then caught myself. I wasn't questioning him out of nostalgia. I was searching for a murderer. Could this tall block of a man be the one? How well did I really know Chris Moore? The old images that came to mind were all stereotypes. Chris Moore had been that rarity, a straight shooter. The high school basketball star who hadn't drunk or wrecked his dad's car. Mr. Clean Cut All-American Beauville. He and I never hung out in the same crowd, but we knew about each other.

It didn't seem likely, but something this brutal seldom was. And I'd seen how he looked at Delia, how he'd moved in when he felt I was threatening her. Clearly, the fires still burned. But were those fires hot enough to turn this man from a high-school hero into a cold-blooded killer? Those wounds had been vicious, claw-like slashes. Three, at least, side by side. For someone to tear open Charles' throat like that, not to mention stage a scene that would frame an innocent animal, there was more than momentary passion at work.

I sized him up, trying to see him as a stranger would. Like Detective Creighton. With his broad features and that short-cut hair, Chris still looked like a small town poster boy. Creighton seemed young enough to know him from school. Maybe he'd seen him play, cheered him on. But the muscles beneath my hands were iron hard. And Chris had the height and the reach to overpower anyone I knew.

He cleared his throat, and I realized I'd been staring at him. Would he think I was sweet on him? That could be useful, but for now I dropped my hands. "People are going to wonder." I heard the chill creeping into my voice. I couldn't help it, not with these new thoughts racing through my mind. "Particularly now, when she doesn't exactly seem to be broken up over his death."

"Hey, she's a *friend*. Do you mind?" He pulled back, and I was struck again by his size, by his strength. "I don't know what she saw in him. I never understood what was going on with them, but it was her choice, and I respected that, okay?"

"Okay!" I raised my hands in a placating gesture. He had the temper all right, but he also sounded honestly wounded. I started to think of dog tricks. He needed soothing. I could do this. But as I reached out, more slowly this time, he spun on his heels and stalked off. I turned around and saw that the remaining crowd was staring at me. I plastered a fake smile on my face and waved, before making my own retreat.

I took my frustration out on my old Toyota, gunning its tiny engine and leaving rubber on the corner. Something was going on here that I didn't understand, and I hated being played like that. Even by a good-looking man who seemed to enjoy flirting with me.

My mood hadn't lifted by the time I got home, and I threw my bag with such force onto the kitchen table that Wallis jumped up with alarm from her post on the windowsill.

"Sorry, Wallis." I mumbled. The anger was beginning to wear off.

"I was awake anyway." She stretched. Possibly all cats, certainly Wallis, like to pretend they're on top of every situation, despite the fact that, as obligate carnivores, they sleep three-quarters of the day. "I've been waiting for you to come home."

"Oh?" I pulled off my boots and waited for her to comment. The fact that she didn't convinced me that she really must have something on her mind.

"It's that kitten." Wallis rearranged herself on the windowsill as I looked around. "She's upstairs, asleep on our bed."

I slid into a chair and waited. I could use more coffee, but Wallis found the grinder annoying. She also likes to build drama.

"I wonder if there might be something wrong with her. Developmentally." She licked her paw in a desultory fashion. I waited. "I'm having trouble coming up with a better diagnosis."

"What's she saying, Wallis?" I didn't know how seriously to take my cat's concerns. After all, she had a vested interest in being not only the smartest one in the room, but also the only cat in the house.

"It's partly the fixation on the box." Wallis tucked her paw underneath her chest, her distaste showing in the way she drew her head back. "It's overdone. And the constant crying for her 'Mama.' I mean, really, Pru. She's been weaned."

"Maybe she's homesick, Wallis." It's rare when I'm the sentimental one in the conversation, but my heart did go out to the little orange kitten.

"Like that *dog.*" Wallis sniffed and turned away. I'd been dismissed.

With a sigh—I really did want more coffee—I pushed myself out of the chair and headed up the stairs. With Lily out of immediate danger, I might as well try to put my own house in order. Sure enough, the kitten was asleep on my bed. She'd propped herself up, sphinx-like, with her feet tucked under her. But unlike Wallis, she didn't yet have an adult cat's sense of balance. While her body held the "meatloaf" pose, all four feet tucked under, her head had fallen forward so that she was sleeping on her face. For a moment, my heart melted. Then a flash of panic kicked in. Could she breathe?

"Kitten!" I raced over to the bed, but before I could grab her, she'd woken. Two blue eyes blinked up at me. "*Mama?*"

"Sorry, honey." How can anyone be cross around a kitten? But even as I settled on the bed beside her, I saw her mood shift as she woke fully.

*"I didn't do anything wrong."* The woeful mew was so soft I had to bend forward to hear her. *"I didn't."*

"Of course not, kitten." I stroked her back. Compared to Wallis, she was a mere handful of fur. Touching her, I picked up the sadness and confusion behind her protest. This wasn't a developmentally challenged animal. Something bad had happened—and she felt responsible.

I felt her relax a little under my hand and took a gamble. Scooping the tiny body up, I held her to my chest. Not that long ago, she'd have been nursing, and I counted on the warmth and the beat of my heart to calm her.

*"Mama."* The cry was silent now, the plaintive wail of her heart, but it still made my throat close up. I continued stroking her as I thought about posing my next question.

"You're a good girl. Yes, you are." Murmuring softly into the downy fur of her back, I tried to think in images, to let the emotion behind the words color my memories of her using her litterbox, eating from her dish, and finally of her asleep on my bed. "A very good girl." I felt her relax, and decided to try my question. "Why do you think you're bad?"

The tiny body tensed. Damn, this was so much easier with Wallis. "You're a good kitty. Yes, you are." I cooed and stroked another few minutes, finally perching on the edge of the bed. This wasn't going to be quick by any means. "Very good."

Time to try again. "Who yelled at you? Who said you were bad?"

*"They both did."* The thought came quick and strong. *"They were loud. Very loud. I didn't do anything wrong."*

The small face lifted to me and the tiny red mouth opened in an almost silent mew. *"Mama? Why, Mama? Why?"*

◇◇◇

There really wasn't any answer I could give to that, and I lay back on the bed, holding the small kitten until she fell asleep again. Sunday afternoon, I had no work pressing. Nowhere to be. At some point, I felt a thud as Wallis joined us. Coffee is a great invention, but sometimes a nap with your cats fits the bill.

# Chapter Twelve

"I'm here about your cat." It was not quite eight when I rang the doorbell, but the short, sharp-looking woman who answered the door already had her coat over her arm. I'd called on Saturday, and the message waiting for me after the funeral had asked me to come "as early as possible" on Monday. For most people, that means nine-ish, so I'd walked the bichon and made more coffee before swinging by the new development known as "Overlook Ridge." I was glad I hadn't waited any longer. The woman at the door looked like I'd caught her on her way out, dressed in a smart grey suit. The skirt ended just above her knees, and the shoes were the kind that out here we call "city." She must have been forty-five, if a day, but her legs were up to it, and I got the sense that she knew they were her best feature. There wasn't anything wrong with the rest of her either. Underneath a helmet of sleek, black hair she had skin like ivory, so smooth I knew it couldn't all be natural, with only a slight puffiness under her dark eyes to give the game away. She knew how to play it though. Her face was made up, down to the lip liner, but not overdone, and her expression was blank as she blinked at me.

"You're Eleanor Shrift, right?" I was waiting for her to register me as human, and the wait was putting an edge in my voice. "You have a black Persian with Doc Sharp?"

She nodded, not a hair moving out of place.

"I'm a behaviorist. I work with animals that come into the county shelter." I held out a hand. She glanced down at it. "My name's Pru, Pru Marlowe."

"A behaviorist? But why?" We were still standing at her front door. I was beginning to feel like a Bible salesman.

"You do have a black Persian, right?" I'd be damned if I said "owned." "A beautiful cat with some behavior problems? I mean, if he's not your cat—" I started to turn away.

"No, no. That's my cat. I just, well. I thought the vet could give him some Prozac or something. I mean, he has this *wound.*" She fluttered dark lacquered nails at her own cheek, and I nodded, mainly to get her to stop. "It's disgusting, that's why I brought him in."

"He's in distress." I heard the edge in my own voice. This wasn't an issue of aesthetics. "That's why I'm here."

"But he's doing it to himself!" I opened my mouth and paused. I'm much better at communicating with animals. Always was, even before. But she didn't give me a chance to form the words. "If this is some kind of new service, I'm all for it. Not now, though. I've got an eleven a.m. flight."

I bit my lip. She'd been the one who'd said Monday morning, and then neglected to set a time. Truth was, the cat was better off in the shelter. But I don't like to give an inch to types like this. "When will you be back?" I made the effort to keep my voice steady. "Because as soon as possible, I need to talk with you, to see the living situation and try to figure out what is making that poor animal so unhappy."

"Unhappy?" I saw a flicker of something behind the mascara. For a moment, even with the Botox, Ms. Shrift looked human. "I didn't think—"

I waited. This was getting interesting. And possibly useful as well; this wouldn't be the first time an unhappy person had inflicted pain in some way on a pet. She must have sensed my interest because she stopped talking.

"No, most people don't." I was beyond politeness. "Look, when can I come back? We need to talk."

"Tomorrow, I'll be back tomorrow." She turned to close the door, but I had my foot in it. Her former poise was gone, something had shaken her. It made my job easier.

"Wanna set a time this time?" She was signaling fear or some kind of distress, her breath coming short and fast between those dark red lips. "We'll need about an hour."

"I'll be getting in around midday." Her eyes were darting around like caged sparrows. "Come by anytime in the afternoon. We can have drinks!" From the upward lilt of her voice, it sounded like drinks were often the highpoint of the day. This would be a business call for me, and I was in no mood to chill out with an animal abuser. I grunted something that sounded like assent and backed off, letting her slam her door shut.

I sat in my car for a few minutes, just for my own curiosity. Sure enough, within five, she was out the door, her purse banging against her hip and one of those rolling carry-ons bumping along behind her. Wherever she was going, I hoped she'd have a chance to pull herself together. The flawless ice queen who'd first greeted me had been cracked.

◇◇◇

Since I was doing so well with people today, I decided to head on over to the pound. By the time I'd get there, it would be nearly ten. Even if Albert wasn't in, someone should have opened the office by then.

Albert was getting out of his own car as I turned into the small lot. The junker had been a muscle car at some point, but it had as much wear on it as the animal control officer himself. Today, he'd topped the customary flannel—a red plaid—with a tan down vest. A splotch of duct tape showed where the nylon shell had been ripped.

"Hey, Albert," I called as I pulled up to a space.

"Oh, hey, Pru." He was juggling a large coffee and a grease-spotted bag. More donuts, I guessed. Or maybe some roadkill he'd picked up on his way in and planned on reheating for lunch. "Go on in."

I nodded, but waited by my car as he opened the trunk and rummaged around, balancing the coffee mug on the fender. I didn't think it likely that he'd keep his pet in the back, no matter how spacious it was, but I still felt a sharp stab of disappointment when he straightened up with only a bunch of papers in his fist. As he struggled to close the trunk, I raced over to grab the bag and he jerked back, nearly spilling his coffee.

"Relax, Albert. It just looked like you needed a hand."

"I've got it under control," said Albert, as best I could tell. He was holding the bag in his teeth and had the papers pressed against his body, the mug in his hand, as he reached up for the heavy trunk lid. "There."

"Suit yourself." The idea of handling the bag after it had been in his mouth went too far, even for charity, and I followed the big man through the glass doors. He dropped the bag on his desk and shoved the papers into the lower drawer. I peered over the desk top, hoping to see a familiar masked face. "No Fr— Bandit today?" It didn't seem likely, but the possibility did exist that Albert had been in early and simply gone out for donuts.

"Why're you so interested in my ferret, Pru?" He beamed and I smiled back, letting him enjoy his little obscene allusion for a moment.

"I'm always drawn to the most intelligent male in the room."

"Ha. Ha." His face deflated. He then put his feet up and took a long draw of his coffee. Clearly, I was being punished.

I wasn't going to ask. Instead, I strolled over to the ledger over and started looking through it. No further sign of Delia Cochrane, but neither, I realized, were there many other visitors.

"Business slow, these days?" I flipped back another page. Only three people had come by on a Saturday?

"What?" Albert pretended to be absorbed in whatever he was reading, but the desire to appear important was too strong. "No way, we were packed all day. Those new people, they don't know how to winterize, and they come to me when they get squirrels in their attics."

I made a sympathetic noise, ignoring the chance to point out that nuisance animal removal was, in fact, part of his job. So not everyone who came by signed in. Considering all I knew about Albert, I shouldn't have been surprised. Why had Delia signed in, then? And who might have just walked by the open log?

"So, uh, do you want to see the keychain thing?" In my preoccupation, I'd outwaited Albert.

"Sure thing, Al." I smiled up at him. "Bring it on."

I was curious about those papers, but he shoved them back in the drawer, and I told myself that they might actually be related to his job. At any rate, they were out of my reach. I watched as he took a key out of the top drawer and opened the locked bottom file of the tall file cabinet, pulling out a metal box, the kind people keep their important papers in.

"I wanted to keep it safe," said Albert, as he dusted off the little box and placed it on his desk. If it weren't for the cleanliness issue, I realized, Albert really would resemble his ferret.

I pulled up the guest chair and waited as Albert opened the box and began poking through its contents. "Lots of stuff in there?" I tried to keep my voice neutral.

"It's not just Bandit," he sounded a bit defensive. "People leave stuff all the time." He took out an envelope that had been folded twice to fit, and I wondered what letter had never been posted. "Ah, here it is."

Licking his finger, he reached in and pulled out a small, grey oblong, about the size of an eraser. Even as he held it, I could see the broken silver ring that must have once held the drive onto a keychain. I held out my hand, and with an audible sigh, Albert relinquished his treasure.

"Thanks, Al. This looks like mine." I wasn't lying; I had a portable drive just like it with all my class notes. "So, um, you didn't take a peek at the files?"

Albert smiled. "Got your diary on it, do you?" His voice had taken on the tone of that smile, and I resisted the urge to cut him dead. "Wonder who I'd find in there, Pru. Your old boss?"

"Charles was a client." I turned the drive over in my hands. The USB port seemed intact, and I couldn't wait to leave. But before I did, I had a few more questions that needed answering.

"What about Mack then?" he asked.

I did my best to impale Albert with an icy glare. Small town gossip needs to be plucked out by its roots, like a tick. "What about Mack?"

"You two seemed to be having a little tiff yesterday. Lovers' quarrel? Did you expect our Mack to change his ways for you?"

"Change his ways?" From Albert's broadening grin, I knew I'd said the wrong thing, and waved him down. "Never mind. No. We're not an item. Never were. We were talking money." I was improvising now, but I knew that if I didn't give the gossip gods a different story this one would dog me. "He was Charles' business partner, and I'm owed for my services." I caught myself. "For my dog training. He was telling me I had to get in line behind other creditors. Once we find out who inherits."

"Lots of luck with that." Albert was positively grinning now. What didn't I know? I'd brought up my unpaid bills as a distraction, but in truth, I could use the dough. The question was, how could I find anything out without giving anything away?

"Well, that's the problem." I was stalling, trying to think of a way to use the little I did know as bait. "I knew they were getting close to launch, and Charles was always going on about how successful they were."

"From what I heard, Charles was the *last* person to talk about money."

I waited, but he didn't say more. "Well, we each have our own sources."

"Yes, we do." Well, that was intriguing.

"Speaking of, I was hoping to get in touch with Delia." I nodded toward the open logbook. "Has she been back?"

"Nuh-uh," Albert shook his head, forlorn. Her visit must have been the high point of his day. "I don't think she likes me much."

What a surprise. "Who knew? But I was sure she'd been in the other day."

"Yeah, but I had to send her to the shelter." He was poking through the box now. "Her cat wasn't here."

That made me sit up. "Her cat?"

"Yeah, she lost a kitten. I told her the coyotes probably got it."

"A little orange and white thing?" Poor woman. Her boyfriend and now her pet. I felt sorry for her, but I had to be sure. Albert nodded, and I was. Now I had a new problem: how to explain that I had her kitten—and that I had broken through police tape to find her. "I'll keep my eyes open. Where did she lose it?"

"She didn't say, but I'll tell you, she was looking daggers at that dog. I'm wondering if she and Chuck had a falling out, and he fed it to that animal."

"Not likely." I'd have to think of a way out of this, sooner rather than later. My heart went out to anyone who thinks she's lost a pet, even someone like Delia. And that kitten was now evidence. What kind of evidence, I wasn't yet sure of. But Albert had also given me my opening. "So how is Charles' dog?" I should have dropped by over the weekend. Man, I was growing soft.

"It's calmed down some. Let me guess, you want to visit." He opened the drawer to replace the box, sparking me out of my pity party.

"Yeah, I do. But first, Albert, you said something about an earring?"

He looked a little peeved—maybe he was more magpie than ferret—but reopened the box and dug around.

"Here it is. One's not much use, though. Unless you have someplace special pierced." He leered, and I scowled in return. But even as I reached for the hanging sparkler, I gasped. As he held up the long earring—easily two inches of glitter—it caught the light. It might as well have caught fire. Gingerly, I laid it flat on my fingers and held it up close to examine the multi-pronged setting. This earring was no cheap rhinestone doodad. The delicate setting, the artful safety catch, the cut—these all signaled the good stuff, or at least a killer copy. If this was the real thing, then what I held in my hand was worth most of what I owned, my mother's house included. Someone would be missing this.

# Chapter Thirteen

If only the rest of my day turned up more treasure, but I couldn't count on such luck. And as much as I wanted to examine that flash drive, after a short visit with Lily, I stuck it in my pocket and drove over to the county shelter. I was probably on a fool's errand, and I knew it. Plus, I was putting more miles on my little Toyota than I'd done all summer. But I was running short of paying clients, and nobody was racing to pay my overdue bills. Besides, now that I'd met Eleanor Shrift, I felt even more for her beautiful mess of a cat.

I could have saved myself the trip. The black Persian didn't know I was there. Didn't know he was there, either, I suspected. That hard-looking Eleanor Shrift must have gotten through to Doc Sharp, or else the vet was desperate to stop the cat from hurting himself further. He was so loopy on some combination of antidepressants or tranquilizers that I couldn't get any sense out of his smooth black head. *"Here, here, here,"* he kept repeating, his third eyelid half closed, masking unfocused eyes. *"Here."*

"Where, kitty? What are you trying to say?" I took the inert body into my arms, trying to listen in on what was happening. All I picked up on was an urge to groom—a sense of sleek fur and of the comfort of a regular pattern—and so I stroked that midnight head until he fell into a deeper sleep, with dreams too subtle for me to read.

I sat with him a few more minutes, just enjoying the gentle bulk of him. Ever since Wallis and I had started communicating,

I'd felt a little odd about holding her. It seemed at once too intimate and vaguely disrespectful. You might hug a friend in greeting, but did you heft her onto your lap? No.

The third time the vet tech came into check on me, I put the Persian back. The good news was that Pammy had other animals for me to look at, requests from Doc Sharp. With Charles out of the picture, I needed all the referrals I could get. And so the rest of my afternoon was filled with routine. A bored spaniel who had taken it out on her person's sofa. A mixed-breed puppy who loved the shrieks and squeals when he bit. As always, the people, not the animals, needed their behavior modified, although I'd learned how to pose the problem as an issue of training.

"Don't yelp. Don't hit. Just walk away." How often had I told some clueless human that? "What he wants is the attention. He thinks you're playing. If you simply leave him alone at the first sign of aggression, he'll stop doing it." I'd be seeing them again within the month, if that puppy didn't get put up for adoption first.

"Be good." I whispered to the tiny creature as I put him back in his carrier. How much did he understand? I wasn't optimistic. In puppy terms, he *was* being good. He was playing; he was learning to hunt. That was his role, and he was perfect for the world he knew. If only these stupid humans would quit messing him up.

All of which brought me back to Eleanor Shrift and her suffering cat. Under the influence of the drugs, the open sore was scabbing up. With luck, the fur would grow back, too. But the underlying problem was driving me as nutty as that cat. What had that woman done? I peeked in on the sleeping cat one more time, getting nothing for my troubles but the image of a hand stroking him, and drove home with more questions than I'd gotten answers for. That black Persian was a puzzle, but I'd get to the bottom of that. Eleanor Shrift might look tough, but as soon as she returned she was going to have me to deal with, not some sad cat. More urgent, at least in my mind, were the questions of the kitten, the flash drive, and the earring. How could I tell Delia that I had her cat, when the cops had seen me during what was supposed to be my last visit to Charles' house?

Could I pretend I'd found it outside? What excuse would I give her for being outside her boyfriend's house? And why had she brought that little creature to Charles' house anyway?

And what about that earring? As soon as I realized the potential value of that sparkler, I'd wanted to claim it. Albert had been too smart for me. He'd seen the shock on my face and slipped it from my hand before I could tuck it away. "Bring the other and its yours," he'd said. Too smart, or too covetous. I wouldn't be surprised if that earring ended up in an Albany pawn shop, sold for the value of the stones. How could someone lose a jewel like that and not be looking for it high and low? I thought of the yelling that the kitten had overheard. Sounded like Delia and Charles had a lot to fight about.

What with the kitten, the Persian, and that drive, I was afraid I'd given Lily short shrift. Albert was right, she had calmed down. But although my cursory visit showed me that, yes, the poor dog had stopped hurling herself against the bars of her cage—and, in all fairness, her enclosure did seem to be cleaner—I couldn't stop thinking about her as I drove back to Beauville. Lily was suffering, and her environment wasn't helping. I'd spent a few quiet minutes with her after my chat with Albert, but I didn't know that it did any good. Even when I took her out back for a quick walk and a pet, she barely acknowledged me, only stopping to do the necessary and paw halfheartedly at the ground. All I got were images of Charles, and I had the feeling that these were fading fast. I'd bought her a reprieve, finding that certificate, but she wasn't as tough as she appeared and incarceration was taking its toll. As I looked into her eyes, trying to make some kind of contact, I knew it was up to me to come up with a way out.

"I hear they're looking for the killer finally," I had whispered to her, rubbing my thumbs against the velvet base of her ears. "We'll get him." The eyes that looked up in response were huge and sad and lost. *Home?* The whine was barely audible. *Home?* I shook my head. "I'm sorry, puppy."

I did my best to shut out thoughts of that poor beast as I pulled up to my own home. Wallis would never be sympathetic to a dog, and I had other work to do that I might need her feedback on. Fingering the keychain drive in my pocket, I unlocked my front door to find the stout tabby waiting.

"Finally." She gave me the unnerving, unblinking stare cats use so well. "You owe me."

"Oh?" I walked by her toward the laptop I keep in what had been my mother's formal living room. Nice thing about walking by an angry cat. She has to trot to keep up, and it cuts into her dignity.

"That kitten." I stopped dead in my tracks and looked down at Wallis. She paid me back by proceeding to wash her face. I knew this game. I waited. Finally she put both paws back down on the hardwood floor. "I don't know what you unleashed, but she's been crying all day. Something about a fight. No, don't get all excited." I didn't know if she'd read my mind or my face, but I shut my mouth, swallowing the questions that were forming. "Nothing specific. Just that there were loud voices—that's voices, plural—and that it scared her. If I hear, 'I didn't do anything wrong' one more time, I will not be held responsible."

"Thanks, Wallis." I turned her report over in my head. "And I'm sorry." There wasn't much new here, but the fact that two people had been arguing confirmed some of my suspicions. The raised voice hadn't been on the phone, the fight was in the house. Delia must have brought her over to Charles' house and then forgotten her after the fight.

" 'Salright." Wallis shifted a little on the hardwood, a precursor to kneading. She was in a good mood, and I was glad for the company.

"Do you want to look at this with me?" I didn't expect much, but flattery works, and she leaped to the desk top with an unfeline enthusiasm. I plugged the keychain drive in, and we both watched the screen, eager in anticipation. "I'm not sure what we'll find here," I warned as the laptop whirred.

"Is that it?" An icon had shown up on my screen, and Wallis' quick eyes, attuned to small movements, spotted it first. I clicked on it and breathed a sigh of relief to find it wasn't password protected. As I opened the first file, Wallis came closer, her soft fur brushing against my hand.

"What's that?" She stared at the screen, and I enlarged the image with a few keystrokes. Wallis is slightly myopic, as much as she denies it.

"A spreadsheet," I murmured in response. "God, I hate spreadsheets." We both leaned in, and I felt the tickle of whiskers on my cheek. "I don't really understand, but it seems someone was doing accounting online." Wallis said nothing, but I felt her warmth next to me as I opened one form and scrolled down columns of numbers. "This could be anything. A budget, a mortgage statement…"

"Mouse tracks." Wallis' voice was low, but I could tell by the angle of her ears and her whiskers that she was concentrating. "It seems like…mouse tracks. Or maybe the dirt after the sparrows have had their dust baths."

I looked over at the tabby. "You're kidding, right? I mean, I don't know what they're for, but…"

She turned, her green-gold eyes alert, and then she blinked. "Well, *you* said you didn't understand those markings. I thought I'd give it a try."

"Wallis, I meant I didn't know what the numbers signified." She blinked again. "You do know they're numbers, right? Symbols for money or something that's been measured." Another blink, and I sighed. "You don't, do you?"

I should've been more careful. I should have noticed that in the last few seconds Wallis' black-tipped ears had tilted back, that her paws had stopped kneading. That, in fact, her claws were already partly distended. If I'd been working with her, as a client, I'd have been more alert, but the truth was, I'd forgotten to think of Wallis as a cat and had just started to think of her as a friend—a human friend.

"I'm sorry, Wallis, I forgot—" As I spoke, I reached up to pet her, hoping to smooth her ruffled fur. But she was too fast for me, and I'd gone too far. With a hiss, she swiped at me, her eyes staring and wild. "Wallis!" I pulled my hand back and sucked at the scratch, a red line in the meaty base of my thumb.

"Stupid numbers. Stupid *humans.*" Her ears were still back, but she had settled down, and was grumbling to herself on my desk. "Why don't you ask a *dog* to read those scribbles? Why don't you get that *kitten* to make sense of it? Am I the only nonhuman sensible creature you know around here?"

"Okay, I'm leaving now." I knew better than to mess with a pissed-off cat. I reached, gingerly, for my laptop as Wallis turned her back, allowing me to retreat. Setting the computer on the kitchen table, I found myself staring at it without really seeing. My relationship with Wallis felt so tentative, and I realized, sitting there and watching the shadows reach across the table, how much I relied on her. I'd wanted company, sure. I'd also wanted a second opinion, unsure of what I would find. Was I asking too much of a cat? Had this blowup been in the works?

I shook my head to clear it. Worrying about such things was a luxury I couldn't afford. What I needed to do was find out what had been going on—with Charles, with Delia. With Mack, for sure. And, yeah, maybe with that cop Creighton, too.

If Lily had indeed been cleared of Charles' death, my relationship with Creighton could relax a little. I could think about passing along the few things I had learned. I'd have to come up with some kind of explanation, but I'd find a way, some way, to let him know about the yelling downstairs, about the strange, sweet scent. Delia's kitten might be some kind of proof, and Lily's memory of that morning, the sight of something horrible happening just outside her crate. That had to be worth something. They'd be searching for a person now—

With a shiver, I felt the other shoe drop. If Creighton and his colleagues were now looking for a human killer, they might just be looking at me. Creighton had implied as much, but at the time, I'd not taken him seriously. Now, though, I'd have to.

At the very least, how would I ever be able to explain why I had Delia's kitten?

I was in a mess, and this time Wallis wouldn't—probably couldn't—help me. I fixed my eyes on the screen, the weight of my situation sinking in, and watched the numbers roll down. The movement was hypnotic. Soothing, until something caught me eye and woke me from my musings. There: a date, 9/21, and a number, 210. I scrolled back to 9/01 and saw it again, and then back some more. It didn't mean anything; these were numbers, not signatures. But the dates matched up to the ones on my invoices, and the amounts were my city rate. I was perusing Charles' budget, or some part of it, and my little bills were by far the smallest amount entered by a power of ten.

As soon as seemed reasonable, I headed back to Happy's. It wasn't that I needed companionship, though Wallis was still not talking to me and had, pointedly, sent the kitten to ask for their dinner cans when I started putting together my own meal. Nor was it the warm buzz of alcohol I craved, though I did perk up at the thought of a good stiff drink. No, what I needed were answers, the kind that only other humans could give me. And while the telephone is a lovely instrument, I somehow suspected that catching people unawares, and possibly under the influence, would give me the best chance of uncovering the information I needed. Besides, the phone works both ways. If Creighton had more questions for me, he could come looking, too.

Just my luck, then, that neither Delia nor Chris nor Mack were visible as I entered the dark bar. Yes, it was a Monday, but that didn't seem like any reason for this trio not to drink. I had no idea what Chris did for a living, but Mack seemed to be a private investor—and out of a job. And Delia should still be grieving. I took up a post at the far end of the curved wood bar, where I had a clear view of the front door and close enough to the back to hear if anyone was stepping in. I indulged myself in a Jameson's, neat, and settled in to wait.

Two drinks later, I was getting sick of the bartender's taste in music. I'd pushed myself off my stool to feed some quarters into the jukebox and was just deciding between Tom Jones and Lou Reed—Happy's was nothing if not eclectic—when I heard the back door swing open. I turned, too, realizing belatedly that the third whiskey had probably been a mistake.

"Hey, Pru. You all right?" It was Albert, and he was coming toward me with his arms outstretched.

"I'm fine." I straightened up. "Thanks." I made my way back to the bar. The place was empty, but Albert sat right beside me. Ah well, I wanted to talk.

"So, Al, how's the ferret?"

"Hey, Haps, she's asking about my ferret!" This occasioned much laughter from Albert and a humorless grin from the bartender, who brought over a Pabst without asking.

"He's not the real Happy, you know." I sipped my Jameson's, then made myself put the heavy glass down.

"But I bet he's real happy you're here." Albert leaned close, and I tensed to keep myself from recoiling. I wanted information. "So, you celebrating?" My face must have answered his question. "I mean, getting your drive back?" He emphasized the word "drive" just a little too much for my comfort, and I shot him a look. "A girl could say 'thanks,' you know."

"I did, Albert. Even though it was your ferret that stole it."

He accepted the truth of that, and we drank companionably for a while, him finishing one beer and gesturing for another. Me sipping as slowly as I could. At some point, he noticed and nodded toward my half-empty lowball glass. "You waiting for someone?"

I must have appeared confused, because he answered his own question. "Mack, maybe?"

I started to wave him off and then reconsidered, remembering our earlier conversation. "I wasn't, but that's not a bad idea. I mean, maybe he's going to take over the business." I was fishing—Charles owed me, not his company—but the bait was a core of truth. "Of course, my bill is probably small potatoes for the proprietor of a software company."

"We'll see if any of those bills get paid." Albert leaned back on the bar and took a long swig of his beer. He was playing me, I could tell. But we weren't in the office now, and I had all the time in the world.

I tried not to sound too curious. "Really?"

He took another swallow and wiped his sleeve across his mouth. "From what I hear, the business was going belly up before it could take off. I also hear the cops are asking questions about the finances."

His imagery was making my head hurt, but he'd raised a good point. "I was wondering about the cops." I spoke slowly, as if I didn't care. "Like, why are they now saying it was murder?"

He shrugged. "Maybe they think Mack killed him for the start-up money. I've seen him here after hours, you know." Albert leaned back on the bar, and I had the distinct impression that he was striking a pose. "And that cop was poking around asking questions about Mack. About you, too, Pru." I didn't respond to that either, and after a few minutes, he gave up and finished his drink. Pulling a five from his wallet, he waited while the bartender brought him change. With a half smile, he counted through it, leaving fifty cents and a few pennies. "I mean, they're saying it's murder now, but I didn't hear anything about a weapon. Maybe they think you sicced the dog on him," he said, without meeting my eyes. "You know, when he couldn't pay up."

# Chapter Fourteen

I tossed and turned for much of the night, trying to reconcile what Albert had told me with my own confusing discoveries. I scared him, I knew that. But I couldn't disregard his threats. They meshed too well with my own worries, and, besides, there seemed to be other connections at work that I should be paying attention to. Still, whether it was my drinking or some gap in my knowledge or understanding, I just couldn't make a comprehensible whole out of it.

What I didn't know was tantalizing, made worse by my own slivers of knowledge. Not just about Lily—or why Charles' death was now being called a murder, but the smaller things. The things within my grasp. For instance, I didn't know enough about spreadsheets or finances to make out if Charles had really been in trouble. I hadn't even examined the other files on the drive. I did recognize my own invoice in that list, and I knew it was by far the smallest amount there. Mack's role in all of this was another question mark. Clearly, Albert was jealous of Charles' partner, maybe because of some unrelated interaction with him in the after-hours world of Happy's or beyond. But I couldn't completely discount what the fat, flannelled animal control officer had said about him, either. I knew myself well enough to know that when I felt sparks, they often came from a loose wire. Mack might be shady. He might just be a ladies' man. The verdict was still out on the handsome financier—or whatever he was.

Thoughts of Mack, those knowing eyes and that generous mouth, were a welcome break from fears of the cops, but they only increased my restlessness. The whiskey didn't help, nor did the absence of Wallis. The kitten came and went throughout the night. But each time I woke, feeling for Wallis on top of the comforter I was reminded again of our squabble. She'd become such a friend to me, a companion instead of a pet, and the only true confidante I had. Had I expected too much? I found it hard to lower my estimation of the tabby. Clearly, I'd pushed too hard.

Tangled dreams finally dragged me down, and I woke at dawn as tired as when I'd retired. My dreams had been full of animals, mostly cats. All of them talking, but in phrases and tones I couldn't understand. I shook my head to clear it of the incipient hangover and looked down at the foot of the bed. I had a headache, and the fog didn't clear. And Wallis was nowhere to be seen.

Sometimes routine can be a good thing. The necessity of showering occasionally, dressing, and feeding myself—along with Wallis' coaching—had gotten me out of bed not that many months ago, and it worked again this morning. Before I tackled the bigger issues, I needed to work out what had actually happened with Wallis. I probably owed her an apology. But in order to keep food on both our plates, I also had a bichon frise to walk and something like a business to get in order.

◇◇◇

"So now they're saying it's murder, did you hear?"

I grunted something noncommittal as I bent to clip on the bichon's lead. I was in no mood for gossip, but I'd take information from wherever I could get it. Tracy Horlick took a deep drag on her cigarette and kept on talking.

"Can you imagine using a dog as a deadly weapon?" The little dog wagged his tail at the concept, and his owner recoiled in mock horror, dropping ash on the floor. "And we let them sleep with us!"

"Is that what they're saying now?" I shouldn't have said anything. I'd been nearly out the door. But ignoring her own pet's obvious desire to run, if not relieve himself, the old gossip dragged me back indoors, surveying the empty street outside dramatically before closing the door.

"I don't know the details." She leaned in and I smelled alcohol, though, come to think of it, that could have been my own breath. "Just that it's murder. And they're having the coroner do an *autopsy*."

She said the word as if it were an obscenity, softly and with glee. I pulled away and tried to hide my own pleasure in disabusing her. "That's standard, Mrs. H. Whenever someone dies unexpectedly, even when they're just hit by a truck." I couldn't help it. I smiled.

It didn't help. She leaned in closer. "I knew you'd know about these things." The booze might not be hers, but the stale cigarette smoke was. "Seeing as how you've lived in the city and all."

"It's not that different out here." I pulled away. "Only, my clients in the city never got killed." That set her back a bit, and before she could recoup, I lifted the leash and reached for the door. "And now I think Bitsy has to go." A little bark emphasized someone's impatience, and I made a mental note to give the miniature dog an extra good run as thanks.

"You'll let me know if you hear anything, won't you?" Tracy Horlick leaned on the doorframe, the bright sunlight showing how faded her housedress was. "I mean, if you learn anything from that dashing young man of yours."

I nodded and waved. There was no point in arguing, and besides, the bichon really did have to go.

"Come on, Bitsy." Poor dog. With any other animal, I'd have made an effort to learn its private name, what it called itself. But this little creature was such a tiny thing, and, I had to admit, I associated it so strongly with its owner. "Go, puppy, go!"

Once we were down by the river, I unhooked the bichon's leash. He took off like a superball, and I followed behind, letting the crisp morning air wipe out last night's fogs. I pretty much kept him in sight, but still, when I heard a small yelp, I jumped.

"Bitsy?" A rustle and a small white face looked up. Good. I owed the dog for extracting me, but if he were taken by a coyote or, hell, even a fox, I'd probably have to leave town. But another yelp followed, and when I crouched down to his level, I saw the problem. Burrs the size of my thumb had gotten into his pretty little curls. One of them must have worked its way under his fur, and I had a hell of a time keeping him calm while I teased them out. Patience wasn't either of our stronger suits, and I finally pulled my knife, slicing through his silky undercoat to remove the last two. First time I'd used my knife since leaving the city.

I had to confess, I had mixed feelings about being in Beauville. On one hand, I'd gotten used to the space. My mother's house, as rundown as it was, felt like the right amount of room, these days. Especially when Wallis and I were at odds. On the other, if I simply took off, went back to New York, maybe I could leave this whole mess behind me. The idea of returning to my former haunts was no longer quite as scary as it had been. I didn't know if I was feeling better, really, or if Beauville had just become too complicated for me. Not just Charles' murder—or Creighton's possible interest in me. This town was all gossip, all the time—and even the wide open hill country seemed too close for anyone to keep secrets for long.

As if on cue, Delia Cochrane came into view, jogging down the path. I flipped the knife closed and slipped it into my jeans.

"Hey!" I raised a hand in greeting. I had a ton of questions for her, none that I'd figured out how to ask. But when she slowed down and circled back, I realized that this might be my best shot.

She slipped off her headset. "Pru. I've been meaning to call you. Thought I'd get you at the funeral, but…" She raised her hand in the universal symbol of frustration.

"It seemed like you had your hands full." What it hadn't seemed like was that the supposed girlfriend was mourning. "How is Charles' mother?"

Her pretty face tightened up in thought. "Not great. I guess it's the shock. The funeral—and what that cop told her—really knocked her for a loop. I took her car keys, and I don't think she even noticed. Except for her garden, she seems really out of it."

I nodded. That, to me, made more sense than Delia's apparent nonchalance. I saw my opening. "It must be really hard on both of you."

Delia looked off down the trail, and I wondered who she was expecting. Chris Moore, perhaps? "Yeah, well, nobody deserves to go that way. Charles was a good guy."

"Yes, he was." We could agree on that. "I guess I didn't know how serious you two were." I was fishing, but it seemed better to approach her this way than to say her kitten had told me they'd been arguing. "That you were engaged."

"It wasn't official. Not really." She shrugged. "We'd talked about it. So, yeah, sure, I'd have married him. Chuck had a good heart, you know?" She must have seen the question in my eyes, cause she went on. "I met him when I was temping, helping out his mother after her fall. He took in strays, you know that."

Did she count herself among those strays? I couldn't think of a way to phrase the question, but her lack of grief seemed to be out there, like the autumn sun.

"Excuse me for saying so, but you don't sound like you were keen on the idea."

Another shrug, which made her honey-toned ponytail bounce. "Maybe I'm in shock, too." She turned back to me and, I swear, she batted her eyelashes. "We made a good couple, though. Don't you think?"

I nodded, but thoughts of the homely programmer's warm heart kept me from saying any more. There was something wrong with this scenario, and I needed to find out what. "So, if you two had an arrangement, do you know what's going to happen to his business?" It was crass, but it was the best I could come up with on the spur of the moment.

"Jesus." Delia wrinkled up her nose. "You sound just like the cops." She pushed the headset back on her head and adjusted the volume. "He left everything to his mother. The lawyer came by after the funeral with all this paperwork. He wanted to take care of her, you know. Chuck, I mean. He was much cooler than any of you could imagine," she said, and took off down the path.

"I didn't get to tell her about the kitten." I was talking to myself, but as I did, I realized the glossy black eyes of the bichon were on me. "Did you get all of that, Bitsy?" I didn't expect an answer, not from such a frivolous little thing. But Wallis' words came back to me. Maybe it was time for me to start talking with a wider range of animals. If Bitsy was half as gossipy as his person, maybe she'd have seen something I could use.

"So what do you think?" I crouched on the path and reached out to the fluff ball.

In response, he sniffed my hand, his nose cool and damp. As he did, I got flashes. Wallis, her thick fur rubbing against these fingers. The dark, rich smell of coffee. Last night's pizza. This was hopeless. I'd have to find out more about Delia and then talk to her again. I pushed myself to my feet.

*"Find out who the father is."* I spun around so fast, my head spun. The little dog was looking up at me and panting, as if eager for more play. *"The father,"* the tiny voice rang in my head. *"Anyone with half a nose can tell she's pregnant."*

I was dying to ask the bichon more, but after that bombshell, he shut down. Could have been the surroundings; we'd reached an oak tree that had been marked by every dog within ten miles. Could have been the dog. I still didn't think bichons had much concentration. But for the first time, I found myself wondering if it was me. My special sensitivity was so new, I'd never questioned it. How it worked, what impression I was making on the animals with whom I could now communicate. None of that had ever come up. Maybe it should have.

I tried to be a little more responsive on the walk home, letting the little dog take me on several detours that seemed important to him, though by the time we got back to town, I was wondering if I'd been naive. I know that Tracy Horlick was ready to spit when we finally returned.

"Well, there you are. I was beginning to wonder if you'd run off with my Bitsy."

"Not likely." As soon as the words were out, I plastered a fake grin on my face. "I mean, he'd be more likely to run off with me. He just seemed extra curious about everything today, so I wanted to give him a chance to sniff around."

"Hmm." The dog's owner sniffed as well. "Curiosity must be in the air."

I didn't want to ask, I really didn't. But it did occur to me that Tracy Horlick might be able to expand on Bitsy's bombshell. Kicking myself just the tiniest bit, I gave her what she wanted. "Oh, really?" I asked.

She smiled, a horrible sight. "Really." She paused for another drag on her cigarette and held it for effect, but I just couldn't bring myself to beg. "Someone has been asking about *you.*"

That was my cue. I knew it. But when push came to shove, I looked at that face and thought of the dog. No wonder Bitsy didn't like people. "I'm listed." I tried for breezy as I hung Bitsy's leash on its hook, and headed for the door.

I'd gone too far. "You think it's that dashing Mack Danton, don't you?" Her voice had gone from syrupy to harpy sharp in seconds. "Everyone knows you've set your cap for him, but you don't know the half of it."

"Bye, Mrs. Horlick. See you tomorrow." I refused to rise to the bait.

She barely paused in her tirade. "He's the one you should be keeping on a leash. Sneaking around."

I smiled and started to close the door. Just in time to hear her parting shot. "But it's not him! It's the police."

"What?" The question was out of my mouth before I could catch it. Damage done, I turned back toward the door, only to be rewarded by that thin smile. "The cops were asking about me?"

She had Bitsy in her arms now. The dog's black button eyes fixed on mine, but I didn't have the time to focus. "They wanted to know what your habits are. How *stable* you seem." That grin would've fit a crocodile. "Seems they've been looking into your past."

"Great," I muttered to myself. To her, I tried for a brave front. "I guess they've got to worry about anyone who comes back to this town."

The old harridan sputtered for a moment, during which I remembered that she was now one of my only regular paying clients. With a deep sigh, I set about to backtrack. "But if I hadn't come back, I'd never have met you and Bitsy."

I reached over to pet Bitsy's fluffy head, and as soon as I touched him, I got it. *"Watch out for the old ones, walker lady. They bite."*

I confess I was a little shaken as I drove back home. Tracy Horlick's venomous sputter hadn't told me anything I hadn't expected, but hearing that the cops were asking questions about me so soon still made me uneasy. Maybe they didn't have much else to focus on in this godforsaken town, but this was going fast. Too fast.

Bitsy had given me a lot to think about, too. So Delia was pregnant? She seemed awfully calm for a potential single mother, especially if she wasn't inheriting from Charles. There might be something else—something she wasn't talking about, like insurance—but I had to wonder if she'd already lined up another potential mate. That could lead to motive, too. If she had been seeing Chris while Charles was alive, he might have found out. Maybe—I mulled this over as I waited at one of our town's two traffic lights—maybe Chris was the father, and Charles had learned the truth. As I started up the mountainside to my house, I played that scenario over in my head. Perhaps she'd planned on deceiving Charles, getting a moneyed husband for herself, a better father for her baby, and he'd dumped her. A pregnant woman, hormones running mad...could she have torn his throat open like that? Stabbed him repeatedly with something sharp and lethal? What if she'd sprung the news on him—and then found out that he was having money problems?

Along the same lines, Chris Moore might have a motive for killing Charles, especially if paternity or custody of a child-to-be were involved. He seemed like an old-fashioned type, the kind of mug who might get involved in something dirty if he thought his honor or his woman's was involved. Or, if my mind was running along these lines, was there a third man in Delia's life? I'd seen the stir she caused. It was possible.

I pulled into my driveway, thinking that all bets were off. "Wallis, I'm home!" I called. I needed some support here, someone to figure out my options with. But the only answer was a small peep. The orange kitten came bounding down the stairs to twine around my ankles.

"Hey, kitten, what's up?" I lifted the kitten and felt a purr starting as I looked around for my adult feline companion. "Wallis?"

Nothing, but as I carried the kitten into the kitchen, I got a flash of thought. *The big one doesn't like me.*

"Wallis? That's not true," I lied and put the kitten down. Reaching for the can opener, piercing a can of imported tuna in olive oil. No matter how nonchalant the tabby liked to seem, she rarely missed a meal, and the fish was fragrant. I raised my voice, "Wallis!"

Still no response, so I fed three-dollar tuna to the kitten and went into my office. The laptop sat there, accusingly. I'd not gone back to the information on the keychain drive since the fight. Playing with it seemed preferable to worrying about the cops, so I opened it up again and poked about some more. Maybe the adrenaline had sharpened my wits. On second viewing, I located two spreadsheets, and both seemed pretty clear. These were definitely someone's budgets—Charles' most likely, given that my invoices showed up with regularity on the smaller of the two. What I didn't see were deposits—on either of them—and both accounts were running low. Of course, Mack had said that the company was near launch. At this point, it was probably running off its startup capital. No wonder it looked like the bottom lines were sinking. So, was the company viable? In this economy, any kind of funding had to be tight. Still, a good idea, low overhead...what was Charles' great idea, anyway?

I didn't have anywhere near enough info, and I really didn't want to spend another night lurking at Happy's. A bit of poking about and I turned up a phone number for one Malcolm Danton.

"Mack, it's Pru. Can we talk?" A part of me wanted more than information, not the least because I'd been warned—repeatedly— about the dark-eyed stranger's bad-boy ways. But I'm not the girly type, never been good at flirting. And I did have questions I wanted answered. I left my number and figured he'd call me back. He hadn't given me the impression that he wanted to avoid me.

Wallis, however, was another matter. After she didn't show for lunch, I started poking around what I'd thought were her usual hiding places. Back of the closets, under the bed. I knew the old tabby could hold a grudge, but this was getting ridiculous.

"Wallis? Are you around?" I called from the top of the stairs. "Look, I'm sorry! Come on, let's make up, can we?"

Nothing. I checked the kitchen clock and saw that I'd managed to waste a good chunk of the day. And so after a few more minutes of fruitless searching, I grabbed my coat and headed out once more.

◇◇◇

"Oh, it's you."

This wasn't my day to make friends and influence people, but still I'd expected something a little better than a dead-eyed stare and that toneless greeting. Eleanor Shrift had run to the door quickly enough. I'd heard her call as she fumbled with the lock and had a flash of a smile as the door came open. As soon as she'd seen who it was, her face had fallen, and she'd turned and walked back into the neat split level.

"Ms. Shrift," I raised my voice as I walked in behind her. "I don't mean to intrude on your valuable time." I wasn't doing a very good job of hiding my sarcasm. But then, she wasn't being particularly polite either. "You've got a beautiful cat wasting away at the shelter, and I'm here to find out why."

She turned toward me, cigarette in hand, and muttered something as she lit it.

"Excuse me?" We were in some kind of entrance hallway. The living room, to our left, had a fake fireplace and an abundance of overstuffed furniture, all in shades of cream and white. I wondered if the cat were ever allowed on any of the chairs.

She took a long draw, and I waited while she let the smoke out. "I said," she looked up at her own smoke as she spoke, "'you've got him now. You deal with it.'"

"Yeah, well," I looked around and walked toward a snow-white sofa. "That's why I'm here."

I sat and waited. She didn't shoo me off, which was a good sign. Instead, with a deep, theatrical sigh, she picked up an ash-tray and joined me, settling herself into a matching armchair. "So?" she asked.

"Your cat's problems aren't physical. They're emotional." She rolled her eyes. I kept on talking. "Something in his home environment is upsetting him. That's why I'm here. For starters, can you tell me how long you've had him?"

"He was a gift." Another drag. "From a friend."

I noted the emphasis. We don't usually get gifts from our enemies.

"I'd just moved in. I guess it was, what? June?" Another drag and suddenly Eleanor Shrift was grinding the butt out as if she wanted to kill it. "You want a drink?"

"Sure." Something was going on, and I followed her into a pristine kitchen. No sign of a pet here. No sign of any kind of life. "Do you travel much?"

"What?" She cracked an ice tray open into a shaker and reached for a bottle of vodka. "Oh, yeah. Travel. I cover the East Coast, sometimes Cleveland. I'm a detail woman. Pharmaceuticals?"

I caught myself before I declined that offer but took the proffered martini. "Have you been traveling more recently, or been away longer?" The black Persian's excessive grooming could be a stress reaction.

She looked thoughtful. "No, not really." She took a sip, a big one, and gestured me back into the living room. I noticed that she took along the shaker.

We sat. Properly medicated, Eleanor Shrift looked almost relaxed, her porcelain face less strained. I took a chance. "Look, Ms. Shrift. It's simple. Something changed for the cat. Maybe something you're aware of, maybe not. But something set him off. Can you think of what that might have been?"

"Something set *him* off?" That tight look was back and I noticed how her makeup sank into the lines around her mouth.

"I'm sorry, did I say something wrong?" I wasn't sure why this woman was so edgy, but for the Persian's sake, I'd find out.

"It's nothing." She shook her head and then looked at me, hard, as if seeing me for the first time. "Maybe you didn't know."

I waited, always a good strategy with animals.

"You're too young." She refilled her own glass without offering me any. Just as well, I put my glass down on an end table and let the silence build.

"You still—" She stopped. A few more sips, another minute of silence, and then those black lashes fluttered and the steely voice cracked. "He called it off, okay? My 'friend.' We had a perfect arrangement. No strings, no expectations. He said there wasn't anyone else, but I'm not a fool. A man like that..." She glowered at me as if I were responsible. "You probably think I was too old for him."

"Hey," I raised my hands in surrender. "I'm just here about the cat." It wasn't three o'clock yet but I'd begun to have the feeling that this wasn't her first shaker of martinis. I needed to bring her down. "I don't know the guy."

"Oh, really? And everyone so interested in *you?*"

"It's not what you think." I didn't know what she'd heard, but I didn't want to get into this. "Look, I can sympathize." I thought of Leo, the chef. We'd said "no strings," too, and it worked for a while. Until he started trying to keep tabs on me. But I was willing to talk if it would help. I was just about ready to start reminiscing about Leo, with his scarred hands and his wild laugh, when she gave a little sniff. For half a moment I was afraid she'd start crying. I needed to cut into this and fast.

"Your guy, did he have a lot of interaction with the cat?

"With the *cat?*" She was angry now. In a way, that was easier. "Yes, he had a lot of interaction with the *cat*. Smoke was my pet, but he was always the one petting him. Always the one picking him up and carrying him onto the furniture. Even into bed. The *cat*."

"Well, that explains it." She looked up at me and blinked, and it occurred to me that Eleanor Shrift had no idea what she'd said. "Your cat, that gorgeous black Persian. What did you call him? Smoke? He misses your friend, and since you travel a fair amount, you probably haven't taken up the slack. He's over grooming himself because he's lonely. Smoke wants comfort."

"My *cat* wants comfort. Great." Eleanor Shrift stalked off into the kitchen. Usually, at this point, I'd start talking to the pet owner about alleviating the problem, trying to find ways to get the human to modify her behavior, at least temporarily. Once you name an animal, you start thinking of it differently. And the animals themselves are extraordinarily adaptable. I suspected that with just a modicum of affection, the Persian would return to normal—and be thrilled to be back in familiar surroundings. But right now Eleanor Shrift was hurting and angry. She seemed about to jump down my throat for being younger, and she wasn't about to forgive her cat—whom she barely acknowledged—for getting more attention in her grief.

Attention, that was key, I thought as I got up to leave. I might sympathize more with the Persian, but there was a lesson in his behavior that applied to his person. Eleanor Shrift might not be capable of love, but she wanted attention. She was hurting in part because her affair hadn't been acknowledged. She'd been someone's secret, and she'd still been thrown over. The Persian had found a way to make his sorrow public, and she envied that. Well, I'd discovered the source of the black Persian's problems. But finding a remedy for the situation when the owner saw herself as competing with her cat was going to be a bit more difficult. Especially when the cat was still in his prime.

# Chapter Fifteen

Wallis didn't show for dinner either, so maybe I sounded a bit eager when Mack called me a bit after eight. I mean, I like attention, too.

"Hey, doll." There was a warmth in his voice that I didn't quite trust. "Good to hear from you."

I could have kicked myself. Wallis would have made some cutting remark, if she'd been there. But as I looked around, all I saw were the kitten's guileless eyes.

"You still there?" Was that a chuckle?

"Yeah, Mack." I took a breath. "I've got a few questions I was hoping you could help me with?"

"Aw, gee. Is that all?" The tone of mock disappointment wasn't as endearing as he thought, and I grunted in response. He got the hint. "Okay, happy to be of service then." He wasn't giving up entirely. "Can we do this over dinner?"

I was glad then for the meatball sub I'd wolfed down, alone. Dinner sounded too much like a date. But some questions were best asked in person. Mack was smooth enough without the distance of a phone line. "I've eaten. What say we meet at Happy's?"

His short, sharp laugh—traces of Leo—sounded so relieved I was sure he read me wrong. At that point I didn't care, and we agreed to meet at the bar. I gave the house one last scouring, even checking under the old lawn furniture on the enclosed back porch. Nothing. I called out a greeting to my missing tabby and took off. At least if Creighton came looking for me, I'd be out, too.

Happy's looked like Happy's, and if the bartender nodded when I walked in, that only made me feel like I'd rediscovered a little bit of home. Mack was sitting in one of the back booths when I got there, nursing the kind of whiskey I'd grown fond of. I hesitated a moment before joining him in such an intimate setting, then realized the privacy would serve my needs as well.

"Jameson's," I called over to the barkeep. I couldn't bring myself to call him Happy, but if this kept up, he was going to have to give me a name. As it was, I nodded back and left a five before taking my drink to Mack's booth and sliding into the bench opposite.

"I hear you're becoming a regular around here." Mack leaned forward so I got a good look at his dark eyes.

"It's not like there's much else in this town." I took a healthy swallow and thought about how to start this conversation. "I wanted to ask you a few questions." Direct seemed best.

"You and the cops." He must have seen my interest, because he laughed again, more softly this time. "Thought that would get you."

"Hey, they've been asking about me as well." I stopped myself as I reached for my glass. The night had gotten chilly, and it would be too easy to throw the whiskey down. I needed to keep my focus. "Probably questioning everyone in Charles' life."

His eyes narrowed at that. "And what have you been telling them?"

Now it was my turn to smile. I'd wanted to disarm him, but I wasn't going to be grilled. "Everyone in town knows that I found him. But I found some other stuff, too, that you might want to know about."

He leaned back against the wooden booth, and I found myself examining him. With his pale skin and dark hair, he was my kind of handsome. Not as muscular as Chris Moore, or put together like Jim Creighton, but a good-looking man, broad in the chest. His arms, where he'd pushed back his sweater sleeves, were covered with thick, dark hair, and I fought the urge to trace them with my fingers. Mack Danton wasn't a pretty boy. Wasn't a gentleman, either. So why had my offer of information set him back?

"Of course, I don't have to tell you." I ran my finger around the rim of my glass instead. An old move, but an effective one.

"But you want to." He was leaning forward again, those bare forearms edging close across the table.

"What I want," I paused for effect, "is to know more about your startup."

Mack made a face. "Could have fooled me, Pru. But since you asked, it is—it was—language recognition software, and we stood to make a bundle."

"*Language* recognition?" I'd heard of voice-recognition software, the kind of device that turned speech into typed words, but Mack was shaking his head.

"Like an automatic translator, but a good one." He rubbed one large hand over his face. "Or it would have been. Like I've said, Charles was the brain. I'd seen enough so that he convinced me it had solid applications, real-time business translation. Shit like that. Now…" He shrugged and lifted his whiskey.

I took a hit off my own drink to buy time to think.

"So if the idea was so good, what did he need a money guy for?" The idea had thrown me, close as it was to my own strange gift. But there was something I wasn't seeing.

Mack shook his head and put down his drink. "You think you come up with a good idea and that's it? No, not Charles." He turned to get the barkeep's attention. "You see, he was sort of an idealist. An idealist or a loner. You want another?"

I nodded and when the bartender came over he free-poured a healthy shot into my glass as well. I might be recognizable, but Mack was definitely a regular.

"You see, a software developer who works solo will usually sell his work to one of the big firms. But Chuck wanted to keep it private, license it himself."

"He wanted to maintain control." I could see the appeal.

Mack threw back most of his new drink before answering. "In his dreams, yeah. Low overhead, no corporate connections. Dip into the nest egg to pay the bills. That was the theory, anyway. But even if he didn't mind living on nothing, he has his mother to take care of. And, of course, every stray animal that comes his way."

"Just Lily—I mean, the pit bull." I still hadn't found a way to explain that kitten. "But if the idea is so hot, why was he having money problems?"

That big grin came back. "You heard that, too? Let's just say Charles needed me around. He was thinking small, but I had some ideas of what he could do. For a genius, the man had no more money sense than, well, a kitten."

I swallowed. Maybe he did know something. But the best defense is a good offense. "So what were you doing for him?"

"Setting up investors, trying to come up with a reasonable budget for development and marketing. A realistic budget. Trying to keep Charles from nickel-and-diming himself into the ground. He would've, you know." For a moment, Mack's large features took on the bemused expression most of the world gets when confronted by a dreamer. "No sense at all of reality."

"I'd say he got a good dose of it, at the end." The more I learned about my former client, the more I liked him. And no matter what Mack said, the files I'd seen showed that Charles was very well aware of his expenses. He wasn't a bookkeeper, but he'd kept track of every cent. "So, did you have any big investors yet?"

"Anyone screaming for his money back, you mean?" Mack focused in again. He knew I was fishing. "Anyone besides you?"

"I'm small potatoes." Now it was my turn to lean back. "But maybe somebody didn't like his business plan."

"Ah, like Miss Delia Cochrane?"

We were thinking along the same lines. "Well, that is an interesting situation, is it not? Everyone's idea of the perfect couple." I watched his eyes. Did he know about her pregnancy?

"He was devoted to her," he said at last, sadness coloring his words. "And Delia? Well, Charles didn't owe her any money, that's for sure. And even for our golden girl, he was a better bet alive, don't you think?"

I waited, but he was done.

"I don't know what she thought—or who she owed." He stared into his glass. "And frankly I don't care."

I couldn't read anything in those dark eyes except fatigue and the warmth of whiskey. But waiting worked. "I don't think he owed anyone really," he finally admitted. "Except you, Miss Small Potatoes. And me. I mean, I'm the one who had the plans. I'd set everything up. And, no, I don't benefit. I've heard it's all going to his mother. Not that there's much of the business. Everything was still in Charles' head. And now…" he threw up his hands. "Pfft. It's gone."

"Well, Delia is still around."

"You think?" He laughed, that short dry bark of a laugh again. "Like I'd trade a going business concern for a blonde?" He leaned in. "I've got no interest in green girls."

I smiled, as I knew I was supposed to. From a man like Mack, that was a compliment, supposed to make me turn all fluttery. It didn't work, but it did give me pause. From what I'd seen, Delia might be younger than I was, but she seemed to know how to twist everyone to her whistle. Was Mack one of her victims, maybe protesting too much after the fact? I eyed the dark-eyed charmer and tried to play it out in my head. It was possible. As I sipped my whiskey, another thought hit me. Maybe Mack wasn't comparing Delia to me at all. Maybe he really did like his women older, not to mention more solvent. And Eleanor Shrift had spent her summer with some young stud. Maybe I didn't fit into the picture at all. There had to be a way to find out.

"Somehow, I wouldn't imagine that there's a huge selection out here." Let him think I was flirting, if it got him to talk.

"In beautiful Beauville? Don't underestimate yourself." That smile turned conspiratorial as he leaned across the table. He saw me raise my eyebrows and wisely drew back. "Besides, I'm not talking specifics. I'm too much of a gentleman. Just, generally."

"I'll be sure to keep that in mind." Happy—as I was beginning to think of his current incarnation—had come over again with the bottle. He refilled Mack's glass and looked over at me. I raised mine and nodded. I have a good head for liquor, and besides, I needed to keep Mack talking. "I've got a client, a very fine looking lady, who is recently single."

"Oh?" Mack was humoring me, I could tell by his tone. "Do tell."

"Professional woman, dresses to the nines." I toyed with my glass, looking into the amber liquid, and put it back down. I've got a high tolerance, but not that high. "Might be in your target demographic, too."

He lowered his voice and leaned in. "You sound like you're trying to sell me something."

"Just thinking out loud." I raised my glass and looked across it, trying to hide the fact that I was watching Mack's face. "Eleanor's a good-looking woman."

"Eleanor Shrift? You think that's my 'target demographic'?" He was laughing. I was trying to figure out if the laugh was real or a cover. One thing was certain, he knew who I was talking about. In response, I simply shrugged—and rewarded myself with a sip of whiskey.

"Sheesh, so you're trying to play matchmaker now." With that, Mack leaned back against the side panel of the booth, putting both feet up on the bench beside him. He looked comfortable, so I did the same. But if I was hoping for more info, I was to be disappointed. Dodging any further questions about Delia or Eleanor—or his business—he started grilling me about mine.

"So, what do you do with a dog that bites?" He'd politely avoided any questions about Lily—or any further queries about the police. Instead, he'd moved on from nervous barking to more serious crimes of the canine kind. His voice had gotten a little sloppy by this point, his gestures a bit broad. But I wasn't thinking that clearly either. I wasn't drunk, far from it, but I couldn't work out how to turn the conversation around.

"You try to find out *why* he bites." Then it hit me. "So, Mack, why won't you answer my questions?"

"Maybe I like to take the lead." That smile had only gotten broader, and it hit me that perhaps I had drunk too much.

"Okay, I think it's time to call it a night." I stood up and grabbed the edge of the table. I was not going to let him see me stagger. "Happy?"

"I've got it." Before I knew what was happening, Mack had pulled out his wallet and weighted down a couple of bills with his empty glass. Then he was helping me into my coat. "Maybe I should give you a ride home."

"I'm fine." I was. I just needed some air.

"Uh huh." He donned his own jacket, and walked with me to the back door, turning to wave off the bartender. "I'll be the judge of that."

"Oh come on!" I'd been having a good time. Mack was a charming man, but this was too much. I grabbed the door as he reached for it and pulled it open to storm out to the back lot. "You're not my father."

"No, I'm not." He was up against me, then, pushing me back against the rough brick wall. His mouth tasted of whiskey, hot and inviting, and I felt myself melting into the kiss.

"Mack." I pulled back, but he had me pressed against the wall. The night air had gotten frosty, and I found myself very aware of the warmth of his body. "This isn't what I meant."

"Why not?" Eyes closed, he leaned in, and I felt myself responding. That laugh had made me lonely for Leo. For Stevie. Lonely for any man with a smart mouth and knowledgeable hands. Why not indeed? I'd done worse, and in this parking lot, too. I ran my hands up his back, inside his jacket, and felt him tense up in response. He looked lean, but I felt muscle.

"This is how you like it, isn't it," he said.

"Shut up," I said, and kissed him again. Just then, the back door pushed open and two more laughing revelers passed by, caught up in their own booze-fueled drama. Mack was saying something. "My place," was all I heard.

And that's when it hit me. "No," I said, my voice lost in his mouth. "I can't." I pulled back and put my hand up to his mouth to stop him. "I've got to go home."

His eyes focused then, and I stammered for a moment trying to find the words.

Wallis, that was why not. As much as I thought of her as a friend, our fight had reminded me that she was in fact a cat. A cat I hadn't seen in close to twenty-four hours. A small domestic animal. Taking a deep breath to sober up, I made myself see the reality of the situation. Wallis might see herself as my caretaker, but in reality I was hers.

"I've got to get home. You see, I have a cat." How to explain the situation with Wallis?

"A cat, a kitty cat." He leaned in to kiss me again, but this time I pulled away for real. My hands were between us now, and I was pushing him back. "I see." He dragged the word out, a clear sign that he didn't.

"No, really. She went missing yesterday. I think, well, something upset her." No way could I say more. "I've had her for years. She's elderly. Older, anyway and I'm worried. So, I should go home and look for her."

"Hey, I understand. Cats and me." He held up his hands in mock surrender.

"It's not what you think." I was laughing now, almost sorry that he didn't ask to come along. But he didn't, and I found myself thinking better of him as I drove, very carefully, home.

Thoughts of another type crowded out Mack as I pulled into my own gravel drive and parked my old car. It was late, close to midnight. I hadn't seen Wallis since the night before. Should I have come home earlier? Persisted in looking for her? As much as I'd wanted to respect her privacy—we were more roommates than owner-pet at this point—the concerns I'd voiced to Mack began to resonate, loudly, in my head. Wallis was an elderly tabby. Round and out of shape. She'd grown up in the city, where the main dangers came from humans, in the form of cars and crazies. I'd stopped monitoring her movements since we'd transitioned into our current relationship, but had I also abdicated responsibility? She seemed so wise, but did she know about coyotes? Hawks? Wolves or whatever wildlife prowled these Berkshire woods? More than the drink was making my hand unsteady as I fumbled for the key.

"Wallis?" I finally managed to get the door open and called for her even before I hit the light. "It's me. Are you home? Are you there?"

I reached for the light, but as I stepped into the dark, I felt something beneath my feet. I froze, trying to make sense of my space. Trying to listen, to see in the dark. Nothing, and I shifted, taking a slow step. Whatever was underfoot crunched like gravel, and I heard an answering movement. "Wallis?" My voice cracked, as much as a whisper can crack.

Nothing. I held my breath and with a movement as slow and quiet as I could manage, I reached over for the wall and flipped on the light.

"Took you long enough." Wallis was sitting on the back of my sofa, black-tipped tail wrapped around her white front feet. All around me on the floor shattered glass glittered like sand.

"What happened?" Now that I saw her, alive and evidently unharmed, I found myself getting angry. "Why didn't you say anything."

She jumped down from the sofa back and made her way toward me, stepping daintily between the fragments. "I forgot you couldn't see that well," she said, not even trying to hide the smug tone of her voice. She stopped about five feet away and looked at the glittering mess between us. "So much for your so-called humanity."

I sighed. She had reason to be pissed, but I was tired. "Look, Wallis, I'm sorry. I said I was sorry last night and I am. But I've had a long day. If you can tell me anything about what's happened here, I'd appreciate it."

She began washing her front paw, an obvious stalling tactic, and so I went to get the broom and dustpan from the mud room. As I swept, she continued to groom, jumping back a little ostentatiously as I swept up the nearest glass fragments. By then, I'd noticed the small window by the front door was shattered, a chill breeze chasing after the path of a large rock, which had skidded under the sofa.

I retrieved it with the broom and looked it over. It was a rock, which is to say, nondescript. "Seriously, Wallis. Do you know anything about this?"

She looked up. I waited, but it's nearly impossible to outwait a cat. "Please?" I added. The scare, the night, and now this. I was exhausted.

"I was upstairs when that came in." She looked at the rock and I held it out for her to sniff. "A car drove away, and the night birds sounded nervous so I suspect it was driving too quickly. Interesting." She sniffed at it again, then recoiled.

"What? Are you getting anything?" I didn't like that someone had thrown a rock through my window and then driven off. That sounded personal.

"Only that godawful alcohol." Her ears flicked backward.

"I'm sorry." I didn't want to rekindle our fight. "I needed to ask someone some questions."

She sniffed again, this time moving her wet leather nose more to my fingertips. "I can see that." Her whiskers angled forward in concentration, and I felt a wave of self-consciousness. How much of what happened would be revealed by my pheromones, my sweat?

"Well, you're always after me to begin dating again."

"*Dating.*" She sat back and licked her chops. "So that's what you call it."

Wallis went back to grooming. I lowered the hand with the rock and waited. "Well, maybe not 'dating,' per se," I said finally. I was too tired for this.

"Clearly." She started on her ears, working that same paw roughly over the black-tipped velvet. "And I know this is a small

141

town, Pru, but still couldn't you find a different man? That perfume." She shuddered and set to work on her white bib. "I don't know if you'll ever be rid of it. And I wouldn't have thought you'd want a man who smelled so much like her."

# Chapter Sixteen

I cleaned up the mess, taping a sheet of cardboard over my busted window, as Wallis explained. She confirmed that, yes, according to her sensitive nose, Mack had spent some time with Delia Cochrane, who had, in turn, passed her scent onto the kitten. Whatever was going on between them, she couldn't tell. But it was strong enough to put my discerning tabby's ears back.

What that meant to me could be very little. He'd been her fiancé's business partner. They probably had a lot of loose ends to tie up. Hell, it was a small town. He could have been carrying her groceries or fixing her pickup truck. He could have been catsitting the kitten. But I doubted it. Denials aside, I'd pegged Mack Danton for a womanizer, and Delia was as tempting as an August peach. Whether he'd also been involved with Eleanor Shrift was anybody's guess. The older woman believed that her lover had left her for another woman, so it could have been Delia—or even me, I realized with a laugh. Mack had been making, or planning, his moves for a while now. Or it could simply have been boredom that led her backdoor Romeo to abandon his somewhat overripe Juliet.

I placed the stone on a bookshelf with the vague idea that I'd think about it again in the morning. The glass I dumped in the trash before finally dragging myself upstairs. My bed beckoned, but I detoured to the bathroom. With its deep, claw-footed tub, it was possibly my favorite place in the house, and as I filled it with an intemperate amount of hot, hot water, I silently thanked my mother for never wasting the money on renovations.

Wallis joined me, keeping the running tap at a distrustful distance, and once I sank carefully into the steaming water, she caught me up on the kitten's antics. If I didn't know better, I'd have said the older cat had been amused by the marmalade baby's battle with a late season moth. I didn't dare voice such thoughts aloud, however, and instead told Wallis about the bichon's jaw dropper. As I'd unwound, she'd settled down on the closed toilet seat, her front paws tucked under, and appeared to mull that over. "Pregnant." She closed her eyes. "Yes."

I didn't know if Delia's hormones could really be carried, third hand, along with her perfume, but I was learning better than to question my housemate. "So maybe Charles was the father. Or maybe Mack. Or, hell," I stood and reached for a towel, "maybe Chris. That seems to be who she's spending the most time with these days. The question is, would one of them have a reason to kill Charles?"

I stepped from the tub, dripping, careful not to stand too close to Wallis.

"No." She jumped down and led me from the bathroom, tail up. We were back on good terms then. "The question is, would Charles—would any of those males—have cared?"

I was mulling that one over as I toweled off my hair and pulled an old T-shirt on. "Most guys would," I said, as much to myself as to the stout tabby, who had jumped up to the foot of the bed. The kitten was already asleep on the other corner. Warm, clean, and still buzzed, I longed to join them, and was having trouble even combing out my wet hair. Three swipes later, I gave up, laying my towel-wrapped head on a pillow as a stray thought coursed through my mind. "Of course, some guys are just dogs."

"That reminds me," Wallis kneaded the comforter. "You got a phone call. Something about that dog."

With an effort, I pulled myself out of bed and down the stairs to where my old answering machine sat blinking. What with all the fuss and broken glass, I hadn't thought to check it.

"Pru, it's Albert." Great. I longed to hit the sofa as he rambled on, but I doubted I'd be able to make it back up the stairs if I did. "The coroner's report came back. Cause of death was 'inconsistent with canine attack,' it says, and I passed the rabies thingy along, too. So, I guess the dog is free to go. That is, if anyone wants it. Otherwise." He made a noise that was either supposed to be a knife sliding through flesh or a wad of spit. Albert was always a classy guy. "And, hey, Bandit says hello. Maybe you and me and him and your cat can double date sometime. Heh, heh."

I was glad I didn't have to respond and hit erase. At least Lily had been cleared of Charles' death. Maybe I could find a rescue group, I thought as I climbed back up the stairs, ready to fall into bed. It was not to be. As my eyes adjusted to the dark, I saw the kitten curled up, back toward me, on one pillow. Wallis stretched out on the other, eyes half closed, and smiled up at me.

I managed to get under the blankets and between the two felines before passing out. Sometime during the night, Wallis jumped down for her usual nocturnal rambles, and I reclaimed the pillow, point taken. She ruled, and I was to respect her dignity.

By the time I came down for breakfast, late for me, she was already in the window, supervising the birds in the yard.

"Hey, Wallis." I measured out coffee beans on automatic pilot and set the water to boil. "I meant to ask you, can you keep an eye on the kitten today?"

She didn't turn, only lashed her tail.

"It's just that I should have someone come by and fix that window, and I don't want her to get out." Another lash. "I mean, she's not the brightest bulb."

That got her. "We'll manage." She twitched an ear. "But at some point, Pru, we're going to have to talk about long-term plans for that child."

"I know, Wallis." I stared at the kettle, willing it to boil. I was late. "But don't worry, I know who she belongs to— with, I mean." It wouldn't do to antagonize the tabby now, but she turned back to her window and I was able to pour the steaming water over the ground beans without any more apologies.

"Her 'mama'?" I carried my mug over to the window in time to catch Wallis' question.

"Well, I don't know about that, but that scent you picked up? Delia Cochrane did lose an orange kitten."

Wallis flicked an ear. "You're having a territorial dispute with that female, aren't you?" There was a note of amusement in her voice that I had no patience for.

"That's not going to happen." The strong, hot brew was waking me up. "I gave shelter to her kitten, that's all. And I don't want her man."

Not anymore. The thought came so quickly, I didn't know which one of us it originated with. For now, I was happy to let it go and join Wallis in staring out at the front yard. "So, you didn't see anything last night?"

"Just because I have excellent night vision, doesn't mean I'm always watching for intruders." From the edge in her voice, I wondered if Wallis had been frightened by the attack. "I heard a car. A nice one, not too loud."

"Thanks, Wallis. That may be useful." I finished my coffee and went back upstairs to dress. I didn't know why someone had broken my window or what it meant, but at least I could check out what people drove. First, however, I had dogs to take care of and a living to make.

◇◇◇

As soon as I saw the smile on Tracy Horlick's face, I knew I was in for trouble. Twenty minutes late to walk Bitsy, she shouldn't be smiling so, unless there was hot gossip warming her insides.

"Good morning, Pru." She greeted me with a syrupy tone at odds with the cold glint in her eye. "And how are you this morning?"

"Fine, thanks. Sorry to be running late." I tried to walk past her to grab the bichon's leash but she blocked me. I bit my tongue. This was going too far. I didn't want to be her source on anything. To top it off, her poor dog was already bouncing up and down, too well trained to take advantage of the door her person held open. "Mrs. Horlick? The leash?"

She stepped aside, but as I reached for the lead she laid a conspiratorial hand on my arm. "I'm not surprised you were running late. I heard you were out last night."

I looked from the little dog to his owner. Her heavy lipstick was already cracked over her dry lips. The cigarettes didn't help, but as I watched her tongue darted out to lick those lips I'd be damned if I were breakfast. Mack and I might have been seen drinking together by anyone at Happy's last night, but only the other couple, the ones who had come crashing out the back door, could say for sure we'd been locking lips. If I'd learned anything from Wallis, it was how to keep a straight face.

"Don't know what you're talking about, Mrs. H." I leaned over to snap the leash on the poor bichon's collar. "Maybe you should get out more yourself."

Her mouth was gaping open like a goldfish's as I clucked to the dog and we trotted down the steps.

◇◇◇

"So, Bitsy, I've been meaning to ask." I'd waited until the small dog had relieved himself and we were out of sight of his house. "What do you know about Delia's pregnancy?"

The small dog sniffed a tree, whizzed and sniffed again, aiming high on the riddled bark. I'd been talking out loud and tried rephrasing my question as a clear thought.

"*Sammy. Tiger. Wolf.*" It took me a moment to realize the animated pompom was cataloging urine scents. Out of curiosity, I walked him over to a white birch that I knew Lily had favored. He sniffed without comment, then moved onto a hydrant. "*Gerald! That kidney trouble again?*"

"Bitsy?" I resisted the urge to tug on the leash, even gently. My new insight might help in some ways, but it certainly went against my former training. I tried to think of the small dog as I would Wallis, as ridiculous as that seemed. "Please?"

"*You don't listen, do you?*" I got a flash of Tracy Horlick's sharp voice and stale, ashy smell. He'd warned me about her. Then it was back to that German shepherd and—what?—some kind of hound. The small dog's wet nose was still busy moving around the tree. *"And if you please, it's Growler."*

◇◇◇

I had to bite my tongue from saying anything to Tracy Horlick when we returned. From the way she fussed over "Bitsy," I felt I understood the small dog's insistence on his masculinity and male associations. At least the fussing kept her from lobbing any more innuendoes my way, and I was able to slip away relatively quickly.

Driving over to the pound, I found myself thinking of gender and identification. Poor Growler. Just because we neuter our animals, doesn't mean we deprive them of their identity. Just because a dog looks like a plush toy doesn't mean he doesn't feel as butch as a bulldog. Then again, we do the same thing to people, don't we? I couldn't help thinking about Delia—and about Mack. Both were used to a certain kind of attention. I was guilty of reacting with my hormones, that's for sure. But where did they really stand in all this?

And how, I pulled my thoughts around as the brick building came into view, would any of this help me place the animals in my care? I still wasn't sure what to do for the Persian, but as I made my way up to Albert's desk, I had some very clear ideas for Lily.

"Hey, Albert, I'm here for the pit bull."

Granted, I'd sort of stormed in. Still, the face that looked up at me was more distracted than usual. I looked over the desk and saw two sharp dark eyes. "Hey, Frank."

"It's Bandit. Uh, you got my message?"

"Yeah." I sat and held out my hand. The ferret jumped up on Albert's desk and ran to sniff it. I didn't care about the man, but it seemed only polite to greet the ferret.

*"Cat, cats plural. Interesting chow, dry though. Not moving… "*

I turned my attention back to the human. "So, if the investigation has moved on, I can take the dog."

"Well, not exactly." Albert straightened his jeans, tucking today's flannel into a loose waistband, and I wondered what exactly he'd been planning for the ferret. "The dog is still in my custody."

"Yeah, but you don't want her. And you don't need to keep her away from the public anymore." As if he had to before. I was pushing it, but I was impatient. Lily had been victimized by fools like this one long enough.

"Well, there's still the question of ownership. I mean, I can't just be giving dogs away."

I'd thought this one through. "Actually, she belongs to Nora Harris. She's part of Charles' estate. I thought I'd bring her over there, get the two of them acquainted."

"You think she'll want it?" He grimaced.

"She has a house and a garden. Perfect for a dog. And the dog didn't do anything."

"Well, nothing that can be proved."

I opened my mouth to respond when it hit me once again. Lily hadn't killed Charles, and the cops knew that now. But someone had worked hard to make it look that way. Charles hadn't been stabbed or shot. His throat had been torn out. Who could have done that? What would have made such vicious wounds?

*"Claws."* I looked over at Frank. His nose was twitching as he answered my silent question. *"When I dig, I tear away at the earth, rich sweet dirt. Sometimes, I rip into my dinner before I can swallow it. That's not good."*

I nodded an acknowledgment. I didn't think any other animal had clawed Charles to death. I was looking for a human perpetrator, but the small ferret had been trying to be helpful.

"Still, that's a big dog. What if she doesn't want it?" Albert reached into his pocket again and pulled out a peanut. Frank stood up, but Albert popped the nut into his own mouth.

I felt Frank's frustration. "We'll deal with that if it happens."

Lily still seemed too out of it to register much as I freed her from her cage and attached a leash to her collar. I got a flash of Charles' hands on her, doing much the same, and a wave of sadness. *Home?* That was it. I'd been thinking of taking her out the back, but remembered, just in time, the questions I had for Frank.

"What are you doing?" As I followed the muscular white dog into the front room, Albert panicked, shoving his chair back into the wall and jumping up in fear. "Get that thing out of here!"

"We're on our way." Frank was standing and sniffing the air with a look of concentration. I tried to focus on his small, intense mind and was rewarded with a wave of images, all dog related. Blood. Dirt. *Home?* I forced myself to address Albert. "I wanted to say 'bye to your ferret."

He sputtered, and I knew I'd have to work fast. I turned toward the small animal, trying to fix my eyes on his.

*"Where did you get that earring from?"* I framed the question silently, staring into the ferret's black button eyes. *"The diamond earring?"* Nothing. I changed my tack: *"Shiny, sparkly, dangling..."* I was running out of associations.

*"The cold fish? In the cave."* I got a sudden flash of a denim pocket, a man's hand, and an enticing flash of sparkle. I'd been right, up to a point.

*"The face? The person?"* Nothing. Lily had seen a squirrel outside, and I felt her lean against the leash. She was too well trained to pull, a necessity with a bundle of muscle like hers. But she wanted to go out. She'd earned it. I stepped forward, but that only made her pull a little harder. *"What about the keychain drive?"*

Nothing. Frank had seen the movement outside and sensed the dog's impatience. He was getting a little nervous, and I struggled to to rephrase my question. *"The dangler, metal..."* I did my best to picture the small, flat oblong.

*"The dog..."* Frank was too focused on Lily. I wasn't going to get an answer.

*"Please?"* I didn't know how that would translate. Frank wasn't Wallis. I visualized the drive, the open metal end that fit so neatly into my computer.

*"The dog... but there was a cap. Red. Tasteless."* I got an image of color, some kind of protective covering and, in a flash, a literal interpretation of the last comment as small teeth bit into the bright plastic. And in Frank's question, I saw how the cap had attached to a metal ring—and from there to a dog's collar. Lily was panting to go out, her body taut and eager. It had been too long since our last run. Only my training and her innate good nature kept her from dragging me out the glass doors. I looked from the ferret, who now regarded me quizzically, to Albert, who was now cowering, and back to Lily. Against her snow white fur, the dark leather collar stood out like badge. I'd noticed the lack of tags. That had been why I'd had to dig up her rabies certificate. And now I remembered that recurring image. Charles reaching for Lily's collar, fixing something to it. Hanging a plastic and metal drive the one place where nobody was likely to steal it. The tags, along with the drive, must have broken off in transit—I didn't like to think of how Albert and his thugs might have handled her—but another question remained. What was it about that drive that made Charles put it on Lily? What about it was he so set on keeping safe?

# Chapter Seventeen

I wanted to let Lily run the moment we were outside, but I didn't dare risk being seen. Instead, I trotted with her down to the river and then gave her a length of lead, trying to imprint on her the necessity of staying close to me—and away from any strangers. She'd been cooped up too long to deprive her of this, and the vivid images I got in return—a quail rousted from its bed of leaves, turtles buried in the mud, field mice under the leaves, and a hawk casting its shadow on some trout—hit me like one of those cheesy three-dimensional greeting cards. I'm not sentimental, far from it, but that dog's sheer joy could have brought me to tears, if I didn't have so much else on my mind.

"What was Charles thinking?" I was asking myself, as much as Lily, when she came back to me with a birch branch. I threw it and watched her lope off, happy for the moment. "Was he hiding something, or just trying to keep his records safe?"

*"Command!"* The thought sprang into my mind so quickly, I turned around, expecting to hear someone. Lily was waiting in front me, though, a dry, forked branch in her mouth. *"Loud, loud. Now!"*

I took it and poised to throw. "So someone was shouting?"

But her attention had shifted.

*"Stick, stick. Stick."* I threw the branch. She'd waited long enough. But as she came bounding back, the piece of wood in her mouth, she rewarded me with an image, what I now recognized as an important memory. Charles, seen through the bars

of Lily's cage, his voice loud. *"Home."* The thought wasn't from Charles, and it filled me with sadness. *"Home. Home. Home."*

The rest of the words were incomprehensible, but Lily—and I—picked up on the tension, the shouting. Then, once again, the longing, and Charles was leaning over Lily, cooing at her, and fixing something to her collar. It was the keychain drive, it had to be. Who had Charles been fighting with?

Another round of toss and fetch, but Lily wasn't any closer. Charles shouting. Charles tense. Charles with his hands on her velvet ears, on her neck, on her collar. I'd heard it said that to a dog only one person ever really exists. Right now, I wished that loyalty was a little less literal. Still, I'd found out a lot. Forty-five minutes later, when Lily had finally collapsed on a bed of fallen leaves, I felt I'd put another piece of the puzzle in place. Now to try to find Lily what she really wanted: a home.

Lily pressed her nose to the car window until we left town. Then she lay down to sleep on my Toyota's back seat. I guessed she'd seen enough new sights to last her a lifetime. Me, I enjoyed the ride out to Raynbourne. All those years in the city had inured me to lots of things, but overnight the cold air had worked its magic. The mosaic of color as the trees turned on the hillsides was something else again. In truth, it reminded me of a bad shag carpet we'd had once, when I was a kid. Ragged patches of orange, yellow, and improbable red, next to a few stands of evergreen. On the carpet, it had probably been described as avocado. I don't know. I was taking a dog to her new owner—to what I hoped would be a new home. I was in a good mood.

Nora Harris must have been, too. Despite the chill in the air, the sun was beating down, and she was out front, on her knees on some kind of kneeling pad.

"Hey, Mrs. Harris." I motioned for Lily to stay and let myself out, walking up the path to meet the older woman.

"Oh, hi. Prudence, isn't it?" The gray-haired woman blinked up at me, holding one gloved hand over her eyes to shield them from the sun. I smiled back, and she put down her trowel on a neat plastic mat, lining it up with a hoe and a weeding fork. "Would you mind? I'm not as steady as I once was."

She reached up and I took her forearms to help her to her feet. She was wiry, with enough corded muscle to pull herself up easily once I gave her a hand. The gardening, I guessed. But she wasn't a large woman, and clearly the events of the last two weeks had taken their toll. Bad enough to lose a child. To lose a child to murder…I couldn't imagine what she was going through.

"Lovely garden." I had no idea what I was seeing, but the bushes looked healthy. What wasn't already autumnal red was glossy evergreen, with lots of berries.

Whatever I said, it was the right thing. She nodded as she looked over her handiwork. "It keeps me going. I've finally finished up the last of the bulbs for next spring. Hyacinth. Crocus. I'd already put in a bunch of tulips over at—" She caught herself and swayed a bit before straightening up. "Over at my son's house. He never cared for planting much, and it gave me pleasure."

"I'm sure it gave him pleasure, too." I tried to conjure up the landscaping at my former client's and failed. I guess I was as oblivious as Charles. "He was a good, gentle man." That much was true.

"Gentle, yes." She seemed lost in thought for a moment, her mouth set, and I let her be, ready to catch her if necessary. "He— well, it's all past, isn't it? He took good care of me." She looked up at the neat little house and I followed her gaze. Had this been Charles' family home? The McMansion next door was already casting a shadow toward us, costing the side yard its afternoon sun. But the little house, dwarfed by the newer building, looked more solid than its pricey neighbor. Whatever its age, it had been well cared for. The windows were double glazed, the paint job new, and the shingles on the roof neat and complete. In fact, the whole building had the spic and span look that said no corners were cut in its upkeep. I wondered how Nora Harris would fare with her son gone, how ready she had been to move in with him. She stood to inherit his business, but what did that really mean? Thirtysomething software nerds probably weren't the best at estate planning.

"Well, maybe you might have a chance to return the favor." It was an awkward transition, but I was feeling a bit lost.

"Oh?" Clearly, she'd been distracted, too, and with more reason. For a moment, I wondered about the legality of what I was about to do. Nora Harris was the legal beneficiary, but should I have gotten her consent before bringing over this particular bit of the estate?

Nothing for it now. I walked over to my car and opened the door. Lily still had her lead attached to her collar and jumped up when I said her name. In a moment, she was on alert, and I was struck again by the amount of muscle packed into that small body. *Dig! Stick!* She was quivering with excitement, her whip of a tail thumping against the door. Good, she wanted to play.

"You remember Lily, don't you?" I wasn't going to continue that "Tetris" nonsense. This was a fresh start for everyone. A chance to begin anew on the right foot. I held the lead close, but Lily was doing her best to impress. At attention, head up, she looked at the old woman with curiosity and sniffed, whining a bit to be petted. "She was Charles' dog and she's gotten a clean bill of health, so I thought—"

A soft thud made me look up. Nora Harris had collapsed on the grass.

"What the hell were you thinking?" A denim-clad sprite dashed out of the front door and over to the fallen woman. I was still frozen to the spot, holding the leash of the now audibly whining dog. "Put that animal away."

"Come on, Lily." With those words, the white pit jumped back into the car, the low, high whine contrasting with the tail that still wagged hopefully. "Delia, what happened?"

I'd recognized the younger woman after half a second and come over as she helped Nora Harris lie flat, with her knees up. She was awake, her eyelids fluttering, but seemed beyond speech.

"You don't just spring something like that on someone." Delia was whispering, a tight, angry whisper. I didn't think Mrs. Harris could hear us, but what did I know? "A pit bull. Christ."

"I'm sorry." I was on my knees beside them, and I took Nora Harris' hand automatically. It was cold and smooth, and made me think of my own mother's before the end. "I wasn't thinking. I just thought, well, the dog needed a home and it was her son's. She's a very gentle dog, you know. Very loyal. Gentle as—" I almost said "a kitten," but caught myself. Another time.

Delia nodded anyway, her attention on the older woman. "Yeah, I know. I'm sorry I snapped. Don't worry, she'll be okay." She looked over at the prone woman. "Won't you, Mrs. Harris?"

"If I could just get some water, dear?" The voice was weak and reedy, but those blue eyes were clear.

Delia gave me a look, and I got up. She'd left the front door open, and it was easy enough to find a glass and fill it. By the time I came back out, Nora Harris was sitting up, Delia beside her for support.

"Here you go." I knelt in the grass beside them. "I'm so sorry." I glanced over at my car. Lily had wedged her nose into the narrow window opening.

"It wasn't you. It was just a shock." Nora made to rise, and Delia supported her. "Seeing that animal again. Charles' animal. Probably too long in the sun, as well." She gave a small chuckle. "Would you come inside?"

"Sure, thank you." I looked back at Lily, her broad snout quivering and quizzical. I'd confused her by bringing her here, and now, thanks to my lousy timing, the odds of finding a home for her here were nearly nil, but I'd make the case if I could. I turned to follow the older woman and her aide, very aware of the looks Delia continued to shoot at me.

◇◇◇

"Have a seat, Mrs. H." Delia hovered like a mother hen, and Nora accepted the attention without comment. I took the seat opposite and studied her. She hadn't seemed particularly frail when she was digging in the dirt, but I remembered Delia's comments about her "spells." Maybe there was something I was missing. Delia filled a tumbler from a pitcher. Lemonade, by the looks of it. I nodded at her questioning glance, and it was probably just my imagination that she slammed it down on the formica table.

"Won't you join us, dear?" Nora looked up at the younger woman. Did she see her as an employee, or as the daughter-in-law who would never be? I wasn't to find out.

"If I don't get that laundry folded, it'll dry all wrinkly." Delia wrinkled up her own pert nose in illustration and left us alone.

"Mrs. Harris," I began again, "I really am sorry to have barged in like that." Even as I apologized, trying to work my way around to making my case, I was thinking about rescue groups. Who would take a two-time loser like Lily?

"Young lady, you're not listening. I won't have that."

I stopped. She was right, and for a moment I saw the steel that had kept her going. "I'm sorry, Mrs. Harris. What did you say?"

"I said, I would try to take the dog. If you think it would be happy with me. Charles loved it, you see, and, well, I feel so bad." She started to mist up, and I froze. I didn't want her to collapse—or to back down. "Excuse me." She left the room, and I sat there more than a little stunned.

I was still sitting there when Delia walked back in a few minutes later and poured herself a glass of the lemonade

"Hey, I really mean it. I'm sorry." I was in apology mode. "I didn't mean to make your job harder."

Delia took a healthy swig of the sweet-tart drink and leaned against the wall, giving me her first real smile of the day. "Don't sweat it. Nora's pretty easy lifting. She had a minor stroke about a year ago, and the agency sent me over to help with the heavy stuff. She fades in and out, occasionally. She forgets things, and it frustrates the hell out of her. To be honest, I think I'm company more than anything else most days. I mean, I keep an eye on her and do the errands, but she keeps saying she wants to drive again. Gets pretty pissed when I tell her she shouldn't," Delia shrugged. "What the hell, she's got the healthiest perennials in the Berkshires."

"So, the dog?" I didn't know how to phrase it.

"Yeah, I'll end up taking care of her. But that's cool, I love animals."

Despite myself, I was beginning to like this woman. And then I realized, if I was ever going to confess, now was the time. "Speaking of animals, Delia, I think I have your kitten."

"Tulip?" Delia set her glass on the window ledge. "How—"

I raised my hands to cut her off. "I'm sorry. I didn't realize she was yours. You see, I found her at Charles', and I thought, well, she had been left there." How could I explain being there after the murder? Maybe I didn't have to. "Alone. Anyway, I took her home and then I heard from the city pound that you had lost a kitten, and it all came together."

Delia pulled out one of the spindle-back kitchen chairs and sat down with a thud. "Oh, thank God. I thought she'd gotten out. Or, maybe even, Charles' dog…" She swallowed hard.

"No. No way." She didn't have to finish. Some trainers bring out the killer instincts in fighting dogs by giving them cats. Any other dog, I'd worry. But Lily, I knew, would never willingly hurt another animal, never again. Delia couldn't know how I knew that, which raised another question. "But if you were scared, then how—" I paused to collect my thoughts. "Why was your kitten at Charles' place?"

She shook her head, the relief still sinking in. I felt guilty for having kept the truth—and her pet—from her so long. I still wanted an answer.

"I couldn't—" She stopped herself. "I had a friend, who—" She tried again. "It was Charles, you see. He was such a softie, and he needed a pet more than I did. Needed something to hold, and that dog…" She looked toward the front window. She was talking at least, so I kept my questions to myself. "That dog was always in her crate. Charles needed a real pet."

"But Charles loved Lily." And Lily was only crated at night, or for training purposes. Wouldn't Delia have known that? More important was what she'd started to say. "Never mind, you were saying, something about a friend?"

"Oh, here you go." Nora Harris had shuffled back in and was blinking at both of us in a slightly unfocused way. Delia jumped up to help her to a chair. "Why don't you sit down, Mrs. H, and I'll go with Pru to see about the dog."

She settled the older woman in with a fresh glass of lemonade and waited for me to proceed, but I had my doubts. The day had clearly worn on Nora Harris, and Lily was a young and active dog. Still, as we stepped outside Delia seemed genuinely pleased to see the white pit bull. Lily, in turn, heeled on command, only pausing to sniff at the newly turned earth, and I, trying to be generous, swallowed my questions.

"Look at her," said Delia, taking the leash as Lily's stumpy tail thwacked on the ground. "Have you ever seen anything like that?"

"Only with every good dog who gets a second chance." She smiled at that, but I couldn't help glancing back up at the house.

"Don't worry," Delia spoke softly as she held the front door open. "I want to. You know, because of Charles. And I can handle her."

I nodded. But as I drove away, I had to wonder which of her charges she meant.

# Chapter Eighteen

"Oh, please." Wallis drew her head back in disgust. "Don't you ever wash?"

I held up my hands. Guilty as charged. I'd been so distracted that I hadn't thought of all the dog scent clinging to me after my time with Lily. Instead, I'd raced in, eager to hash over my latest discoveries with Wallis. She knew something was up and sat there, watching me, as I scrubbed my arms up to the elbow at the kitchen sink and filled her in on my morning. I concluded by asking her where the kitten was.

"So, I thought I'd pack her up, and then see what I can do about that poor Persian." I checked the sofa and ran upstairs to my bedroom. Delia had said she'd swing by around five to pick up the kitten, and I was looking forward to asking her some questions when she did. But first things first: the little marmalade was conspicuously absent.

"You're not handing the infant over to that woman, are you?" Wallis had followed me and stood silhouetted in my bedroom doorway. With the light behind her, I couldn't see her eyes, but her tone was cool and her tail, always her "tell," was twitching ominously.

I should have expected a grilling. I had to admit, I felt a certain reluctance, but I turned toward my cat and tried anyway. "But, Wallis, it's her kitten." Her tail began to lash. Animals have very strong opinions about the whole ownership question. "She misses her." I tried again. "Delia loves that kitten."

"Do you really believe that?" Her voice was low, but the tone of scorn unmistakable.

"I—" I couldn't finish my answer and sat back on the bed. I didn't know what I believed. In truth, I didn't have any real sense of Delia. I could tell she wasn't mourning Charles, not as I thought of mourning anyway. I was seeing her everywhere with Chris Moore, and according to what Wallis had sniffed out, she'd spent some time with the rakishly handsome Mack Danton, too. Either could have been the "friend" so enigmatically referred to. And yet when she spoke about the dead man, it was with respect and a certain affection. Had he been the father of her baby? Maybe she was one of those women who simply want to have a child? That seemed unlikely, but what were the other possibilities? That there had been another man in her life even while she was with Charles was the most likely. Had it been Chris—or Mack? Had either of them killed Charles?

One good thing about living with cats is that they assume victory graciously. Wallis leaped to the bed and tucked her feet under her, a self-satisfied expression curving her facial stripes ever so slightly upward. As her eyes closed, I started making preparations as quietly as possible. Wallis had a point, but Delia was going to come by. I didn't see how I could avoid handing over the kitten.

I had my head under the bed when the phone rang. Of course, I smacked it trying to get up.

"Yeah?" I rubbed my head as I sat back on the bed. Wallis was watching me and, I swear, laughing. "What is it?"

"Oh, hi? Pru?" It took me a moment to place the girlish voice. The snap of gum brought me round.

"Hi, Pammy." It was the shelter. I needed the work, but right now I didn't want to hear about another animal in distress. "What's up?"

"It's that cat you were seeing?" I waited. "The black longhair?"

Hell. I stood up and started pacing. I knew I shouldn't have left him there that long. "What's wrong? What happened"

"Nothing, Pru. Sheesh. You're a bundle of nerves." I didn't rise to the bait, and the girl kept talking. "It's just that we need to decide something. Doc Sharp got a call. The owner says she doesn't want the cat back unless it's 'fixed,' and the doc didn't know what to tell her."

Damn Eleanor Shrift. "I'll handle it, Pammy. I'll come get the cat. I think it's just an anxiety issue."

"Cause she said, you know, we could put it up for adoption or get rid of it."

"I said, I'd handle it." I looked at my alarm clock. Half past three. If I moved fast, I could pick up the black Persian and be back before Delia dropped by for her kitten. What I'd do next, I didn't know.

Absentmindedly rubbing my head, I turned back to the bed. Wallis' eyes were slits, but I knew she'd been listening to every word.

"So, well, I guess I'm going to be bringing another cat over." No response. "It's just going to be temporary, Wallis. I swear it."

She stretched. "You know what they say about women like you, single, a loner, taking in all sorts of cats."

"Stow it, Wallis." I reached for a heavier sweater. My car keys were still in my jacket pocket. "And while I'm out, if you could round up that kitten, I'd appreciate it."

In response, she turned her back toward me, tucked her nose under her tail, and went to sleep.

◇◇◇

I was almost out the door when the phone rang again.

"What is it now?" I really had no time for this.

"Whoa, there, girl." It was Mack, laughing. "Catch you at a bad time?"

I relented, slightly. "Kind of, would you call me back?"

"Sure. Just wanted to see what you were doing tonight." I opened my mouth to answer and then shut it. What did I want to say? He was attractive. I was lonely. But if he was involved with Delia, I really didn't want to go there. Besides, I had my hands full.

"Look, I don't know. Call me back, will you? I've got to go see a girl about a cat."

He was still laughing as I hung up.

When the phone rang again, I should have ignored it. On the off chance that it was the shelter—or Delia—I picked up.

"Ms. Marlowe, Pru, glad I caught you." It was Creighton. Shit. "I thought I'd tell you that our investigation has moved on, but I gather you'd already heard."

"Yeah, look, I'm sorry. I'd just been working with that dog, and I wanted to spring her."

"Commendable, Ms. Marlowe. And very quick. Our coroner only ruled on Saturday that the wounds were not canine." His voice sounded a little too even. There was something going on. "But that's not why I called."

I had expected this, but that didn't mean I had to help. I waited, turning his own technique back on him.

"Because our investigation has progressed, I've got a few more questions for you. I'd appreciate it if you could come down to the station this afternoon."

"No, I can't." I was feeling pressured already, with too much to do in too short a time, and that always helped me build up a head of steam. "Believe it or not, some of us have to work for a living."

This time it was the young detective's turn to fall silent. I looked at the clock. Three forty-five. The shelter was a good half hour drive. "Look, Creighton, you know everything I know already." An image of the keychain drive flashed through my mind. Those financial records. The cops must have found copies. The info had to have been on Charles' main computer. It wasn't my job to help them, and anything I said would just make me look bad. But Creighton's efforts had probably helped exonerate Lily—and somebody had done a very nasty job on her person. I sighed, and gave in. "From what I hear, Charles was in financial trouble. Maybe you should look into that. See who he owed money to."

"Funny you should say that." Creighton didn't sound amused. "You see, we've been going over Charles Harris' files and bank statements, and it seems like your invoices are some of the only ones he ever paid. Until recently, that is."

Three forty-eight. "Look, I really have to be someplace. Can you come over here in about an hour?" Maybe he'd show up when Delia did. Maybe that would be interesting.

Instead of an answer, I heard a small bark of a laugh. "That's got to be the first time anyone has invited me to her home during an investigation. Don't get me wrong, Pru. I'd love to come by. But if you're busy today, why don't we say first thing tomorrow?"

I murmured something that I hoped sounded like agreement, but before I could hang up, he sprung the trap. "I'll be very curious to hear how you know so much about the deceased's finances, Ms. Marlowe. Extremely curious."

I probably drove too fast over to the shelter, but I was peeved. Besides, after years in the city, I kind of enjoyed hitting the gas. Enjoyed the scenery as well, the slanting afternoon sun backlighting the leaves like some kind of stage set. The occasional sparkle—a bit of open space, or reflection from a mica-flecked rock—only made the colors glow more vividly, and I let myself fantasize that I was cruising through a gemstone kaleidoscope, all color and shape. Maybe that daydream blinded me, maybe it was that tricky, slanting light. It wasn't until I neared the town line that I saw the cruiser behind me. I lifted my foot, ever so slightly, to let the car slow. No sense in getting pulled over. But as I studied my rearview mirror, that dappled light played me again. I couldn't see who was in the driver's seat. When it turned off, soon after I passed into Raynbourne, I was left wondering if the meet up had been accidental or if my speed had prompted it. Or if someone was checking to see where exactly I'd been headed.

"Hey, Pammy." I burst into the shelter with no time to waste. "I'm here to pick up that Persian."

"Ms. Marlowe." Her tone alerted me. I looked around and realized we weren't alone. The veterinarian, Dr. Sharp, was sitting with a young family in the reception area.

"Hey, Doc," I called over and waved. This should be routine. No need to bother him in the middle of pet counseling, or whatever was keeping him out front here.

"Pru." Pammy lowered her voice as she came over. Taking my arm, she led me to the far side of the reception area. "I didn't realize you'd be over so soon. I would have said something."

"Said what?" I glanced up at the big industrial clock. It was only a little past four. I'd made good time, but not enough to waste any here.

"Well, some policeman came in and talked to Doc Sharp earlier. I think he was asking about you." She looked up at me, and I realized how young she was. How scared. "They're saying weird things about you, Pru. About you and animals."

For a moment, the room spun. I closed my eyes and waited for everything to settle. This is what I'd feared second most. Next to losing my mind was having everyone believe that I had lost it. I made myself look straight at Pammy, focusing on her blue eyeshadow and those wide, open eyes, and tried to think. Had someone heard me talking to Wallis or, God forbid, to Lily? Had Albert squealed on me about his ferret? Had I said—or done—something that revealed too much? I tried to form a question, but my mouth was too dry to speak.

"It's because of that dog, Pru. The one they thought killed the guy?" Pammy was whispering now, and the relief that flooded through me must have surprised her because her concern quickly shifted to irritation. "Well, that's a big deal around here, Pru. Maybe not in the city."

"No, no, it's not that." I was nearly laughing with relief as I took Pammy's hands. "I don't mean to make light of that. It's just, well, there's been a lot going on, and I didn't know if, I don't know, I'd lost my license or something." I was improvising. I had no license to lose.

"Yeah, well, that's another thing." She looked over her shoulder, but the vet was still preoccupied. "They were also asking about your qualifications. Doc Sharp thinks the world of you, but he had to be honest. He told the policeman that you weren't actually certified as a behaviorist. He said he thought you'd left the city in a hurry. He didn't know why."

"My mother was sick." Poor woman, I used her as an excuse a little too often. But Pammy was nodding.

"Yeah, I wanted to remind him of that. I'm sorry, Pru. I guess Doc Sharp didn't know the whole story."

You bet he didn't, I thought to myself. And then the vet was walking toward us.

"Pru, thanks for coming in." The grey-haired doctor looked uncomfortable. Old Yankee stock, he didn't take well to confrontation. "I wanted to talk to you."

"Yeah?" Damn it, I could hear the defensiveness in my own voice. I tried to soften it with a smile. I was too busy for a lecture, and as I saw him gather his thoughts, I took the offensive. "I think I've reached a resolution with that Persian. It's anxiety, like we thought." Like *I* thought, but I hoped that inclusive "we" and my stuck-on smile would get me out of here faster. "The owner's had some lifestyle changes, but I'm sure with some home visits, I can make everyone happy."

I started toward the kennel area, but with one raised hand, Doc Sharp stopped me. "Now, Pru, I trust you. You know I do. You have an unerring instinct when it comes to certain animals." I bit the inside of my lip to keep from cracking wise. The lecture was coming whether I wanted it or not. Better to get it over with. "But working with animals isn't all about *instinct*."

"You said it." The words slipped out. But the elderly vet was on a roll and either didn't hear or didn't care.

"I've been giving a lot of thought to your qualifications for the work we do here. Some concerns have come up." I waited. He didn't mention the cops. If he wanted to take credit for the brainstorm, that was fine by me. I could handle Doc Sharp. "Questions, really. Some questions about certification."

"You know I left the city before I finished. My mother was ill." That was my story, and I was sticking with it.

He waved me down. "I know, Pru. I know. It's just that we have a responsibility to the animals here. To the *community*. And, well, you're not even certified as a vet tech."

I saw where this was going, and I didn't like it. The cops had scared him, and he was going to dump me. "Dr. Sharp, you know perfectly well I'm more qualified than half the volunteers you have working here." I thought fast. "If you need me to take the technician certification exam, I will. But a working practicum is part of my degree. It's quite legitimate, considering my background, to have me here helping out with the animals."

"But you're not properly supervised here." He looked up at me and then away. Something else was coming. "And we're paying you."

So that was it. Money again. But I had one more card to play. "If it's the pay issue that bothers you, I can always go freelance. Charge clients directly. Set up a placard; take out ads."

"No, no, no." That feeble waving let me know that he was done with me. I'd become an annoyance. "Don't take on so, Pru. I just wanted to bring it up."

And I just wanted to quash it. "I'm going to finish my degree soon, Doc." I'd throw the old man a bone. "But right now, I'm going to reunite one sad kitty and his person."

The black Persian was asleep when I got to his cage, his breathing regular. His dreams, the little I could pick up, seemed benign. A small feathered thing—either a toy or a bird—hovered just out of reach, but the chase was enticing. His paw pads twitched for a leap.

"Come on, kitty." I opened the door and scooped up the solid body. "Time to go home."

"*Home.*" The sleepy cat was slow to wake up, but even so, I was pleasantly surprised by his placidity. "*Home is for pets.*"

Something had changed, and for the better. If I had time, I'd have tried to figure it out. As it was, I hoisted the cat into his carrier and hit the road.

◇◇◇

Wallis bristled a bit when I slammed in, as much from my own noisy entrance, I suspected, as from the black stranger in the green plastic carrier.

"Sorry, sorry." I swung the carrier up on the kitchen table and shed my coat. Wallis jumped up and, back ever so slightly arched, approached the newcomer. "Wallis, this is…" I paused. I had no idea what the black Persian called himself. Perhaps introductions didn't matter. Wallis hissed, and the Persian backed up as much as his carrier would allow.

"Okay, maybe this was a bad idea." I swooped the carrier off the table and looked around for a place to leave it. The air outside was too cold to even consider my car, but from the way Wallis was looking at me, I knew no counter would be high enough. "Hang on."

I ran the carrier upstairs and left it on my bed, closing the door behind me just as the doorbell rang. "Hang on!" I called again, this time for a different audience, as I raced down the stairs and flung the front door open. Delia Cochrane looked up at me in surprise. Behind her, blocking the light, stood Chris Moore.

"Sorry." I was apologizing to everyone today. "I just got in and, well, I had to sequester a cat. Please, come in." I held the door as the couple walked in. Delia looked around, frankly curious about her surroundings, as I ushered them both toward the living room.

Chris, however, was staring at Wallis, who had assumed her sphinx pose on my dining room table. "What a lovely cat." Too late, I realized his intentions.

"Good cat." He reached one large hand out.

"No!" Wallis hissed and with a swipe, a line of red appeared on the back of Chris' hand. "I'm so sorry." I reached for Wallis, but she'd jumped down. Instead, I took Chris into the kitchen, where he let me wash the scratch. "She's had a bad day. I had to bring another cat into the house and she's riled up." I lowered my voice, not sure where my feline roommate had run off to. "Wallis can be very territorial."

"I understand." Chris nodded, but his ordinarily stolid face looked stunned. Not much experience with cats, I figured.

"Well, then, how is everybody?" I led him back into the living room, where Delia was now examining my bookshelf. Too late, I realized, the door to the back room—my office—was wide open. My laptop was in plain sight, open and, as always, on. A quick glance reassured me that the keychain drive was, in fact, attached. "Anyone want a drink? Cup of tea?" Hospitable was the last thing I felt, but there was an odd tension in the air, and I felt guilty first, of having swiped a kitten, and second, of having let Wallis attack Chris.

"Interesting." Delia pushed a hardcover back into place. "But no thanks. I think we'll just get my kitten and head home." She turned with a smile that I guessed was supposed to make up for her snooping. "I've had a long day."

"That's right." I fought the urge to apologize again. "How was Mrs. Harris?"

"Nora? She's a brick." Delia turned toward me, and I realized she'd made no move to remove her jacket. "But she's, well, she's not taking her condition all that seriously. She misplaced some of her gardening tools a while ago. She's very particular about them—they're specially made for all the roots and rocks around here—and I guess she felt embarrassed about that. So she drove herself into town to buy new ones, even though she knows I'm there to do her errands. Turns out, she had an extra set of car keys hidden away. We had words about that." She shrugged. "It's a process. That dog is a handful, though."

"Lily's not misbehaving, is she? Because if she needs any further training, you can call me." I could feel the tightness of panic in my throat. If Delia couldn't keep Lily, I'd be hard pressed to find another home for her.

"No, she's fine. She's fine." Delia stepped toward me. "She just seems a little needy right now. She cries, if you can call it that. But it's a new place, and Charles...." She left the sentence unfinished. "She'll settle in. But right now, between Mrs. H. and the dog, I'm wiped. My kitten?"

"Oh, of course." I hadn't had a chance to ask Wallis where the kitten was hiding, and I didn't think such a query would be welcomed now, even if there weren't human witnesses present. "Let me just see where she's gotten to."

I motioned toward the sofa, but neither Delia nor Chris sat. Instead, they watched as I went into my office, chirping and calling for the kitten. No sign of her, and I used the opportunity to close my laptop as I walked by. "She must be upstairs."

Inwardly, I cursed my own haste. Not only had I missed a chance to have the kitten packed up and ready to go, if I hadn't rushed the Persian inside, I could have asked Wallis to treat the visitor kindly. Maybe she'd have been able to find out more about the black cat and his distant owner.

I checked the second bedroom. With my bedroom door closed, I thought Wallis might have come in here to sulk, but her usual place on the windowsill, right by the night table I'd used all through grade school, was empty, and there were no felines of any kind under the bed. She and I were going to have to talk later.

For now, I opened my bedroom door. Sure enough, the orange kitten was on the bed reaching toward the black Persian in his carrier. This time there was no hissing, only a strong sense of curiosity. I stood watching, and heard Delia behind me.

"Oh, isn't that adorable." She stood beside me, both of us watching as the two cats touched noses. "Tulip has made a friend."

"What's up?" Chris still moved like the athlete he had been. I hadn't heard him come up the stairs.

"Look." Delia nodded toward the scene. I stepped into the room, as curious about the feline dialogue as I was ready to move these two humans on.

"So, look, I can lend you a carrier for Tulip." Stupid name. I picked up the kitten and got a sense of dislocation. The tiny kitten had been enjoying the larger cat. *"Stay here?"*

"No problem. I can hold her." Delia reached for the kitten. I hesitated. Cats can react badly to cars or sudden movements. But, then, I was hardly in a position to protest, seeing as how I'd lifted her kitten. *"Pets?"* At least the kitten didn't mind.

"So, you're not going to have a problem keeping her now?" I hadn't bought her story about why she'd brought the kitten over to Charles. "You don't need me to find another home for her?"

"Of course not." Delia lifted the cat to her face and nuzzled it, her own tawny mane falling over the orange and white fur. "*Delia! Pets!*" The kitten started purring. Her person looked up at me. "What gave you that idea?"

I didn't get a chance to answer, and hearing the kitten's enthusiastic reaction to the embrace, I'm not sure what I would have said. Instead, I was distracted by Chris, sprawling across my bed. "Hey, buddy." He reached to unlatch the carrier door.

"That cat isn't used to people." I reached for him, not wanting to see a guest scratched twice in one day. But if I expected the kind of reaction I'd gotten when I'd first started seeing the black Persian, I was proved wrong. The mellow mood of earlier seemed to have continued, despite the drive and the run-in with Wallis, and the large black cat came out willingly, letting Chris heft him into his lap.

"Wow, that's amazing." I watched as the Persian strained his head up into Chris' large hand. "That cat's been having some behavioral issues."

"Not anymore, are you buddy?" Chris' face was turned down, but I could see the cat's paws reaching out to knead the air with pure pleasure.

"That's so strange." Two cat lovers, two happy cats. Something was off here.

"Not really." Chris looked up, as happy as the cat he held. "I'd seen this guy in the shelter, when Delia was looking for her kitten. I've been visiting him."

I nodded. "Good to know. I'm supposed to be reuniting him with his owner. However, if that doesn't work…"

"We have Tulip back now." Delia's words were more for Chris than for me, and with a sigh he placed the large Persian back in his carrier. "Thank you so much, Pru."

I followed them back down the stairs. I'd been hoping to have some more private time with Delia, but maybe some of my questions had just been answered. Clearly, she was planning on making a life with Chris, whatever the story of her pregnancy. I watched them head out, Chris holding the door. Delia tucked the kitten inside her suede jacket for protection. She'd probably be a good mother, much as I didn't like to admit it. Then it hit me. All those first few days, that kitten had been crying for her "mama." But she hadn't said anything like that when Delia had picked her up. Maybe she was young enough so that she'd already forgotten the woman who'd adopted her. Maybe the parent she was seeking wasn't the blonde charmer at all.

# Chapter Nineteen

One cat down, one to go. I called Eleanor Shrift's number, wondering what kind of program she'd go for, and left my number on her machine. The Persian, meanwhile, had curled up for a nap in his carrier. I couldn't leave him in that forever. If his person was on another business trip, things might get crowded here. For now, though, he looked so peaceful, I decided not to disturb him. Instead, I went downstairs to make peace with Wallis—and make sense out of those files.

It took a while, and I wasn't entirely successful on either front. On the plus side, by the time Wallis emerged, I'd done what I should have from the start. I'd copied the files on the keychain drive to my own computer and begun to look through them in earnest. What Creighton had said was disturbing, but not surprising. Charles probably paid my bills because they were some of the smallest on there. That, and maybe he cared more for his dog than for his suppliers or distributors, whoever they were. But if I was going back to the cop shop, I wanted to know for sure what was up. Businesses go belly up lots of times, even those founded on great ideas. Nobody ends up dead.

"No one you know, anyway." Wallis landed by the keyboard with a thud.

"I wish you wouldn't do that." I'd been staring at a screen too long, and her sudden appearance had startled me.

"What, land abruptly?" She began licking one paw. "Or read your thoughts?"

"Either. Both." I pushed the laptop back. "I'm having a hard time making sense of any of this."

"Maybe because there's no sense to be had." She stared down at the keyboard, and I remembered our previous fight. I needed to change the subject.

"Wallis, I wanted to ask you about the kitten—and also about the black Persian."

She sniffed and started closing her eyes. "You're changing the subject."

"I need the break. And I did mean to ask you. Wasn't it odd how the kitten greeted Delia Cochrane?"

One eye opened. "I wasn't in the room. Remember?"

Actually, I hadn't been sure where she was. "Well, it was. After all those days of crying 'Mama,' the kitten called her 'Delia.'"

"Who knows? I got a whiff of that woman. Her perfume is enough to knock the sense out of anyone. Maybe the kitten got over her. After all, we've been taking care of her."

Had Wallis begun to soften toward the marmalade kitten? She shot me a look. "Forget about it."

"Sorry, but what about the Persian?"

She shifted, a stalling technique that I recognized. "What about him?"

"Why the abrupt turnaround? He'd been grooming himself bare less than a week ago, and now, well, you saw him."

"We didn't exactly converse." I remembered the hiss. Maybe this wasn't a good topic, but Wallis didn't let it drop. "He was lonely. I got that. Someone had broken his heart. You know the type: always ready to fall again. A real lap cat."

I looked over at the tabby and realized again how alike we were. "Maybe that's not a bad way to be."

She tucked her nose into her tail, giving me one last green-eyed glance. "It's a sucker's life."

I had no answer to that one. "Well, he's bunking down with us until I can get him home." I didn't mention that I'd closed the bedroom door behind me. She'd find out soon enough. Perhaps she already knew, because she turned away and went to sleep.

Me, I went back to work. An hour later, Eleanor still had not called, and I was still clueless. I rang her again, kicking myself for not asking whether this was a landline or a cell number.

"Eleanor, it's Pru again. Would you call me? Anytime." I hung up, wishing I could've worked some more warmth into my voice. I both wanted her and didn't want her to claim the big old boy I had upstairs. If she would give us both the time, I thought I could make it work. He deserved a home. Hell, he deserved better than to be abandoned.

With that in mind, I went up to check him out. He was still sleeping, though he'd shifted around some, and so I left him to it and returned downstairs to scrounge around. Although I sensed Wallis watching me, I grabbed one of her cans and a couple of bowls. Food, water, a makeshift litterbox. It was the least I could do, seeing as how I'd sprung the black Persian from the shelter without making any other plans.

Without waking the big cat, I opened the latch on the carrier door. For a moment, I considered reaching in. Perhaps with a touch I could get something. Listen in on a dream. But just then the feline shifted and sighed. He'd been through enough. He deserved some privacy. Instead, I returned to my office and those financial files. Why had Charles put this on Lily's collar, and had it gotten him killed?

A few clicks and I found my way back to that first spreadsheet, the one that seemed to function as Charles' checkbook. Now that I knew my way around, I was able to make sense of more of the expenses. Monthly deductions—I was guessing heat and hot water—showed up in red, as did the odd twenty or forty dollar withdrawal. The running averages were to the right. Once I got the hang of that, I clicked over to the next file. The numbers were definitely bigger here. Some of them, quite large—and most of them in black or a glowing green that made me think of speculation. If I hadn't known better, I'd have wondered if these were projections, the kind of puffed-up estimates that entrepreneurs mock up to show investors. "In the first year, we expect one hundred and thirty percent return," and all that. This kind of hard sell didn't fit with the Charles I'd worked with, the Charles who wanted to stay small—stay in control—and that made me think of Mack. Were these numbers that he had thrown out? Pie in the sky plans designed to entice Charles to go public or seek out venture capital? Pitches for cash that Charles didn't want, but that Mack might have waited for like payday?

What was Mack's role in all of this anyway? Beauville was a small town, but I still had trouble seeing the smooth-talking townie with the geek.

As if on cue, the phone rang. Wallis woke and jumped off the table. I grabbed the phone. It was Mack.

"Hey, babe."

When did I become his babe? "Hello, yourself." I scrolled down the spreadsheet. If I could get him talking, maybe more of this would make sense. Then again, I'd tried that the other night and ended up with a hangover.

"You doing anything?"

"No," I lied. Nothing I wanted to tell him about.

"Wanna come out and play?"

Wallis woke up. We made eye contact. "Play," we both knew, was synonymous with the hunt. "Happy's again?"

"Nah, I've got someplace classy in mind. Why don't I pick you up?"

"You know where I live?" Wallis lashed her tail.

"This is a small town, babe. Everyone knows everything here."

◇◇◇

Two hours later, Wallis butted up against me to alert me to a car pulling up outside. I'd painted my face, as much as I ever do. I refused to change out of my jeans, despite the look Wallis gave me.

"Too late now." I reached down to stroke her sleek head as the doorbell rang. Then, remembering to close the laptop, I went off to greet my date.

"You look scrumptious." I'd opened the door to find Mack moving in. I stepped back automatically and kicked myself for it.

"Let's get some dinner, I'm starved." The man didn't understand subtle.

"Not going to show me around?"

I'll confess the high wattage smile started to thaw my resolve. But when I heard a thump coming from my office, I came back to my senses.

"I have a cat. You don't like cats." I nodded toward the door.

"Whatever made you think that?" He looked down, and I followed his eyes to see Wallis approaching. "They like me well enough."

"Wallis!" I scooped her up before she could reach him and got a quick flash. *Put me down, fool. Let me do my work.*

I almost dropped her after that, startling Mack who, finally, backed up toward the door.

"Whoa, watch it." He stepped away as Wallis, her dignity affronted, began to groom. "Well, shall we?"

"Sure." I motioned for him to lead the way and reached back to lock the door. *He didn't pet me, did you notice?* I nodded once to her. "Later," I said.

◇◇◇

We made the kind of small talk people do, when they've nearly had drunken sex behind a bar but don't really know each other.

"Nice place you got." He was driving into town, and I wondered if he'd changed his mind about Happy's.

"Thanks. I grew up there." This was very small talk. I was really thinking about the significance of what Wallis had said.

"Yeah, I remember you." That got my attention. "You were a few years younger, but you had a reputation."

"Oh?" Wallis had nothing on me when I wanted to freeze someone out, but Mack only laughed.

"Relax. I'm talking kid stuff." We drove through the night. "Still, it got my attention. I guess that's why I decided to look you up when you came back to town."

I turned toward at him. This was news. "*You* decided to look me up?"

"Yeah, babe." He turned toward me, smile at full power. "You think I always hang out at Happy's?"

We rode in silence after that, and at some point, Mack flipped on the radio. There was a college station in the area, and he tuned in some blues, low and mournful. I liked it; it helped me think. We parked in front of a glass storefront that had held a hardware store when I was growing up. By then, I was ready to start again—with our conversation if not with my queries—but Mack walked me up to the glass door, and I realized that in place of tools and sundries, the storefront had turned bistro, its plate-glass window blocked halfway up with thick curtains and its fluorescent aisles now occupied by small, candle-lit tables. We stepped inside and a young waiter, apron wrapped around his waist butcher style, came up and escorted us to a deuce. We'd just given him drink orders—red wine for me, a beer for Mack—when Mack excused himself. I contented myself with reading the menu. A free meal is a free meal, and I liked the look of this place. The menu convinced me that Beauville hadn't changed that much. The steaks and chops might come with pedigrees, but this was meat and potatoes, fancy trimmings or not.

Don't get me wrong. I love a good burger, and I used to be able to put away a steak that would scare a full-grown man. But ever since I've started being able to hear what animals say, I've had problems with the obvious cuts of meat. Wallis would laugh at me, for sure, if she knew. She was one of the reasons I still cooked with ground meat and brought home the occasional chicken. On my own, however, I preferred to avoid the issue. I scanned the menu. An eggplant lasagna seemed to be the one vegetarian offering, a sop to former city folk like me. I resigned myself to something thick and tasteless and closed the menu to wait for Mack's return. As if on cue, Officer Creighton appeared and took the seat opposite me.

"Good evening, Officer. Are you going to be our sommelier tonight?" Maybe it wasn't witty, but it was the best I could do.

"Don't get mouthy with me, Pru. I've been trying to talk with you." He leaned forward and I fought the urge to pull back.

"I said I'd come in tomorrow, Officer." I emphasized my words. He wasn't going to see me quake. "Now, if you don't mind?"

"I do, actually. I heard that one of the activities that was keeping you busy was scaring poor Mrs. Harris half to death."

"What?" I was pissed now. "She's a tough lady. She was out digging in her garden before I left." Not exactly true, but close enough. Another thought struck me. "Who's been telling you these things?"

"Delia Cochrane." As he spoke, I saw Mack come up behind him. He heard enough to suss out what was going on.

"Ah, Delia." I forced myself to smile. This was beginning to make sense. "And you and Delia are close?" Behind Creighton, Mack smiled for real.

"Delia's a good girl, Pru. She's not out to cause any trouble."

I raised my eyebrows at that one, but Mack took his cue. "Delia's a real sweetheart, Jim. But if you'll take my advice, you'll stay clear of that particular honeypot. Now, if you'll excuse me?" Only Mack could be menacing with such charm. Whether it was the bigger man leaning over him or his own sense of propriety, I couldn't tell. Creighton stood up and nodded to me. "My office, first thing."

"Good night, officer." I waggled my fingers at him.

"Can't leave you alone for a minute, can I?" Mack took his chair back. "Now, where are our drinks?"

An hour later, I was warm, full, and mildly astounded. The lasagna had proved a treat, with good cheese and a zingy tomato sauce that played off the eggplant nicely. More to the point, Mack had proved to be better company than I'd expected. I'd learned the hard way that sexy men who are fun in bars don't often clean up so well. But here he was, acting charming and like he was very interested in me. That, in fact, was the big sticking point. I'd been hoping to get some more out of him, but he'd managed to turn it all around. I was a bit of a legend, the way he saw it. The wild child. The joyrider who busted up her mom's car and still managed to graduate top of the class. With a free pass to college and the city, I'd gotten away clean, and yet here I was, back in town. He gave me a look when I pulled out my mom's final illness as my excuse. He sensed something else had driven me from the city. By the time coffee came around, he was probing, both at our shared slice of pie and my defenses.

"So you were this close to your degree, and you came here?"

"I needed a change anyway." I shook my head, turning down a forkful of spiced apples.

He ate it, chewing more thoughtfully than the filling merited. "Who was he?"

I nearly laughed with relief. "There was no 'he.'"

His eyebrows went up. "She?"

"No, I mean, I'm no nun. But, honestly, that's not why I left."

"'Cause I have noticed a certain reticence about intimacy." I must have made a face. "And yes, we do use words like 'reticence' out here. Or was it 'intimacy' that got you?"

I was chuckling out loud by then. He *was* charming. And we'd drunk a fair amount of wine. "It was my cat." Maybe I wanted to tell someone. I didn't think he'd get it.

"Great, another—"

"*Don't* say it." I held up my hand to stop him. "Yeah, I know, I'm becoming a stereotype. But, that's the truth and—"

I was about to say something else. Something about sticking to my story that would allow me to be ever so slightly honest and yet give me deniability later, if I ever could tell him the truth. But just then something caught my eye. The restaurant was small; two rooms, maybe thirty tables tops. We were seated in the second room, away from the front door, but some movement, some flash of color, had caught my eye.

"What?" Mack turned around, but she was gone.

"Excuse me." I pushed back my chair, suddenly aware of just how much I had drunk. "I've got to go talk to a woman about a cat."

I threw down my napkin and stormed into the front room. Eleanor Shrift might blow me off, but she'd adopted an animal.

She was responsible for that black Persian, and I was going to call her on her it. Only thing was, I no longer saw her.

"Excuse me." I reached out to the young maitre'd. "Did a woman just come in here? Dark hair, a little older?"

"I'm sorry, I didn't see anyone."

I turned around, searching for another sight of Eleanor. She wasn't among the diners. "Could she have gone back there?" I glanced toward the kitchen.

"Not if she doesn't work here, and your description doesn't sound like any of our staff."

"Well, maybe she's waiting outside."

The maitre'd looked past me, and I had a nasty feeling that he was about ready to call for Mack. "That's not likely, ma'am. We seated our last party forty minutes ago."

Sure enough, most of the tables were empty. The radio in the kitchen had been turned up, signs of cleaning already beginning. I turned back toward Mack. He looked slightly puzzled. We were, I noticed finally, the only table still occupied in the second room.

"Sorry." I slunk back to my seat. "I thought I saw someone. A client."

"Not Charles, I hope?" He was smiling. Maybe it was the wine.

"No, Eleanor Shrift. I have her black cat over at my place."

"She's got a cat, too? Figures."

I tried to read his face as he settled the bill. Was he having me on? If he was Eleanor's secret lover, he not only knew about her cat, he'd basically broken its heart. I remembered the earring and wondered if I could get anything out of the big Persian when I got home.

"Hey, I should be getting on," I said. I wasn't getting anything out of him, and I had other business to take care of. "I've got a big day tomorrow." For the second time, I stood up. This time, the wine didn't make me sway. The maitre'd came over with our coats, the last two left.

"Jim Creighton?" Mack rose and reached for my arm as he helped me into my jacket. His arm lingered. "Don't let him spoil our night."

"Come on." I pulled away, but softened the words with a smile. "You've already had your dessert."

I couldn't read his face after that, but put it up to disappointment. With only the barest thanks to the remaining restaurant staff, he ushered me out to the street.

"Well, that was delicious. Thanks for a great evening." I knew we had a drive home, but I wanted to make my position clear.

"My pleasure." His smile seemed forced now, his gaze distracted.

He was, in fact, looking over my shoulder. I turned and squinted. Down the street, someone was walking. A woman, with the clipped, sexy gait of high heels. It was Eleanor Shrift.

◇◇◇

The college station had switched to jazz, and I cranked it. I was in no mood for conversation, and besides the DJ was playing Monk. Instead, I gazed out the window as the streets of our small town gave way to trees and hills. Beauville could be beautiful, especially this time of year. But there was too much that was strange going on, and in the headlights the foliage was all bleached to gray anyway.

"Penny for your thoughts?" He was trying, I gave him that.

"I was thinking about this dog I walk." I was. That snippy little bichon hadn't given me anything since he'd told me that Delia was pregnant.

"Come on, Pru. Tell me what's really going on."

I wanted to confide in somebody. Would he believe me? "I'm just thinking of all the animals in this town, Mack. If they ever told all they know, everything they see…"

"You're thinking of Charles, aren't you?" He glanced at me, but then turned back to the road. His voice seemed level and calm.

"Yeah, I am."

"If his dog could talk, huh?" He kept driving. I kept my eyes on him. "What happened to that dog anyway?"

"I took her over to Charles' mother."

He mulled that one over. "So that's what Creighton was on about."

"Well, you know she was cleared."

"The dog, you mean?"

"Of course, the dog. The coroner's report cleared her: the wounds weren't consistent with dog bite."

"But still, does Charles' old mom want it?" He kept going before I could respond. "I mean, I know Charles loved that dog, but, hey, it's a pit bull."

"She's going to give it a shot." The more I thought about the old lady, the more I admired her. She was tough. "And, besides, they both loved Charles."

He nodded a little thoughtful. "I guess it's just as well that dog can't talk then. If she could, she'd be a witness to murder. Someone might try to kill her, too."

# Chapter Twenty

It wasn't what Mack had said. I didn't really think Lily was in danger. After all, nobody had believed her story except me. The combination of his casual reference and the sight of Eleanor Shrift had gotten to me. I didn't know what was wrong with these people. But the animals were suffering for it, and that I wasn't going to stand for.

By the time Mack pulled up to my place, I was steaming.

"Don't bother," I said, reaching for the door. I'd noticed he'd turned off his car engine, and I didn't think he was only planning on walking me to my door. "I'm going out again."

"Oh?" My declaration seemed to put him off balance. "Something I did? I mean, if you want to keep on drinking…"

"No." I was halfway out the door. "I'm going over to Eleanor Shrift's. She never called me back about her Persian."

"Can't it wait? I mean, it's just a—"

"*Don't* say it." Something of my mood must have carried in my tone because finally he seemed to get it. He still got out of the car, and with his long strides caught up with me before I reached my own front door.

"Want some company?"

"No." I fumbled with my key for a moment, but managed to let myself in. Before Mack could follow, I turned back to him. "Thank you for the lovely dinner," I said, and closed the door.

◇◇◇

I didn't mean to listen to him drive away, but as I stood there in the dark I couldn't help but notice how dark and lonely my house was. That is, until I felt the brush of fur against my skin.

"Wallis?"

"You were expecting someone else?" I reached down for the hefty tabby, and, probably sensing my mood, she allowed me to lift her. "Your mind is full of that Persian—and that *dog*."

"I know, Wallis. I'm sorry. Life has gotten complicated."

She snorted, a small delicate sniff. "You always had a choice." I felt the pinprick of claws through my shirt. "You still do."

Wallis must have sensed my intentions, but I was having second thoughts. "How do you feel about letting the Persian stay the night? I mean, I want to talk to Eleanor, but maybe bringing him into it—"

"Wouldn't be the smartest idea?" Wallis drew back to look at me. I had the unnerving sense that those green eyes saw more than she let on. "You getting all heroic on us now? Does that mean you might be getting brave enough to return to the city soon?"

I sighed and put her down on the floor. "It's just, well, I feel responsible."

"For everyone but yourself." Wallis began neatening the fur I had disturbed. "But in answer to your questions, plural. No, I wouldn't mind. That flat face has the personality of an ottoman, but he knows his place." She kept washing, clearly avoiding my eyes. "And, no, he couldn't tell me any more about his person's man. Some big guy. Very hands on. It seems the human had the good sense to prefer fur."

"Oh?" Wallis had more to tell, but she likes to know her audience is listening. "Into bestiality, was he?"

"Please." She twisted around to work on her back. To anyone else, it would seem like she was ignoring me. I knew better. Wallis liked her dramatic pauses. "It was a rebound affair. Burned out quickly." She moved on to her tail. "I gather everything was hot and heavy for a few months, then, well, then he turned his attention to the cat. Sensible human."

I knew better than to take everything Wallis said at face value. Cats, for example, have a very different sense of time. But the rebound factor was something new. I thought of Mack, and of Delia's perfume. If he had been Eleanor's summer fling, maybe he'd ended it because the younger woman had taken him back. Which left me—where? Were Chris Moore and I both serving as beards, while Charles' supposed fiancé and his business partner carried on? Or was the Persian's petter someone else entirely?

I had questions for Eleanor, but I wasn't going to submit that cat to humiliation and rejection—or an unnecessary car trip. I grabbed my keys and, with a nod to Wallis, headed out.

By the time I found that college station, the jazz DJ was winding up. Close to midnight, he'd said, and I wondered for a moment if I was going too far. Sane animal behaviorists don't storm over to their clients' houses at this hour. But, hell, I'd seen Eleanor Shrift up and about not that long before. Besides, my messages had asked her to call me whatever the time. She was back in town. She hadn't called. She had this coming.

◇◇◇

Eleanor's house was dark when I pulled up into her driveway, but the closed garage door kept me from speculating whether she was home or still out. For a minute, I hesitated. Then, sitting in my car, I dialed her number.

"You've reached 413-" Great. All that told me was that Eleanor still wasn't answering her phone. I hung up. No reason to let her think I was stalking her. But after one more tune—something by 'Trane—and the DJ's signoff, I decided to stop wasting gas and try her door.

I knocked. There was no answer. I rang the bell and heard it chime inside, these new houses lacking the solid doors and walls of Beauville's older houses. I tried Eleanor's number again, and once again hung up on her voicemail. At least I hadn't heard it ringing inside the house. Wherever she was, Eleanor likely had her phone with her, and she was choosing not to answer it. With a childish, and yet very satisfying, kick at her door, I gave up and returned to my car. Five minutes later, I couldn't stand the wait. The next show was some kind of ambient techno, and I tuned into an all-night news station as I drove more slowly back to my own home.

◇◇◇

What was going on with that woman? What was the deal with Mack? And what was I going to do with the big black Persian? Wallis and I had something special, I knew that, but I also knew that animals were my soft spot. Was I going to end up taking in every unloved cat in the Berkshires?

"Pru Marlowe, crazy cat lady." As I pulled up in front of my own house once again, I tried that out for size. "Pru Marlowe. Hoarder." Yeah, it could fit. I pushed open my front door. "Hey, Wallis! What do you think—" But before I could finish my question, the oddity of my own action had hit me. I'd *pushed open* the door. Hadn't I locked it before I'd left? Beauville might be a small town, but I still had a city dweller's instincts, didn't I?

"Wallis?" My voice had dropped to a dry whisper. I stepped into the front hall and felt the broken glass crackle beneath my shoes. Great, second time this week. I reached for the light when it hit me. Maybe I shouldn't be walking in here. Maybe I should step back, get out. Call Creighton or one of his colleagues. I hadn't last time. But Wallis had been there, reassuring me. Filling me in.

"Wallis?" Where was she? I'd left her here. Alone, except for Eleanor Shrift's long-suffering Persian. The moment of fear vanished, evaporating into sheer rage.

"Who the hell is here?" It wasn't my smartest move, but I was pissed. "I said—" Before I could go any further, two strong hands grabbed me from behind, clenching down on my upper arms. "No!" I yelled, twisting to my left. The arms pulled me backward, and I let myself start to fall, the movement giving me enough slack to reach into my jeans pocket. Thumb on the button, and my blade was out. It was in the wrong hand, and I didn't have the leeway for a good strike, but using my wrist

I stabbed down hard. My knife has a sharp blade, and I felt it connect with the leg behind me. Not deep, but deep enough. I waited for the smack I knew would come. Most men don't like being stabbed. But instead of pulling me around, the stranger threw me away, toward the couch. I stumbled, trying to keep my balance, and came down hard on one knee. That knee gave out, and I found myself falling onto the glass.

"No!" I yelled out, as much at the glittering floor as at my attacker, and forced myself to roll to the side. I didn't need a face full of glass, and I did want to see who had invaded my home. But even as I landed, rolling up against my worn-out sofa, he—or she—was gone. I sensed as much as saw the movement: a body, a flash of dark, a leg heading out the open door. I reached to push myself up and had to fight back tears. Despite my best efforts, a sliver of glass had wedged itself into the heel of my hand, and something had gone wrong with my knee. By the time I was up, the intruder was gone. Down on the street, an engine started. A car must have been waiting there, in the dark, but I'd been too distracted to notice a strange vehicle. The sound of the car faded away, and I was left standing, in pain, alone.

"Would you mind closing the door?"

I whipped around. "Wallis!" My tabby was standing at the far side of the glittering mess, highlighted by the weak moonlight coming through the remains of yet another of my front windows. The broken glass, I could now see, had been one of the panes, and I found myself feeling absurdly grateful for small favors. At least the intruder had only smashed one pane and used the access to lift the window open. I turned to the plump tabby. I could've hugged her.

She saw my outstretched arms and drew back. "You're bleeding."

She was right. I looked at my open hand and even in the dim light I could see the shard that had gotten me, an angry sliver sticking out of the base of my thumb. "Wow, for a moment I'd forgotten about that." I started to pick at it.

"That's the adrenaline talking, Pru. You've been attacked."

"And now my pet is telling me I'm not in my right mind?" I gave her a look, but I couldn't stop the smile that was spreading across my face. She stared back. "You're right, Wallis. I've got to take care of this." I got up and started toward the bathroom. The knee hurt, but it worked. "But, hey, Wallis, watch out."

"Don't worry." She sidestepped the broken glass delicately. "I'm not a kitten. Speaking of, I trust that the little redhead got settled in all right?"

"I hope so, Wallis." I sensed rather than heard her follow me to the bathroom. She jumped up on the closed toilet seat and watched as I used a tweezer to pull out the slice of offending glass. "Opposable thumbs," I bragged.

"Useful," she agreed. She was humoring me, but the adrenaline had already started to wear off. I washed the wound and slumped to the floor. "So, you probably want to know what happened." She jumped down and walked up to me. I extended my legs, and she climbed into my lap, warm and soft.

"Yeah." My eyes started to close. "Who—" With a start, I sprang awake. Wallis stopped kneading and looked into my face.

"There's nobody else here, Pru. Relax." I closed my eyes once more. "It was a single human, male. I'm not sure who. Once I heard the noise, I decided it would be prudent to stay undercover."

"What did he want?" I was drifting off. It had been a long night. But a thought broke in. "The Persian?"

"He's fine. Slept through it all. I gather that so-called shelter is not the most restful place for a feline."

"No." I thought of the other animals that came in and out. The staff—Pammy—talking all through the day. The bright lights, the institutional smells. "It wouldn't be." My knee was throbbing, and I wondered it some glass had gotten into it as well. I should take my jeans off, check. But Wallis was settling in, so cozy. "So, it— he— wasn't looking for that cat?" The idea didn't make much sense. Neither did I at this point.

"No, he didn't come upstairs at all."

Good. I had few personal treasures. A brooch from my grandmother. My mother's rings. But Wallis was still talking.

"He seemed to know exactly what he wanted. As far as I could hear, he came straight in the window and headed toward your office. He was on his way out when you came in. I tried to warn you, but you weren't listening."

I hadn't been. My mind had been on my incipient future as a cat hoarder. To Wallis, it must have seemed like I'd been absorbed by thoughts of other cats. "I wasn't serious, Wal."

"I was. I'm not entirely sure who this fellow was, but I didn't like him coming in like that. He could have waited till you invited him."

"Excuse me?" I was too sleepy. Wallis wasn't making sense.

"Well, I didn't catch the details, but one thing I can tell you with all certainty, there's no new scent here—in the house, or on you. Whoever he was, you've had contact with him before."

Great. I sat there for a while longer and then finally pulled myself upright, taking Wallis with me as I climbed the interminable stairway up to my bedroom. Whoever had broken into my home was someone I had invited over at some point. Who could that be? Compared to my recent past, I'd been positively nun-like since moving back to Beauville. Still, even counting the casual guests, there was a sizable list. Detective Creighton came to mind, though I couldn't see the straight-laced cop making a midnight raid. Albert had been by, early on, when I was first establishing my bona fides—and I didn't yet realize how obnoxious he could be. Doc Sharp, too, for that matter. Mack had swung by, and dropped me off not—I checked my watch—two hours before. And earlier Chris Moore had come by, accompanying the always-mysterious Delia. My mind flashed on Eleanor. No, Wallis had definitely said "he," and the arms that had thrown me to the floor did not belong to a fortysomething woman, no matter what gym she belonged to. Still, if her secret lover were out and around…No, there were too many possibilities to sort through tonight.

I was about to open my bedroom door when I remembered why I'd closed it. I looked at Wallis.

"It's fine, you know." She blinked twice. "I've let him know how things are run around here. As long as this is temporary…"

Still, I wasn't sure. I turned back to the guest bedroom. Wallis squirmed, and I let her jump down. In response, she reached up with both paws and deftly turned the doorknob, leaning against the door at the same time to push it open. "See?" With a flick of her tail she led the way in.

I should have been asleep as soon as I hit the bed. Maybe it was the adrenaline runoff, but something was wrong.

"Hang on, Wallis." I took a deep breath and headed for the stairs.

"He's gone, you know." She remained on the bed. "It's just the three of us now."

"Three?" I felt myself tense. The pain in my knee didn't help, and I was startled to feel a familiar pressure against my shin. When I saw the thick midnight fur of the black Persian, I made myself relax. "Sorry, big guy." I was very tempted to pick him up, but Wallis was watching. Besides, I needed to check out the first floor myself. "This isn't the refuge I was planning."

I didn't know how much he understood, but with one final head butt, he walked back into the room. I heard a brief hiss— Wallis, no doubt—and then silence. I walked gingerly toward the stairs.

My house is old, built sometime in the late 1800s. But I'd grown up here, and I'd known its quirks since girlhood. It had been a while since I needed to descend silently; there was little need to sneak out at night when you lived alone. And I trusted Wallis' senses, I really did. Still, I hugged the wall as I made my way down, lowering my weight ever so gently on each wooden step.

"Hello?" There was no answer, of course. Still, I found myself breathing easier as I stepped around the broken glass. Wallis had said that the intruder had gone into my office, but through the open door I could see my laptop, closed and silent. Maybe I'd interrupted him before he could decide what to grab. I looked around the back room. Some files, more bookshelves. A folded blanket that Wallis favored for naps.

From here, I could see through the back porch, enclosed since my father's day. It struck me as funny. Twice in one week, someone had broken my front windows. This back room would have been easier to enter. I looked at the old wicker furniture stored there, a settee that had seen better days. A rocker with a shredded pillow. Perhaps my intruder wasn't that smart. Or perhaps he hadn't thoroughly cased the house.

Well, no harm done. Relief came in the form of exhaustion, and I collapsed into my desk chair. On a whim, I opened my laptop. Yes, it woke up, and the screen staring back at me was once again the column of numbers I'd been analyzing earlier.

Then it hit me. The keychain drive. I had everything on it, copied onto my laptop. But the little plastic drive that I had left here, protruding from its side, was gone.

I so wanted to sleep. The damage was done, and I and the cats were okay. But some perverse sense of justice—or maybe simple annoyance—made me call Officer Creighton.

"Yes, I am home late. I thought you should know that someone broke into my house tonight. No," I made a snap decision. "Nothing is missing. Not that I can see." That would give me a little wiggle room in case I changed my mind. "But you wanted to talk to me in the morning, and well, it's nearly three now."

I heard a grunt on the line and wondered if he'd gone back to sleep. I didn't hear any other voices, female or male, and a moment later he came back on the line.

"Don't do anything. I'm coming over."

Unsure about what exactly his proscription covered and too tired to be bothered with cleanup, I sacked out on the sofa, waking with a start when headlights cut through the dark.

"You know, you could have called 911." Out of uniform, his dirty blond hair standing up where he'd run his hands through it—all in all, not an unattractive visitor to have pre-dawn.

"Could I? I didn't know if anyone would respond." I let my hair fall in my face and tugged my shirt down to remove some of the wrinkles.

"Very funny." I'd flipped on all the lights as he'd walked up to the door, but he had his flashlight out anyway, peeking under the sofa and out the broken window to the ground below. "Run me through this again?"

So I did, from arriving home to being thrown onto the glass. "Then he ran."

"And he didn't take anything." Something told me Officer Creighton didn't believe me.

"I didn't see anything in his hands." That much was true. "And I've looked around."

He rubbed one broad palm over his face again. "Okay, well, I'd like you to check in again later, when you're awake. And you can file a report when you come in, too."

"Aren't you going to dust for fingerprints? Take samples or anything?" I gestured at the glittering glass, which by now had been spread further into the living room.

"You been watching too many cop shows, Pru." He looked at me, hard. "This sounds like amateur hour. Maybe some of the local kids. You're getting a reputation, you know?"

"Oh?" Faced with a statement like that, I find it best to stonewall.

"Yeah, first that dog. Now people are talking about you taking cats home." To do him credit, he tried to smile. "You've got to be careful, Pru. They say you're turning into one of those crazy cat ladies."

"They don't know the half of it," I said. As I walked him out, I snuck a glance up the stairs. Wallis and the black Persian sat side by side on the landing, making sure I'd seen the cop out.

"Okay, what's up?" I trudged up the steps, after once again deciding I could leave cleanup till the morning. "Spill, or I'm going to sleep."

"It's Floyd here." Wallis sounded ever so slightly sheepish.

"Floyd?" I looked down at the Persian, who hugged my right. He looked up and blinked. "Okay, hi, Floyd."

The black cat blinked again. I was too tired for this. "Wallis? I think you're going to have to translate."

Wallis sighed. "I told him you were cool." The two cats stared at each other. If there was something going on here, I wasn't getting any of it. "Something about the intruder."

"I know, he's been here before." Right now, I'd have given good money for uncommunicative cats.

"Yeah, but he knows him. It wasn't his person, but it was someone who'd been around. And I heard what that copper said."

A new voice chimed in.

"It wasn't a boy." The Persian's voice was as soft as his fur, hesitant. "It was a man, a big man."

I started to say something. I knew that. I'm the one who had been thrown to the floor. But something about the Persian's tone stopped me. "And there was something else. He was, how would you put it? He was polite."

I shook my head to clear it. My wires were getting crossed. "What did you say?"

"Polite." The big cat blinked up at me. "You know, nice."

"Nice?" Someone had broken my window. Had broken into my house, and had attacked me. My knee throbbed, as did my hand. "Nice?"

I looked at the two cats, but they only blinked and turned away. Great. Now I had two animals in my house who thought I was as dense as a dog.

# Chapter Twenty-one

I still hadn't figured that one out when the phone woke me early the next morning. It was Creighton. Revenge I guess.

"Just making sure you're still planning on coming in." He sounded a little too chipper for the amount of sleep we'd both had.

"And here I was, thinking that you cared." I sat up to keep from falling back asleep and looked over at my clock. I'd have been up within a half hour anyway.

"Oh, I do, I do."

That was a joke, it had to be. But there was still a slight awkward silence while my brain caught up. I remembered what he'd looked like last night, all tousled and buff, and I shook my head to clear it.

"Feeling's mutual, Officer." I reached for my jeans. "But I've got some animals to take care of first. I'll be in by 10."

"Looking forward to it." That wasn't his usual signoff, and I found myself staring at the phone as the line went dead.

I was making coffee when Wallis found me. Something about the curl in her tail told me she was thinking, and I turned toward her, waiting to hear what she had to say.

"You know, I'm not so sure I like this." She sat and fixed me with a look.

"Coffee?" I was playing dumb.

She didn't buy it. "Don't be more stupid than you can help, Pru." Her tail lashed once. "I mean, the translation gig. It's not me, and I'm not comfortable with it."

"Translation?" I stopped measuring beans. There was something I was missing.

She half closed her green eyes. "You don't think that Floyd actually communicated with you, do you?" I shrugged. "He's way too shy. A real scaredy cat. No, I had to, well, *boost* his thoughts."

"Huh." I nodded and continued to measure out spoonfuls. This was news to me, and it made me wonder how often Wallis had been putting herself into my conversations.

"Not often."

"Wallis!" I spun around. She was stretched on the floor.

"Sorry." She reached out to knead the air. "You asked. But usually I just, well, I just give other cats a lift. Help them focus. After all, we phrase things differently than you do. We have a different emphasis."

I was beginning to suspect where this was going. "And you think you misinterpreted something Floyd wanted to tell me."

She turned away from me. "Not misinterpret. Just…a slight difference in emphasis."

"That's understandable, Wallis." I tried to keep my voice calm. "Would you tell me what it was?"

"It was the idea of courtesy. We, as cats, don't really have a concept of manners. We don't need to. But some things are unpleasant to us. Loud noises. Water. Sharp smells that irritate our eyes or noses. Direct eye contact or constant, what do you call it? Petting. I mean, when we don't desire it."

"So 'not annoying' might have been a better translation than 'polite'?" I paused. I really didn't need to set her off this morning. "Perhaps a little more accurate?"

"Something like." She stood up to leave the room. "And don't patronize me, Pru. It doesn't become you."

After that I wasn't going to search for the black Persian. I needed time with my own thoughts. I poured my coffee into a travel mug and hit the road. It was early enough that I stood the risk of waking Tracy Horlick, but I had a busy day ahead of me, and I didn't really care. As I drove over, I started to map out my day. First, the bichon. Then, Creighton. A waste of time, but maybe not quite the waste I'd have thought a few days earlier. Besides, I wanted to find out what the latest was on Charles' case, and I knew I'd have a better chance of finding out in person. At least, I should be able to suss out whether I was still in the hot seat. Then I should try Eleanor Shrift again. It wasn't just that I was pissed at her, or that the black Persian—Floyd—deserved a home. Technically, I had no right to her cat, and she could raise hell for me for taking the animal from the shelter without her authorization. Finally, if I had a chance to breathe in there, I wanted to swing by Nora Harris' again. I'd left her with a dog she didn't necessarily want. A dog that took a fair amount of care, too. And while it wasn't Delia Cochrane's job to take care of Lily, I wanted to hear why she'd been badmouthing me to the cops.

I paused and sat back. Maybe I was overreacting on that one. Maybe that was Creighton, being protective of the young widowette. I sighed. No hiding from your own motives. But, hey, at the very least, I should go by and see how they were all settling in. Offer the grieving mother some obedience training lessons or something.

If I had hopes of waking Tracy Horlick, they were dashed as I walked up to her door.

"Come in! Come in!" My client had on her customary housecoat and slippers, but her face was already heavily made up and underneath some clumpy mascara her eyes shone with anticipation. "Would you like some coffee?"

That was a first, but I raised my travel mug in response. "No thanks, Mrs. Horlick." I didn't trust her brew anyway.

I reached for the bichon's lead, but she grabbed my arm. "I hear you had some excitement last night."

For a brief moment, I thought of Mack. Had she heard about our dinner date already? But the tight-faced little woman kept talking. "First, there's a murder, then a break in. Makes you wonder what's happening to Beauville, doesn't it?" The pure glee in her face undercut any concern in her voice and set my back right up.

"Crime happens everywhere, Mrs. Horlick." I poked around for the dog.

"And once again you're in the center of it." She glared at me, waiting for a response. "It's almost like you're involved."

"Bitsy?" I'd avoided using the cutesy name ever since the little dog had corrected me. But if I were to call for "Growler," old Horlick would have the news about my mental instability all over the county by noon. "Bitsy?"

"I wonder if it's any coincidence." She batted her eyelashes at me, and I had the impression of two spiders fighting. "Seeing as how you were out with that Mack Danton last night."

Okay, my reputation was already shot. "Where's your dog, Mrs. Horlick?"

"What, Bitsy? He must still be asleep."

She turned to glance behind her, and I used the moment to slide past. Once inside, it was easy to hear the scrabble and scrape of small claws on the inside of a locked door. "Growler?" I whispered.

"Oh, there he is!" Horlick had come up behind me and so, without waiting for answer, I reached to open the door. The bichon shot out, then stopped short while I snapped his lead on.

"Guess we're out of here!" I let the small dog propel me down the front steps and toward the street.

"But I didn't get to hear what happened!" Her whine carried down the walk.

"Sounds like you already have," I called, and followed the bichon toward the nearest tree.

"Growler, may I ask you something?" Six trees and as many sniff stops later, and we were well clear of the Horlick house. But even when I repeated my question, the bichon ignored me.

"*Thomas, Marco, Wolf.*" He stopped to sniff at a hydrant. "*Tiger. Hmm.... a new fellow.*"

"Growler?" I thought of what Wallis had said about mediators. Maybe he didn't hear me. Or maybe he simply didn't feel like talking. The more I got to know Tracy Horlick, the more I understood the small dog's reticence around people. I resisted the urge to pull up on the leash and forced myself to remember my training. "Growler?"

Nothing, and so I sat on the curb. I wouldn't pull on the leash, but I wouldn't go forward either. To get what he wanted, the little dog would have to pay attention to what I wanted. Within two minutes, he was staring up at me.

*"What is it now?"* He seemed pissed.

"Growler, I want to talk to you."

With a sigh, he sat on grass. Some things translate across all species lines.

"You told me Delia was pregnant."

*"Anyone with a nose would know that."* He shifted, and I realized he considered that question answered.

"Yeah, well, you were also telling me about Charles." Silence. "You know Charles rescued Lily, right? Well, I want to find out who hurt him. Who killed him. And to do that, I need to know more about him."

I'd lost him. The bichon was on his feet again, sniffing at the air. I got fragments—something about a bird, a whiff of a skunk. Somewhere, a female had gone into heat. I was getting desperate.

"Do you want us to go find her?" I'd have to answer to the female's person, but at this point I had nothing else to bargain with.

*"Do I? What?"* The little dog whipped around and nailed me with a fierce glare. *"No, I don't. I want to keep walking."*

"Okay." I struggled to my feet. The night had left me stiff, and my knee ached. "If we can keep talking."

*"Scout, Tumbler."* His wet nose was quivering. I wasn't going to get anywhere near his full attention. *"Johann."*

"Tell you what, Growler." I let myself be pulled forward. "Just tell me a little about Charles. Just what comes to the top of your head." I didn't know if the idiom translated, but I hoped the intent would. "And I'll take you down to the river again—*and* let you roll in the mud."

Despite himself, the bichon let his tail wag. I had him. *"Good guy. Lots of treats."* Growler had given up on the suburban trees and was pulling me straight toward the river footpath. *"I liked him."*

"And?" Once we got into the wet leaves and wild animal scents, I'd lose him for good.

*"Isn't it obvious?"* He had me trotting now, in his eagerness to get to the river.

"Isn't *what* obvious?" I could have laughed. At least Wallis couldn't see me.

*"He was like me."* And then a blue jay swooped down low, and all conversation ended.

"I was beginning to worry." Tracy Horlick's drawn-on eyebrows bunched together in disapproval. I didn't want to hear it.

"Well, he'd waited for so long, I wanted to give him a nice romp." And butter wouldn't melt in my mouth.

Her mouth bunched up as well, the morning's lipstick already cracking. For a moment, I thought she might cry.

"I'm off. Got to talk to Officer Creighton." I waved and walked off. Might as well throw the old bag a bone. Who knows what I'd hear if I started to shake things up?

I had to admit Creighton didn't look any worse for wear when he walked up to meet me at the Beauville police station. Even with his hair smoothed down and the drab khaki uniform, I couldn't help seeing him as a good-looking man. Which meant trouble, for me. I'd have to be on alert, I reminded myself as I followed him back to his office.

"Thanks for coming in, Pru." At least we'd moved onto first-name basis.

"My pleasure, Jim." I enjoyed the momentary fluster as I took a seat. "So, what's up? Let's start with what the coroner's report said."

He straightened in his seat, like a little boy at school. "If you don't mind, I'll ask the questions. For example, I'd like to know more about that break in last night—and the attempt the other day."

"Attempt?" The broken window.

"This *is* a small town, Pru. When I heard that Ricky was going over to your place to fix a window, I put two and two together."

"And came up with five. How do you know that I didn't do that myself?"

"Throw a rock in? Be real, Pru." He leaned back in his chair. "It's not like you've got money to throw around on home improvements."

I opened my mouth,, but the snappy comeback didn't come. "Is that what this is about? Me and my money? For all you know, my mother left me a fortune."

"I knew your mother, too, Pru. And I've seen some of your billing."

I could feel the color rise to my face. I was steaming. "Look, Creighton—"

"Relax." He raised his hands, and the animal part of me wanted to lash out. The human part remembered that for all our new camaraderie, he was a police officer. I bit my lip. "I'm just telling you I know how things stand. For what it's worth, your penury is in your favor."

"Big word for a cop." I wouldn't storm out, but I didn't have to like it.

"Pru, someone killed Charles. Someone killed Charles in a particularly bloody fashion and tried to make it look like his dog had done it. You were there. You found him, and you'd trained that dog. But it doesn't seem like he owed you that much money."

He paused, and I looked up at him. This was all good, sure, but there was something he wasn't saying. Then he let the other shoe drop. "Unless, of course, there was something not on the books. Like you'd invested in his company. Or had some private arrangement."

The way he said it made me feel greasy. "Maybe you should be looking at Delia Cochrane. Or doesn't anyone want to say anything bad about Beauville's golden girl."

"Hey, you're the one who got away." He chuckled a little, and I could have sworn there was a slight flush on his cheeks. "But, tell me more. Why Delia?"

I wasn't sure how much to say. "Well, she's spending a lot of time with Chris Moore now."

He shrugged. "They were together for years, then they weren't. There were no signs that she was seeing him while she was with Charles."

I wondered how he knew that, and if it could be trusted. "Well, maybe there was someone else, then." I thought of Mack—and what Wallis had told me about her scent. Then, as Creighton shrugged, I found myself considering him, too. The young cop was the right age, and handsome enough to appeal. Especially if one needed an alibi.

"Now, why are you going on about Delia, Pru?" Yes, he definitely was sweet on her. "I mean, she works for his mother, for Christ's sake. She fixed them up."

"Yeah, and she's got Alzheimer's or something, right? That's a hell of a recommendation." I didn't like the way this conversation was going. With a jolt, I realized I was a little jealous. Probably just the attention. "But there's more." Almost before I could stop myself, I blurted it out. "I think Delia's pregnant, and who knows who the father is."

"Now that's going too far." He stood up, and for just a moment, I expected him to hit me. "I don't know where you've heard this, or even if it's true. But the young lady lost her fiancé less than two weeks ago, and here you are accusing her of— of I don't know what."

"Infidelity. Maybe murder." I looked up at him. He surely felt the need to defend Delia.

"For what reason, Pru? What would she gain?" He gained control of himself and sat on the edge of the desk. It wasn't much more casual, but it did allow him to loom over me. I tried not to react.

"Money? Love?" He answered his own question. "Revenge? There's nothing in it, Pru. Nothing for Delia."

"If she had a secret lover…" I let the suggestion hang in the air.

Creighton stood and walked to the back of his office. It didn't take him long, and it didn't seem to drain the anger out of his muscular frame, either. "Chris Moore was seeing someone else until recently." He glanced back at me. "I do know how to do my job. And if there's another man, well, he hasn't stepped forward, has he?"

"Maybe he can't now." An idea was taking shape. "Not if he'd be wanted for murder."

"You're spinning a conspiracy theory, Pru." He walked over to his door and opened it. I was being dismissed. "And what I'm looking at are hard, cold facts. Like money and who had it. When you're ready to talk about your involvement—and that robbery—let me know."

I stood up to leave, but his wording made me pause. "Robbery? But nothing was taken."

He didn't say anything, barely waiting for me to leave before shutting the door with a bang.

I had so much on my mind as I pulled out of the parking lot that I almost clipped the pickup pulling in.

"Watch it, lady!"

I leaned out the window, searching for some choice words, when I recognized Mack in the driver's seat. He looked tired, his eyes half shut. On him, that was a sexy look.

"Fancy meeting you here." I couldn't help it. I smiled.

"You, too. Hang on a minute." Mack parked. I waited as he sauntered over, long legs making the most of his dirty jeans. As he leaned on the roof of my car, he smiled, and I felt myself begin to melt. "Creighton call you in?"

"How'd you guess?" From anyone else, this would have felt invasive. He just made a gesture toward the brick building.

"Hey, I'm here too. Seems the only lead the cops have got is our finances. Such as they were."

"At least he let the dog go."

Mack looked at me, a little too sharp. Behind those half-closed lids something was going on. I had to watch myself. "Yeah, he did that. Hey, how are you, Pru?"

I followed his gaze to my own bandaged hand. "I'm okay." I flexed it and felt my palm throb. "Cut myself on some glass last night."

"But, you're okay, right?"

Sweet, but confusing. "Yeah, I'm fine, Mack. No biggie."

"Good." He stepped back, thumped on my car roof once. "I— Well, I want you to be okay."

I looked up at him, but the morning sun obscured his face. "And you, Mack?"

He bent down and once again I could see that big, lazy grin. "I'm great, Pru. I'll call you later." Another thump on the roof of the car, and he walked away. With a little more care, I pulled into the road.

◇◇◇

Halfway to Eleanor's, I realized I was being inefficient. If the woman was home, I could swing back and get Floyd for her. If she wasn't, well, why waste the gas?

I keyed in her number. Sure enough, three rings later, her voice mail picked up. As I waited for the recording to end, her perfectly modulated tones grating on me like sandpaper, I mulled over what to say. For all I knew, the coifed brunette might have a perfectly good reason to avoid me and my phone calls. And her cat, for that matter. Then again, she might simply be a prize bitch.

On that thought, the beep sounded. "Eleanor, Pru here." With an effort, I kept my language neutral. My voice, she'd just have to deal with. "I have your cat. Call me." Cell phones don't give you the satisfaction of a good slamming hang-up, but I did what I could, jamming my thumb into the keypad. And with a sigh, I turned toward Raynbourne. At least, I could assume Nora Harris would be home.

Sure enough, as I pulled up to her house, I saw the older woman out front, kneeling on her pad and digging with a small spade, a net bag of bulbs by her side. As I got out of the car, the front door opened and Delia stepped out. Dressed in jeans and an ivory wool sweater, she didn't look like she was about to get down in the dirt with her employer. Lily, I noticed, was nowhere to be seen.

"Pru." Delia walked toward me, the question in her eyes rather than her voice. "What a pleasant surprise."

"Unlike yesterday, huh?" I looked around for the dog. "I realized it wasn't fair to dump a young, active dog on you like that. I wanted to offer to help out." Before Delia could say anything, I kept talking. "Continue the obedience training. Maybe lend a hand with walks and exercise." I was digging myself in here. I wanted the best for Lily, but I really couldn't afford to give my services away for free.

"That was Charles' dog." Nora's voice startled me, and I looked over. The grey-haired woman was resting on her heels, having traded the spade for a fork-like cultivator. "I couldn't stop her."

Delia took me by the arm and shook her head ever so slightly. "Don't mind her, Mrs. H," she said, her voice pitched slightly too high. "We're going to get something to drink. Would you like something, Mrs. H?"

"Damned dog." The old woman turned away and started hacking at the earth with a vengeance. "This is my home."

I followed Delia inside. "What's up with that?"

She shook her head. "Turns out, the dog takes after Nora. She was in the garden, digging up some of the new bulbs."

That was curious. Lily had some bad habits, but destructive behavior—digging or tearing at furniture—hadn't been one of them.

"She's just gotten a bit obsessive about that garden." Delia reached for yet another pitcher of lemonade. She must spend half her day making it. "Nora, that is." Setting out two glasses, she answered the unasked question. "I had to take the dog back inside."

"How is she?" I paused, unsure how to ask. "Nora, I mean."

"Charles' death hit her pretty hard. They were everything to each other." Delia handed me a glass and took a deep drink of her own. "Sometimes, I don't know how much she's going to come back. I've talked to her about going into Amherst or Springfield for cognitive testing, but…" Her voice trailed off.

"She doesn't want to give up time in her garden?" It was a guess, but Delia nodded.

"It's the only thing she cares about now. At least, she treated herself to some new tools and all those bulbs. That's good, right?"

I shrugged. "So, where's Lily now?" The house seemed quiet. "The dog?"

"In her crate in the back room." Delia refilled her own glass and held the pitcher out to me. I wasn't thirsty, but the social act seemed to loosen her up. "She seems to like it in there."

"Yeah, it makes her feel secure." I felt a twinge of guilt, as if I were giving away a confidence. But crating is behaviorist 101, and besides, Lily wasn't my client. "Was she really digging?"

"It was the strangest thing." Delia walked into the living room, and I followed. Together we looked out at Nora Harris and her bulbs. "When I let her out, she just went nuts, started churning up the earth. I don't know. Maybe there was a rat or something?" She shrugged, but didn't seem particularly concerned. Delia was, I was finally realizing, cool.

I needed to know how cool. "Delia, are you okay with Lily being here? Sounds like she's taking a lot of work."

"Yeah, I am." Without turning away from the window, she pulled up a seat. Something told me she spent many of her days this way. "Charles really cared for that dog."

There it was, just when I was getting to like her: another of Delia's distant comments, as if Charles had been a polite acquaintance instead of her fiancé and, possibly, the father of her unborn child. I was full of questions, but for once I kept my mouth shut. Let the silence do the work.

"And, yeah, for his mom, too." With her face toward the window, the afternoon sunlight falling full on her face, I could begin to see where lines were just beginning. Delia Cochrane was still beautiful, probably the most gorgeous woman in Beauville. But she'd had some wear and tear.

"Delia, why were you with Charles?" I kept my voice low and soft, but I wanted to hear it. Money, security. A baby before it was too late. "I mean, the dog, his mom…" She turned to face me, and I couldn't help but look from her face down to her slim waist. "I know you're pregnant."

To my surprise, she laughed, a soft laugh, low and relaxed. "I should have known. Nothing stays a secret in Beauville." She patted her abdomen. It still seemed pretty trim. "Charles really wanted a child. Nora really wanted a grandchild."

I waited and, finally prompted her. "And you?"

"I'm a home health aide, Pru. It was my lucky day when Nora Harris introduced me to her son."

"And he fell for you." I said it as a fact, knowing my former client's gentle nature. Even as I did, I saw the smile on her face. And I remembered what a little dog had told me. "He's like me," the bichon said, as he made his rounds, blithely ignoring a female in heat. It hit me like I'd walked into a wall. In a way, I had. A wall built by my own preconceptions.

"Charles was gay."

The look she gave me made me feel as stupid as I sounded. "Well, yeah."

"So, why the cover up?"

She shrugged. "It was for his mom, mostly. He tried to come out, but she never accepted it. She always thought that the right girl…and, recently, her temper has gotten really bad. She blows up over little things. Charles and I liked each other. When she set us up, we figured we'd play along. And Charles always wanted a family."

"So who—?" I nodded toward her belly, not sure how to phrase the question.

"He didn't care." She was looking back out the window again. "Charles really did want a child, you know."

I waited.

"And I was another of his strays," she said at last. "Charles took in everyone who needed him. Poor fool." She put her glass down on the table and stood, still staring out the window. "Probably what got him killed." She walked to the door. "Nora? Nora, I think it's time to come in."

She wasn't getting away that easy. I had too many questions. "Was it Chris?" I called after her as she opened the door. "Mack?" My voice cracked. But even as she slipped out the door to help the frail older woman to her feet, she was saved by my phone.

"Yes?" I was in no mood. Especially if it was Mack on the line.

"Uh, Pru?" It was Albert. I must have scared him. Good work for a monosyllable.

"Hi, Albert." I didn't like the man, but he wasn't the author of my latest problems. At least, I didn't think he was likely to be the father of Delia's baby. "What's up?"

"You like Bandit, my ferret, right? Uh, could you come by? We're having a problem." He paused. "A police problem."

# Chapter Twenty-two

Considering Albert's usual level of articulation, it seemed like getting over there quickly made more sense than lingering on the phone. During the drive, however, I couldn't help wondering what he'd meant. Had Frank dug up some more evidence? Had the small mustalid somehow gotten involved in a crime? He did like his shiny things.

What I didn't expect, when I walked into the pound, was to see Officer Creighton with one hand crudely bandaged in what looked like a handkerchief, the other holding his service revolver. Albert, with Frank clutched to his plaid breast, cowered against the wall behind his desk.

"Okay, what seems to be the problem here, Officer?" I figured levity might be useful, but Creighton turned to me with a face like thunder.

"This isn't funny. That's a dangerous animal, and I want it put down."

"What did you do to him?" Albert had started to protest, but I raised my hand for silence as I stepped in front of Creighton. In the back of my mind, I was hearing a panicked little voice. "*Mine! Mine! Mine! Shiny. Mine!*" "Shut up," I said, barely turning my head.

"I didn't say anything!" Albert was near tears.

I didn't bother to explain. "Officer? Do you mind?" I pointed toward the gun. He lowered it but didn't put it away.

"Sorry."

I wasn't taking my eyes off him. "Shall we sit?"

He nodded and took the guest chair, finally holstering the piece before sitting down. I pulled Albert's chair around to the front of the desk and sat facing him. Behind me, Albert whimpered.

"Now Jim, why don't you tell me what happened?" I was keeping my voice even, holding him with my eyes. He might have put the gun away, but there was more than a little here I didn't like. Mack had been going in to talk to Creighton when I'd taken off, and I knew that man had depths I hadn't begun to plumb.

"I was investigating a complaint." He stopped. I waited. "Look, Pru, this is official police business."

"Jim, you pulled a gun on Albert. And his ferret."

He sighed, and I saw him relax. He was giving up more than the tension of the moment. "Okay, we heard that there might have been something left with that dog's collar. I'm not at liberty to say more. But when we went out to talk to Mrs. Harris, it wasn't there. So I thought, maybe, that I'd swing around here and check it out."

"Thinking, what? That Albert had stolen it?" I knew damned well that he was talking about the disk drive. Given a few minutes to sort through things, so would Albert. I didn't want to give him the chance.

"I was checking his lost and found. Like, maybe it had dropped off, and Albert had stowed it away. And then that rat-thing attacked me."

"*Mine, mine, mine. Thief!*"

"Yes, I know," I said absently. "I mean, I can believe it. Ferrets really love their little treasures, and that was his cache and you reached into it. Probably scared the little guy half to death. And he's not a rat. He's a masked ferret."

"Is that thing even legal?" Creighton just looked sore now. From the way he was holding his hand, it was clear Frank had gotten him good.

"Ask your animal control officer." I couldn't resist a smile. Albert muttered something that we both ignored. "This is his office, you know. As well as the city pound." *"Thief."* Frank was getting distracting.

"Yeah, but shouldn't he be muzzled or something?" The hunky cop raised his injured hand up to his mouth, and for just a moment, I saw the boy he had been. If I hadn't been here, he'd be sucking on that cut, handkerchief and all.

"He's a peaceful sort of creature. Unless—" Frank's insistence finally got through to me. "Did you take something of his?"

"Of *his?*" There was something in his tone. Creighton was lying. I waited. This really was like training a puppy. And like any other young dog, he gave in. With his good hand, he reached into his pocket. When it came out he tossed something onto the desk. There, against the coffee-stained blotter, it shone like white fire. The diamond earring.

*"Mine!"* I could see Frank struggle. Albert, either out of some sense of self preservation or sheer panic, held him firmly.

"Hang on a minute," I said more to the ferret than to anyone else, and reached for the earring. "I just want to look at it." I heard another whimper, either from Albert or Frank I wasn't sure. Yes, this was the pretty sparkler I'd seen before. Strange that nobody had claimed it. Unless Creighton was the one who'd dropped it. He was back and forth between this office and his own often enough. Was the young officer squiring some wealthy woman? Or, I turned the pricey bauble over in my hand, had he come by it some other way? "Was this reported stolen, Jim?"

"Why, no. I mean—" He stammered, and I smiled. This was getting interesting. While the young officer was trying to find the words, I turned toward Frank. His person was no longer holding him in a panicked death grip, but I recognized the resignation in those shiny black eyes. *"Mine."* The tone was softer now. Plaintive. Frank knew he wasn't getting this particular prize back.

"There you are!" We all looked up as a whirlwind of glossy hair and fur whirled through the door.

"Eleanor Shrift." My mystery woman, here at last.

She glanced at me, speechless, but her focus was on Creighton. "They told me you were over here, and I've been looking for you." This was getting so interesting that for a moment I forgot the pretty earring in my hand. But Eleanor had seen it.

"Where did you get that?" She would have grabbed it, but I moved my arm back.

"Officer Creighton 'found' it. Supposedly Albert's ferret had it." I sensed more muttering from the small animal, but did my best to ignore it. I wanted to keep my mind on the drama unfolding with the people here.

"Oh." Eleanor seemed honestly confused, her dark-red lips pushed forward in an unflattering moue of confusion. "But, he didn't…" Her voice trailed off.

"Yes?" Perhaps I should have waited, but I couldn't resist.

"Never mind." She pulled her face back together and reached again for the earring. "Anyway, that's mine."

Creighton interrupted, taking her hand. A little too gently, I thought. "You're going to have to file a report, Ms. Shrift." So they did know each other. Not that this meant much in Beauville. He stood up. "And you were looking for me?"

"Yes, I wanted to complain. That woman has been harassing me." She was looking at me.

"I have your cat." This was ridiculous.

"You see?" She turned toward Creighton. "Among other things, she took my beloved pet."

I stood now, too, feeling the anger rise to redden my face. "She abandoned it at the shelter. I've been trying to reach her for days, to tell her that her 'beloved pet' is ready to come home."

"And did you have authorization to remove the animal, Pru?" Creighton sounded tired. His hand probably ached.

"I've been working with him. He had some serious anxiety issues." If looks could injure, my glare would have pierced even Eleanor Shrift's rock-hard foundation by now. But Creighton was too smart for this particular cat fight.

"That doesn't answer the question, Pru. And by the way," he reached out, palm up. "The earring?"

"You're going to leave the ferret alone, right?"

He nodded, and I dropped the sparkler into his hand.

"I'd love to know how your earring ended up at the pound." I didn't think she'd answer me, but I wanted to ask—just to see if she and Creighton exchanged looks. They didn't, but that could have just meant they were being careful.

"Someone can't keep her hands off others' property." Eleanor practically hissed.

"Me?" I was laughing. "Oh come on, Eleanor. I've been trying to get your cat back to you for days."

"Speaking of cats," Creighton stepped in between us. "Pru? It sounds like you were out of line there. But I'm sure that if you return the animal pronto, this can all be forgotten."

I looked at Eleanor. She smiled, if something so cold could be called that. Now that it came to it, I didn't want to give her the black Persian. Floyd might not be a brilliant cat, but he deserved better.

"I'd be happy to," I lied. "Perhaps Ms. Shrift can come by and pick him up at her convenience?"

The smile sagged slightly. "I'll be there later," she said.

"I'll try to be home." And before Creighton could break in again, Eleanor turned on her three-inch heel and stormed out. Behind me, I caught a low, resigned whine.

"*Thief.*"

# Chapter Twenty-three

To say that something about Eleanor Shrift was still bothering me would be wrong. Everything about that woman was getting to me. Much as I loathed it, I sort of understood her attitude toward Floyd. The black Persian reminded her of the man who had left. Worse, she'd lost him to the cat before he had disappeared entirely. But what did she have against me? And what was the deal with that earring?

I drove home on autopilot, thinking of jewelry and keychain drives. Where did Mack play into any of this, or Creighton or Eleanor, for that matter? I was mulling over the possibilities as I let myself in. I'd have posed some of them to Wallis, only when I went upstairs, I found her and Floyd curled up together, sleeping, on my bed. Rather than disrupt such rare domestic bliss, I retreated as quietly as I could.

But no matter how much I told myself I should at least get Floyd's traveling case ready, I just couldn't do it. Instead, I booted up my laptop. If I couldn't solve one mystery, I'd focus on another. Whoever had broken into my house had stolen nothing but the little drive. And someone—presumably someone else—had gotten Creighton to search for it at the pound. There was something of value in those files, even if I hadn't seen it yet.

As the spreadsheets appeared before me, I cursed my liberal arts education. The only math I'd taken had been to get me through biology, and even then my grades hadn't given me any hope of veterinary school. As I went down the lists of numbers again, I felt rather than heard a soft thud. Wallis had jumped to the desktop and was looking over my shoulder. Remembering our fight, I didn't say anything until she settled in and began to purr softly.

"Floyd still asleep?"

She flicked her ear; the feline equivalent of a nod. "Poor sucker. He's totally wrung out."

I hadn't expected sympathy from Wallis, but I wasn't going to question it. Instead I nodded and kept reading.

"You still trying to make sense out of those scribbles?" Wallis' voice sounded thoughtful, without its usual edge.

"Uh huh." I highlighted one rather large number and tapped on my desk.

"Mouse tracks."

I typed away, not wanting to get into it again. Within a few minutes, I felt whiskers on my forearm. Wallis was leaning over the screen.

"So, explain to me again what those mean?" It was a peace offering. Problem was, I had trouble understanding economics myself.

"Well, each line is an amount of money. Something we barter, like what I bring to the store and they give me chicken." Not that I'd ever had forty thousand in hand, but Wallis was still listening. "And what I'm thinking is that maybe this money didn't belong to Charles, that maybe it belonged to someone else." That didn't fit with what Mack had told me about Charles and investors. But I couldn't think of any other reason someone would care. "Maybe he owed it, and maybe he was killed to get it back."

Wallis stared at the screen for long enough that I began to wonder just how bad her myopia was. I had to give her props. She was trying.

"Where does it all come from?"

"The money isn't really there. This is just a list, a plan, sort of." God, I didn't want to sound patronizing. How much abstract thinking did cats get? "A symbol?"

"No, no." Wallis sat back up, wrapping her tail around her front toes in a schoolmarmish pose. "I mean, where did Charles get all of his money?"

I sat for a moment and wondered. I'd been so focused on the other side of the equation, on whom Charles might owe, that I hadn't considered his sources. Once upon a time, software startups got venture capital. If they didn't, they invested their own money. Presumably, Charles had some kind of job, maybe something high-paying, before he decided to go out on his own. That would've been how he hoped to keep it private. Keep it his. But did he have this kind of scratch? Or was there something funky about his funding—something someone might not want revealed? I looked at my cat and admitted the truth.

"I don't know, Wallis. And that's a damned good question."

To do her justice, she kept her purr subdued.

◇◇◇

With this question in mind, I went back to some of the earlier files, kicking myself all the while. Any of these questions could be inverted. I'd thought, perhaps, that one of Delia's other lovers might have killed Charles in a jealous squabble. And I'd given up that idea on hearing about his sexual orientation. Maybe that was wrong. Just because my late client was gay—and presumably copacetic with the idea of a child fathered by someone else—didn't mean that the sperm donor was happy with the arrangement. And I'd been searching for debts owed. Money due to be paid. But what kind of potential investors would Mack have dug up for Charles—and how much did he want to maintain control?

An unsheathed claw on my forearm made me realize I'd been muttering.

"So, are we fasting for some reason, or what?"

I looked up at the clock. It was close to nine. Eleanor had never shown.

◇◇◇

I had evil dreams that night and was grateful, when I woke, for Wallis' warm bulk beside me in the pre-dawn gray. As my head cleared, I became aware, as well, of a slight snuffling sound—half snore, half sigh—and realized Floyd was curled next to me as well. So deep asleep, his dreams were only vague impressions of grass and sunlight, he was a peaceful addition to our menagerie. I thought again of Eleanor. She didn't deserve him.

The comfort of these two cats couldn't exactly lull me back to sleep, but I may have dozed a bit as I lay there, waiting for full light to start my day. Too much had happened recently, and I had too little say in the craziness swirling around me. It threatened to sweep me up. Listening to Floyd, I tried to steady my own breathing. I'd be damned if I made myself sick again. Sanity—and my freedom—were too important. To give myself some sense of control, I started listing what I knew and, more frightening, what I didn't.

Charles was dead. That was a fact. And Lily hadn't done it. I'd gotten involved to save the poor dog. Now that she was out of harm's way, did I give a damn anymore?

I sat with that one for a bit, listening to the soft vocalizations of the cat beside me. Yeah, I did. For starters, the investigation was still going on—and I didn't want to be anyone's scapegoat. Plus, to be honest, I had to admit I cared. Much as I prefer animals to people, I counted Charles as one of the good ones. He'd taken Lily in. He supported his aging mother. He was a good guy.

I was less certain about Mack. Mack was sexy, and I respect my own animal nature. But he was a little sure of himself, sure of his sway over the opposite sex. And his connection with Charles had too many question marks attached. What exactly did he do in their partnership? Had his charm and easy smile worked on the kind nerd? For that matter, had he been the stud who had sired Delia's child? And, if so, what did either man think of that?

Beyond the personal, there was the professional. People were getting very interested in the financial data on Charles' fledgling company. I'd taken the precaution of carrying my laptop upstairs with me, tucking it under the bed before I retired. I was very aware of it now, aware that if anyone else happened to break in, hiding the damned thing in my bedroom might not have been the smartest move.

But I was sick of being afraid. I'd come back here to simplify my life. To regain some sense of order. Some control. The killer was a cipher. An unknown. And really, who was I going to come in contact with? I could deal with the Alberts of the world. Hell, the poor slob had my sympathy after yesterday. At least his ferret did. And Jim Creighton was a type I knew well. Attractive, not the least because he represented the law—and what's more fun than perverting a lawman?

That last thought made me think of Delia with a grudging respect. She hadn't had the easy life I'd assumed at first, and she had a real-world pragmatism I recognized. She was playing the chips life had handed her. I didn't know where she had placed all those chips—and I wouldn't bet on her to make a sympathetic move for anyone—but she seemed to be a straight shooter, and I had to admire that. Chris Moore, well, if he served a purpose in her life, I wasn't going to worry about him. He seemed to be getting what he wanted now. Had he gotten it before, when she was officially with Charles? Water under the bridge, unless he'd been unhappy being the backdoor man. But he was only one possibility, I realized as the curtain began to glow with dawn's light. And the money might be easier to track. I needed to talk to Mack.

"About the money?" I turned and found myself staring into Wallis' wide green eyes. For a moment, I paused, remembering last night's rapport. Was she still interested in finance? As soon as the question formed in my own mind, I heard the answer. "Please!" She got up and walked to the edge of the bed. "I just don't see any reason for you to keep fooling yourself."

She jumped to the floor and, with a sigh, I pushed myself upright to follow her.

Twenty minutes later, I was at Tracy Horlick's. I was about to pound on the door, the hour be damned, when it opened. A lipstick-less Tracy Horlick nearly dropped her cigarette as she saw me.

"Hi, Mrs. Horlick." I mustered a smile. "Lovely morning, isn't it?"

"You're here early." She reached down to collect the paper and motioned me inside. The house smelled like she'd been smoking all night, but she had a pot of coffee on, so I accepted a cup while I looked around for the bichon.

"Where's Growl— Bitsy?"

If she heard my flub, she didn't react. Too busy lighting her next cigarette from the butt of the last one. "Out back."

I heard yapping from the enclosed back yard and realized that was probably the nightly routine. September, we'd already had frost. I'd have to find a way to make sure she didn't keep him out there once winter came around. Then again, maybe he preferred the solitude, as long as he had some kind of shelter. I wondered briefly if Tracy Horlick was aware of her dog's sexual preference. I doubted it, just as I doubted she ever cleaned up her own dog's waste from the tiny yard.

"I thought I'd take him for a good long walk, since I'm here so early." It must be the lack of sleep. I was becoming a softie.

But for once the old witch didn't grab the advantage. "Did you hear?" she asked breathlessly. She had the second cigarette lit and drew on it like the hot smoke was oxygen. "Delia Cochrane and Chris Moore are getting married."

"Huh." I tried to sound noncommittal. But as she took another long drag, gearing up for what looked like a long spew, I put my mug on the counter. It was too early for her brand of spiteful gossip. I took the lead from its hook in the hallway. "Nope, hadn't heard that. Why don't I get Bitsy now?"

I started to walk by her, eying the door to the yard. She stopped me with a clawlike hand on my arm.

"The dog can wait," she rasped. "We need to catch up."

"No we don't, Mrs. Horlick." I pushed by her. No wonder her dog disliked women.

"But don't you want to know why?" Her voice followed me as I let the small animal in and snapped on his leash. I bit back the temptation to tell her that, yes, I knew why.

"Delia's pregnant." She filled in the blank as the bichon and I headed toward the door. At least I could deny her the satisfaction of responding. "But I don't think he's the father. I don't know if he knows that. You might want to talk to your boyfriend, though. You might want to talk to Mack."

◇◇◇

The fact that her thoughts had followed the same path as mine was no consolation. Still, I waited till I was several blocks away before I got out my cell and dialed Mack's number. No answer. It wasn't eight yet, and I didn't make him for an early riser. But I left a message, as pleasant as I could muster, before marching Growler around the block. His thoughts ran solely to his canine counterparts as we walked, and I couldn't say I blamed him. When I slipped him into his house, my face was enough to silence Tracy Horlick. After that, I went off in search of answers.

Albert wasn't in yet, and the pound was locked tight. So I poked my head in next door and wasn't surprised to see Jim Creighton at his desk, looking rather snazzy in a freshly pressed uniform.

"Sexy boy scout. I like it." I enjoyed seeing him flustered and helped myself to a cup of coffee. "Oh, nasty." That was about the coffee.

"Been sitting there since six." I'd given him the upper hand back with that exchange, and he smiled. "So, to what do I owe the pleasure?"

"Well, Jim." I settled into one of the guest chairs but drew the line at putting my feet up on his desk. I needed him on my side right now. "We never did finish our chat."

He nodded. He could tell I'd come to talk.

"About that earring." I figured I'd start with the easy stuff. "You know that Eleanor Shrift has recently broken up with someone?" For a brief moment, I wondered if I'd overstepped. If Jim Creighton had been her secret squeeze, he might not appreciate this information going public.

"And I care because?" He smiled, but I could tell he was hiding curiosity. Good, it wasn't him. That thought pleased me more than it should have.

"Well, if I lost some valuable jewelry, I'd look to see who had access." I was beginning to sound like Tracy Horlick, and I didn't like it. "I just mean, there may have been other people in her house recently."

"Eleanor says *you've* been in her house." His grin had grown broader now. I'd seen that same expression on Wallis' face.

"Not unsupervised," I backpedaled.

"And you took her cat."

"Oh, come on, Jim." This was ridiculous, and he should know it. "That animal didn't belong in a shelter. I've been trying to return him to her for days now, trying to set up some kind of training sessions with the two of them. By the way, she never came by to pick him up last night."

"Maybe she doesn't know where you live." He was fishing now, and I relaxed.

"And Doc Sharp wouldn't tell her?"

He ceded the point. "I didn't really think you'd stolen that earring, Pru. Or the cat, and you know it. So what does bring you here?"

This was the difficult part. I don't mind lying to cops. I do mind having to confess to such deception.

"You know the USB drive you were looking for?" I felt my voice shift higher, and I tried to cool myself down. Nonchalance, that was the key.

"Uh huh."

"Well, I may have picked it up by mistake, last time I was at the shelter. You see, I'd lost one similar so when Albert told me about one showing up, I thought it was mine." That was a mistake. I'm too good a liar usually to oversell. Jim Creighton was making me nervous, and in response I shut down. But he had gone into cop mode now and sat there, staring and waiting.

Might as well get it over with. "Anyway, when I had that break in?" He nodded once, curtly. "Well, I didn't realize till the next day, but it was gone."

"And you didn't think to inform me of this?" His voice was cold now, all flirtation gone.

But he'd taken the bait, and I pulled the hook in. "Didn't matter much. I'd already downloaded all the information onto my laptop."

"You what?" Creighton was halfway out of his seat.

"Calm down, Jim. It was a mistake." I was trying not to smile. "I've burnt you a copy."

"I'm going to need your laptop." He was using his cop voice again.

"I thought you'd say that, but maybe I've lost it." I pulled a disc from my bag. "Here. Take a look at this first. Maybe this will give you everything you need."

"Everything he needs?" I turned behind me. Albert was pushing through the door, styrofoam cup in one hand, a bag turning translucent with grease in the other. "What about me?" His smile was more sheepish than sleazy. "I saw your car out front."

"Morning, Albert." I was grateful for the distraction. "I thought I'd drop by, but then Officer Creighton and I started chatting."

I turned back to Creighton. He'd put the disc into his desk drawer, but his scowl said I hadn't heard the last of this. "Morning," he growled.

"Seems somebody woke up on the wrong side of the bed." Albert stepped closer and put his coffee cup on Creighton's desk. Milky brew slopped over the top, and Creighton restrained himself with a visible effort. "Speaking of, Pru, I've got something for you." He patted one pocket and then reached to place the bag beside the cup. Creighton quickly grabbed a few folders and pulled them back.

"Here it is." Albert was reaching deep into his opposite pants pocket now. "I was hoping to see you today. Frank told me to give this to you."

"Frank?" My surprise must have shown on my face as he passed me a shiny silver disc about the size of a quarter.

"Yeah, that's my ferret," he explained, for Creighton's benefit. "I'd been calling him Bandit 'cause he's got the mask and all. But Pru has started calling him Frank, and what do you know?

He actually answers to that. So I'm changing his name. From now on, he's Frank. Bandit Frank."

"I like it," I said to fill time. I was looking at the disc. It was an ID tag with Charles' name and address.

"I thought you'd want that, Pru." Albert was staring at me. "Because it came off that computer drive that you took home. You know the one I mean."

"Creighton knows, Al," I said. "Thanks anyway."

"Oh, well, anyway, there it is." He looked crestfallen. Albert was not beyond the potential for blackmail. "I really did get the strangest feeling that Frank wanted me to get it to you."

I slipped the tag into my pocket. It probably meant nothing, now. Lily had a new home. Still, I was glad to have it.

"What is it with you and animals, Pru?" Creighton was staring now, trying to puzzle things out. "There's something weird going on."

"Isn't a girl allowed some secrets?"

Albert reached for his coffee and donuts, and I stood as well. "Let me know what you think of that disc, Jim." I gave a small wave.

"We're not through, Pru. You know that."

I smiled and walked out.

"What was that about?" As soon as we were outside, Albert turned to me.

"That keychain drive, Albert. You were right, it wasn't mine. So I came to turn it in." I left him with his mouth hanging open and his coffee cooling, and drove away.

The tag had been a reminder. I'd gotten involved in all of this because of Lily. Lily was fine now. It was Charles, the man who had rescued her, who was dead and gone, long before his time. Without thinking much about it, I found myself driving over to his place. After a couple of visits to his mother's house, I could see where he got his taste. Like his mother's house, Charles' place was old-school, original Berkshires. Unlike the tiny worker's cottage he'd grown up in, the house I now pulled up to was palatial.

I knew he'd kept up his childhood home, but it would never look like this, set well back from the road, with the wraparound porch and the hillside rising behind it.

I was so busy admiring the vista that I almost didn't notice the car in the driveway. A modified SUV, something built to handle our mountain winters. It could have been anybody's car, but I was pretty sure it wasn't Charles'.

"Hello?" The sun was shining bright, but I was taking no chances. If somebody wanted to make good an escape, I was happy to give him advance notice. "Yoohoo!"

"Hey, Pru!"

Despite my act of friendly nonchalance, I nearly jumped when I heard the voice. Over behind the glossy green of the rhododendrons Delia appeared, pulled along by Lily. She was waving and laughing.

"Hi there." I knelt to greet the dog, taking her head in my hands and rubbing her ears as she surged toward me. "Now, Lily," I addressed the dog. "You know better than to pull like that. I'm sorry, Delia. I thought I had her better trained."

"It's okay. I think living with us is getting to her though. She's pretty much dug up Nora's garden, and I thought it would be good to take her out for a really long walk."

"Good idea." I looked around. "Is Mrs. Harris with you?"

"No." Delia pushed a fall of hair out of her face. She was flushed with exertion. "The dog's a bit much for her."

Lily seemed to be a bit much for Delia, too, and I felt a brief pang of guilt. "I shouldn't have just brought her by." Delia started protesting, but I continued. "At least let me continue her training."

"Sure, that might be good." Delia agreed, still breathing hard. "Especially if you can come by. I don't always have the use of the Wrangler."

I nodded. "I always try to work with animals in their home environments." I looked over toward the tan 4X4. "That's not your car?"

Delia shook her head. "It's Nora's. We've been having it out about her driving again. But my car's a standard, so if I take hers, she's sort of stuck." She had the grace to blush.

"I understand." I remembered my mother's last months. "How is Mrs. Harris doing, anyway?"

"Some days better than others." She gazed out over the landscaping. Beyond the rhododendrons, I could see the green spiked leaves of holly and something else. Mountain laurel? A thick layer of mulch showed where other plants would come back, come spring. "She used to take care of all of this, you know? Right up until Charles died."

Her words pulled me back from the old-fashioned garden. "It was murder, Delia."

She blinked. "I know, Pru. I just, well, he's gone."

Here was my moment, if I was ever going to ask. "Someone killed Charles, Delia. The cops are going through his financials, but sooner or later someone is going to start looking into his personal life. It's going to come out, Delia, that you were his beard. And then people are going to start asking what you got out of it, or if there was someone close to you who wanted to change the arrangement."

That was a conversation killer. Without a word Delia turned away, pulling on Lily's leash. The big dog gave a small yelp. I reached for her automatically, but Delia had already started to walk away. She was heading for the Jeep, and I watched her go, wondering if it was anger or guilt that was making her flee.

"Delia, wait!" I called to her. She stopped short and turned to me. "Look, I'm not accusing you of anything. I'm just trying to figure things out."

Her head bobbed, one short, sharp movement. "I get it, Pru. But you've got to understand, too. It's not just me anymore. I didn't kill Charles. I had no reason to want him gone. Now he is, and I've got to take care of myself."

She had a point, but her plans were all after the fact. I was about to point this out—and point out that whatever her plans, there was at least one other man involved who may have had his own motivations. But just as I opened my mouth, my phone started buzzing. I tried to ignore it, but she gestured to my buzzing bag. "Since you're in everybody's business," she said, her tone sounding more tired than frosty.

With a sigh, I pulled the offending phone from my bag and answered it. "Yes?"

"Well, I thought you'd be grateful that I'd gotten back to you. After all you did." It was Eleanor Shrift, with an attitude that cut through the phone lines. Creighton must have gotten to her.

"Eleanor, I don't know what you're talking about. This isn't about me. This is about you not dealing with rejection." I turned away from Delia, but I knew she was getting an earful. "Now, are you going to come by for him or what?"

"I'll come by when it's convenient." She cut the connection. I turned back to Delia and rolled my eyes.

"She doesn't deserve him." I shook my head sadly. "Not by a long shot."

Delia looked a bit taken aback by the conversation, but at least it had served to break the stalemate between us. And since I was thinking of cats, my followup seemed obvious.

"How's the kitten? What's her name, Tulip?" It must have sounded like a lame attempt to make peace, because Delia sputtered a bit. In truth I was interested. That little kitten had been through a lot.

"She's great. A little snuggle puss." Her face relaxed as she spoke of the marmalade kitten. "And Chris really likes her, too."

"He seems like a real cat person." Except for Wallis, I thought. "Strange, isn't it? The biggest guys fall the hardest."

"Tell me about it." From her tone, I knew she'd moved beyond cats.

"So, are you and Chris..." I waited, intentionally leaving the end of the sentence open.

"Maybe, yeah." She nodded again, slowly. "He'll be a good dad, I think."

I didn't push further. In retrospect, maybe I should have. Instead, I watched her load Lily into the SUV. She'd put a blanket down on the back seat, and Lily climbed onto it and lay down, her stumpy tail thudding against the thick fleece. Nora might not be thrilled about her new pet, but Delia and the dog were getting along like a house on fire.

Waiting for them to take off, I climbed up to the wraparound porch. From here, I could see the spacious living room. There was the sofa, the stone hearth of the big fireplace, and the work area beyond. The yellow crime scene tape was still up, reminding me of why I couldn't take my key and let myself in. Not again, anyway. Anyway, from here I could see everything there was. Except that something was off. The desktop computer was gone; I'd expected that. If Creighton or anyone on his staff had any financial savvy, they'd be going over those files in some sterile lab. But it was something else, too. Maybe the cops had been careless, knocking the furniture over and then righting it again. Maybe someone else had been through the house. Delia or Mack. The cleaning lady who came once a week.

Maybe Nora had started to pack up her son's belongings. Because from where I stood, the house looked a little emptier, and not just from the computer. There were pictures missing from the long mantle. From the wall. One had been of Lily, I remembered. At least one more of Charles with Lily, her tail stilled by the shutter but a big doggie grin echoing her master's. I couldn't remember what else had been pictured. The house was losing its memories. Someone was taking them.

Had Delia gone in for a memento? Had she been searching for something more? I hadn't told her about the computer disc. I didn't know what she was looking for, or if she would find it there. Then I remembered the other disc, the small metal one in my pocket. I pulled out the silver tag and turned it over. "Tetris," it said. The wrong name for the right dog.

# Chapter Twenty-four

My phone rang again before I could get out of the driveway. Expecting Eleanor, I answered with a sharp "What?"

"Hey, babe, what's wrong?" It was Mack. I felt a momentary twinge of guilt.

"Sorry. It's been a day."

"For you, too?"

I made some kind of noncommittal noise and was surprised by the answer.

"I wanted to touch base with you, Pru, 'cause I'm going to be busy for a little while."

"Oh?" Mack didn't seem like the type to get cold feet. "New business?"

He laughed. "No, tying up some loose threads. Though, speaking of new business, I should start hustling."

I bit back my response, but he heard it and chuckled again. "Woman after my own heart. Hey, what about dinner next week? I'll even cook."

The idea tickled me, as did his seeming reticence. "I never saw you as Susie Homemaker."

There was a smile in his voice as he answered. Maybe I'd imagined the uncertainty. "There, you see? I do have some good sides. Why do you think Charles kept me around?"

"It wasn't for your financial expertise?" I paused, recent revelations rushing in. "Or for your rakish good looks?"

"Ah, so you've heard."

There was a pause for us both to recalibrate.

"Well, some things make more sense now." I was treading carefully. I didn't want Mack to know how much I still didn't know. "Other things…"

"He was a good guy, Pru. A lot of people were happy just to be around him."

Being around him hadn't gotten Delia pregnant, I wanted to say. But it was too soon to show my hand. "Yeah, maybe." I remembered Eleanor's call. I didn't need to piss her off any more. I climbed into my car. "Hey, can we talk later? I've got to get home. Eleanor Shrift may be coming by." I hadn't meant to test him, but he'd made it so easy.

"Our own dragon lady! What did you do to get on her bad side?"

"How do you know it's her bad side?" Now he had me curious.

"You said 'Eleanor Shrift.' She only has two sides, and I don't think she'd want to seduce you."

This was getting interesting. "You speaking from experience here?" He paused, and I thought "Gotcha." The idea made me strangely sad.

"Hey, we're adults. We had lives before now." He was digging himself in deeper, and I remembered Creighton's questions. If Mack hadn't set him on me for the computer drive, then who had? The man had the morals of a coyote.

"Gotta run, Mack." I hung up and started the car, the company of Wallis more appealing than ever.

The phone rang again on the way over, and I let it go to voice mail. When it started up as I pulled into my own drive, I glanced over. There was a chance it would be Eleanor. Or Creighton, even.

It was Mack. I picked it up as I opened my front door. He seemed to think we'd been having a conversation.

"Hey, babe, I don't want to leave things on a bad note."

I snorted.

"For Christ's sake, Pru. I like you. Is that a crime?"

I didn't answer. I was going to, but just then a cry burst into my brain. "*Help! Help! Murder! Help!*"

I slammed the phone shut and ran to the back porch. Coming in a tear in the screen was Wallis. In her mouth, she held a grackle. Still alive, but at the end of hope.

"Wallis!" I didn't have any rationale, I just yelled.

And she responded. As gently as a mother setting down a kitten, she lowered the grackle to the windowsill and let it go. We both watched as the bird took off through the ripped screen, a flash of iridescence, purple and black. Then she turned toward me.

"What?" There was a message there, only I wasn't getting it. She tilted her head slightly, and suddenly I did.

"That's different." I knew she would sense my sudden anger, as well as hear it. "I'm not playing with him."

"What's different is, I could have made an honest meal out of that bird." And with that she jumped off the worn settee and sauntered into the house.

◇◇◇

Maybe Wallis had a point. At any rate, I figured I might as well confront my own particular catch. I hit call.

"Mack, I need to see you."

"Now?" If I didn't know better, I'd have said he was cowed.

"We need to talk."

"Well, I was thinking tomorrow night, since it'll be Saturday and all. Or maybe next week."

Who was he avoiding, me or Eleanor? Either had possibilities. "No, Mack. If you want to see me at all, you'll come over now." I thought about adding "please," but I was in a mood. As it was, I heard something that sounded like assent. I ended the call and went to look for Floyd.

By the time the doorbell rang, twenty minutes later, I'd found the Persian. He'd been sleeping on my bed, deep in dreams of a big hand warm and steady on his fur. I sat there longer than necessary, trying to find some identifying mark on that hand. No wedding ring, but that didn't mean much—not in this town. I left him sleeping—and snoring—and went downstairs to answer it, curious as to whether Mack or Eleanor had shown up. If it were both, we might be in for some entertainment.

I had placed my mental bet on Eleanor when I opened the door to see Mack, looking strangely subdued.

"Well, look what the cat dragged in."

He smiled, but when I stepped back to let him pass, he turned away.

"Can we go somewhere?" He wasn't meeting my eyes, and instead seemed focused on a spot halfway down my door jam.

"No, we can't." I tried to read him. If only he'd look up. "Eleanor Shrift might be coming by. I've got her cat."

I would have said more. Would have explained, but at that moment Mack winced. It was a quick reaction, and I wished I hadn't seen it. But I had.

"Eleanor? Mack, really."

"Pru, does it matter so much?"

I shrugged. I didn't know why it bothered me. I'd hardly been celibate before meeting Mack, and the affair was clearly over. Maybe it was his cavalier treatment of the older woman. Then it hit me: Floyd. Eleanor's lover had broken the black Persian's heart, and that I found hard to forgive.

"No, it doesn't." I felt my throat choke up at my lie. "Okay, not entirely. But it does say something about your taste."

"Hey, it was one night. If I hadn't had a good run at Happy's, I'd never have gone for her."

"Such a gentleman." A liar, too. A cat doesn't bond like that overnight. "And you ratted me out to Creighton, too."

"What are you talking about?"

"The drive, the one that was missing from Lily's collar."

"Lily? What the hell, Pru."

I caught myself. Shit, this whole animal thing tripped me up at just the worst moments. "Lily. Charles' dog. The one he called Tetris? There was a flash drive attached to her collar —"

"Hey, come on, Pru." He was backing away now. Something was wrong. Something I didn't understand. "You don't know the whole story."

"Mack Danton." I used my command voice. "Talk to me."

He didn't, but standing there I saw him clearly as I hadn't before, in all my anger. He looked shamefaced, kicking at the ground like a little boy.

"What's going on with you, Mack." I was curious now, my anger on hold. "You look like shit."

"It's nothing." He rubbed his sleeve across his face.

"Yeah, right."

"I don't like cats, okay? Not all cats, but, well, most cats. I've got allergies, and well…"

He looked down. Away. Anywhere but straight at me. "Mack Danton, you're afraid of cats." He didn't look up. He didn't have to. I was connecting the dots. "So you couldn't have been Eleanor Shrift's summer lover," I said. There was something else. Something Wallis had said. Or, no, Delia…but Mack was still talking.

"I told you. That was a one-time thing." He seemed more confused than angry.

"Okay, I'm sorry, hon. I believe you." I moved toward him. Seeing him like this only made him sweeter. Maybe I do have those instincts. "We can go to your place."

I pressed against him, his body warm and hard. He drew back, and I leaned in, placing my hand against his thigh. And he flinched.

"Sorry. Old ski injury." He reached for my hand.

"You didn't mind outside Happy's." I wanted him, but my mind was racing. Making connections. I pulled my fingers out of his and reached down for his hip. He relaxed and moved in to kiss me. But as his lips met mine, I ran my hand down his thigh again—right to where my hand would naturally reach—and squeezed.

"Ow! Hey." He pulled my hand up again, less gently this time.

"What's the matter, Mack? Someone stab you in that thigh?" I pulled back. I wanted my knife hand free.

"Wait a minute, Pru. Just wait. You're jumping to conclusions." He reached out to me, and as he grabbed me, I thought of the arms around me the other night, and I knew that I was right.

"No way," I backed up. "Not again."

It hit me, then. All the charm, all the seduction. It had been Mack all along. Mack had access. As Charles' partner, he undoubtedly had the keys and knew of any alarm codes. Charles wouldn't have expected it, either. How? Well, that would be up to Creighton to find out. Somehow, Mack had torn his partner's throat open and then released Lily from her crate. A wave of fury washed through me. Murder and a frame up. That meant he'd planned it. And here I'd been close to falling for him. I stepped back.

"You killed Charles, didn't you?" I heard my words as if they'd come from somewhere else. Trouble was, they made sense.

"What are you talking about? I loved the guy." He was good, but I didn't buy it.

"Yeah, enough to give him a child. Was it for Delia? Is this all about her?" I thought of the blonde. She could certainly cause trouble. But, no, that didn't fit. Mack didn't care enough. He'd had his fun, but was happy enough to let her run back to Chris when things got serious. I'd seen no trace of jealousy or possessiveness. More likely, he was grateful. For a split second, I felt for Delia. Well, she was making the best of the situation. Mack however…"No, it must have been the money."

"*What* money?"

I stammered. Truth was, I still wasn't sure. Then it hit me. I didn't have to know. He did. "I've seen the accounts, remember? And I have copies of those files."

He shook his head, slowly. "You really are clueless, aren't you, Pru?" To my surprise, he smiled. "There was no money. Never was. I needed those files to find a way out."

"But you're the money guy." None of this was making sense.

His smile grew broader. "Do I seem like a financial whiz to you, Pru? I'm a salesman. Always have been. And there are forecasts in those files, forecasts I could still use if I acted fast enough. At least, I've got to try."

I didn't buy it. "But anything would have gone to his mother. And, besides, if there's nothing there…"

"Nobody knows that, Pru. Nobody but you and me and members of his immediate family. You see, I set up the business plan, and that's what people are looking to me for."

"But if there's nothing done. Nothing built—"

"Still might be enough there to buy me time." Desperation had crept into his voice, giving it a tightness I'd never heard. "You don't get it, Pru. I'm a middle man. I introduced Charles to some people he might not have known otherwise. People who definitely don't know his mother. I mean, folks around here don't have a lot to invest, if you get my drift."

I thought of Happy's. Of Mack's time there, and the gambler who had sold Lily to Charles. "You owe money, don't you?" I swallowed. "A lot?"

"I've had some bad luck." He rubbed his chin. Between the shadow and the puffy eyes, I could see what he'd look like at fifty. It wasn't pretty. Mack wasn't coming out on top.

"You owe, and to pay them off you set up Charles." I looked at him. My point hadn't hit home. "You offered him—his business—as collateral."

It would have made sense. Should have, except that he laughed out loud. "I tried to, Pru. Lord knows I tried! There's not much money out here, unless you're in real estate. But those outside folks can recognize a good investment. Charles would have made money for anyone who partnered with him. Hell, they loved the idea. They'd make him a quick loan under the table, and my debt was going to be forgiven. It should have worked like a charm."

"In other words, you were getting a cut—above and beyond your agreement with Charles." The picture was getting clearer. "Is that why you told Creighton about the drive? Was this whole business a front? Were you laundering funds for some mob?"

"You're not hearing me, Pru. I wasn't. I didn't. I have no idea who told the cops about that computer drive. Maybe if I had…" He shrugged.

I wondered just how much he did owe. "Your debts got Charles killed."

"No." It wasn't a question, but he shook his head. "He never took their money, Pru. The deal fell through, leaving me in the hole for thirty large."

"But why?"

"Because of that dog, Pru. Because of that damned dog." He was meeting my eyes now, and the mix of sadness and humor almost broke my heart. "Charles was only going to the meet because I begged him to, but he wouldn't even sit down with them once he saw that stupid dog out there, Pru. Charles took one look at that dog and made his one and only deal. He bought the dog outright, and then took off. Left forty grand of good money hanging, and left me in the hole. That dog didn't get him killed, Pru. But it isn't doing my health much good."

There wasn't much to say after that. I didn't even need Eleanor as an excuse to say goodbye to Mack and to close the door. I must have had more in mind than I'd admitted to myself, though, because it was with a heavy heart that I climbed back up the steps and collapsed on the bed.

Floyd woke with a start, and I felt the flood of disappointment wash over him as he saw me beside him. Reflexively, he started to groom, and I reached out to stroke him, as much to stop him as to comfort us both.

*"No."* He drew away, and I got another flash of his person. Large, male. Could it be?

Just then, Wallis jumped up beside us. "I was thinking about that child." she said.

"Delia's?" She shot me a look. She meant the kitten.

"What did she hear, locked up in that closet? I mean, that dog didn't have the sense God gave it. Refusing to attack a killer. And that baby sounds like a broken record. What are those animals good for, anyway?"

I sat up with a start. Wallis had put the final puzzle piece down. I reached for my keys, glancing back long enough to see two sets of green eyes watching me as I ran for the door.

*"Mama,"* the kitten had said. Had kept saying, from the moment I'd taken her from that closet till her owner had picked her up. Delia clearly adored that kitten. But the kitten hadn't been talking about Delia.

Too much was piling up. I had to see for myself.

All during the drive over to Raynbourne, I kept repeating, like a mantra, the other options. Maybe Mack had been more desperate than he'd let on. Maybe he didn't know the whole story, and Charles was in debt. Delia was another complicating factor. Did I think she'd done it? No, I didn't want to, anyway. Still, she was a beautiful woman at the end of her tether. Who knows what any of us would do, or what someone would do *for* her? And then there was the complication of Lily and the gambler. Nothing good comes out of mixing it up with small-time hoods. Nothing.

With all of this buzzing around my head, I made it to Nora Harris' house in record time. For once, she wasn't in the garden, and as I waited for someone to answer the door, I tried to work out what to say. There weren't really words for what I was thinking.

"You!" That wasn't the welcome I'd been expecting. But the sight of Chris Moore, red-faced and furious, was enough of a surprise that I pulled myself together. When you see a mad dog, you go into automatic. For me, that meant cool as a cucumber.

"Good afternoon, Chris." I smiled as a way to show him all my teeth. "Are Delia or Mrs. Harris at home?"

"Pru." I heard Delia's voice before I saw her. She spoke to me from behind Chris' outstretched arm. I waited for him to get out of the way. He didn't. "Nora's resting."

"Okay, then." Normally, I would have left then. Clearly something was going on, and I wanted no part of it. Then I saw the left side of her face. Although she had ducked down to hide it, the curtain of her hair couldn't quite obscure an eye already turning purple. The blood on her lip wasn't yet dry, and as I watched, she ran a tongue over the swelling as if she needed the metallic taste to make it all real. "Delia, what's happened? Are you okay?"

I stepped forward, ignoring the big oaf who loomed between us. "Do you want to come with me, Delia?"

She looked up, and her hair fell back. The cheekbone was red and blue, a trace of blood trickling from her hairline down to that distended lip. Her eye was bloodshot, but her voice was calm. "Thanks, Pru. But Mrs. Harris —"

I reached for her hand. "Nora Harris can take care of herself." If what I was thinking was true, she'd done just that pretty recently. "You're coming with—"

"Bitch!" I didn't feel myself being lifted. I only felt the wall come up behind me, and the force that snapped my head back into it and had me crumbling to the floor. "You interfering little—"

I blinked in time to see a fist come at me. The wall doubled the impact, smacking from behind, and everything went black. I couldn't have been out for long, because I woke up choking, my mouth filled with blood. I was slumped in the hallway. People were shouting.

"Wait, Chris. Wait." As my vision cleared, I looked up to see Delia hanging on her boyfriend's meathook arm.

"No!" He grabbed me around the ribs and pulled me to my feet. I tried to kick him, but I hadn't yet caught enough of my breath, and there was no force in it. He shoved me back up against the wall. I fell against it like a ragdoll.

"Chris, no!" Delia was hanging on his arm, but he paid her all the attention he would pay a fly. "She's not the problem, Chris."

He didn't even turn to her. "You. You're the one." His face was right up to mine. I could feel the heat coming off him. "You told Delia." He shook me again and leaned in. I turned away, it was all I could do. Delia was gone. Smart woman. "You told her about Eleanor."

"*Eleanor?*" That wasn't the smartest thing to say, but I'd caught my breath and that was what came out. I'd seen Delia's face. I'd assumed it was about Mack, about her carrying his baby. About leaving faithful old Chris behind to be a beard for Charles with a setup for life. Now it hit me. Chris didn't care about Charles. He knew he was gay. And the fling with Mack wasn't worth more than a smack or two, as long as it was over. What was really eating him up was the idea of Delia leaving him for good. Moving on. And he blamed that on me, on me and Eleanor. On Delia finding out about his rebound fling. "But I didn't say anything."

"Shut up!" He shook me, and I vowed never to work with terriers again if I got out of this. But I hadn't been the rat. Not this time. "I've loved her. Always. And then you show up —"

"Chris, you've got it wrong. I was only looking—"

"I said, shut up!" And with that he pushed me once again. Maybe he thought that would be kinder than hitting me; he always had a rough sort of gallantry to his brutishness. But the effect was more or less the same. I hit the banister of the stair and felt myself tumble, my limbs tangled and unresponsive. Already, I could feel the bruises on my arms from where he'd held me. My ears rang, and, for a moment, the room closed in. I blinked up at a light. The hall light, but it was haloed and indistinct. And then eclipsed. Something dark rose over my face. Oval, no oblong. I could make out the treads of Chris' work boot.

"No, Chris, no!" Delia's voice seemed so far away.

For just a moment, I felt at peace. Poor Delia, she was going to be too late. I let my eyes close. It was over.

But the roar of sound that broke through my unnatural calm had nothing to do with my own hearing—or my face being smashed against those wooden steps. Instead, I heard a scream, a bark, a jumble of noise that startled me awake, and I looked up to see the light. No Chris. No Chris' boot.

When I turned toward the source of the sound, I saw why. Lily—forty pounds of avenging angel—had the big man pinned to the floor. He was clutching his forearm, where she must have grabbed him in her steel-trap jaws, and whimpering, his voice soft and subdued. The big dog stood over him, body tense and trembling, and I didn't need any special powers to hear her fury. Beside her crouched Delia, her hand on the plain leather collar, her hair falling over Lily's quivering back.

# Chapter Twenty-five

"I'm calling the police." I pulled myself up to my feet, my head ringing like a fire truck.

"No, please." Delia reached to help me up. Chris was still on the floor, holding his arm. Lily stood above him, every inch of her body on alert. His arm was bleeding, but it was her growl that was keeping him stone still.

"Are you crazy, Delia?" Her face was turning darker purple, her cheekbone distended. My own head didn't feel much better. As I stood, it cleared, and a thought hit me. "Oh no, you're not getting Lily to do your dirty work for you."

I would've reached for her collar, then, only I wasn't too steady. Instead, I let Delia help me to a chair, and while I waited for the world to hold still, I listened.

"He's not a violent guy." I would have laughed, really. Only it hurt. But the picture she drew made sense. There had been betrayals, and he'd expressed himself the way he knew best, with his hands. The same hands that Floyd recalled so fondly. "He feels horrible about this."

"I bet." She'd gotten me an ice pack by then.

"I do." Chris' voice was soft. "I am sorry. I lost my temper." In response, Lily's growl grew louder. She was tied up to the banister now and not liking it one bit. "Really."

I sighed. These people didn't have the sense of animals. Lily's growl had taken on a new note—*let go! let go! let go!*—that old refrain. I tried to tune it out; we'd had enough violence today.

"What is going on here?" A tremulous voice from the stairwell. I closed my eyes, my reason for racing over was back.

"Mrs. Harris!" Delia jumped up to meet her. The sudden movement must have started her face throbbing, and she held a hand up, as if one hand could cover the damage. I'd have put money on a shattered cheekbone, if I were in the mood for gambling. "It's okay. Everything is fine." She looked back over her shoulder at Chris, at the dog. "We just had a little accident."

"No, we didn't." I pulled myself to my feet. Lily's growl had grown softer, higher in pitch. I tasted blood. My own, probably. Chris wasn't getting off that easily. *Let go! Let go! Let go?*

Delia turned from the base of the stairwell to hiss at me. "Pru! She's been through enough."

"Young lady? You are in my home, and I demand to know—" A wave of dizziness nearly knocked me over. Nausea, the taste of blood. All I could hear was Lily. *Let go! Let go! Let go!*

*Let go?* The scent grew stronger. Blood and dirt. Not perfume, but good, sweet earth.

"No, Delia, she hasn't." Lily's growl was more like a whine now, too insistent to ignore. *Home?* I fought down the nausea and made my way over to the stairs, a little more wobbly than I'd have liked. "Have you, Mrs. Harris?"

"I don't understand." She glanced from me to Delia and back again. "Young lady?"

"She's confused." Delia was keeping her voice soft, but I'd swear I saw the ghost of a smile on the senior's face.

"Yeah, maybe, but not as much as you think." I leaned on the banister. It helped. Maybe I'd needed to be shaken up to put it all together. The whine. The scent. Motive. Opportunity. Everything the animals had been telling me from the beginning. "You see, Mrs. Harris killed her son. I'm not clear on the details, but I know he needed money, and I know that he'd been taking care of her, paying for the upkeep on this house—and for your services—for years."

Delia opened her mouth to protest. I raised my hand to silence her. "But he must have been at his wit's end, wasn't he,

Mrs. Harris? He was so close to launching. He'd run through all his capital, and he'd walked away from his last, best chance at getting more. And here was your house, right where the developers want to expand. But he'd have to act fast, wouldn't he? In this economy, who knew how long the offer would have been good for."

"Young lady, this has been my home for more than seventy years." Her voice sounded clear now. Stern and commanding, all trace of that quaver gone. She paused, though, before adding, "and Charles was a devoted son."

"Yes, he was." I felt my own strength returning. "And I bet he was thinking of you, too. He saw what was happening, how your disease was progressing. He knew you'd need more care soon. He wanted you to move in with him, into his lovely house, didn't he? Old Beauville, with a view of the mountain, and a garden that you had already made beautiful. You were working on it that day, weren't you? Making it all nice?"

"I'm an adult," she said, her lips white with fury. "Not a child. Don't talk to me like a child."

"Okay, so I won't. You didn't like his plan. Maybe it even brought on one of your spells. Or maybe you faked it, so he'd come close and hold you—and you lashed out. Maybe you didn't mean to hurt him; maybe you forgot what you were holding—a garden hoe or a cultivator that would have pierced his flesh and stuck there. Though maybe a spade would have done just as well. You must have been so angry, him making plans for you. Treating you like a child. He must have been shocked as hell. What did he say when he fell? Did he call out to you, call for his Mama? Did he beg you to help him? To call 911?"

"I am not a child. I will not be treated like a child. By anyone. Certainly not by a son who's not even a man." And then the rage passed, as quickly as it had come, and Nora Harris sank down onto the step, burying her face in her hands. "This is my *home.*" She started to sob, and I nodded as Delia went to her.

"You're crazy." Delia mouthed the words over the elderly woman's head.

*Let go!* The whine was softer now. Lily sensed something was happening. In her eyes, a shadow took shape. A slap, a cry. A man falling to his knees. His hands at his throat. What looked like a claw, buried deep, as a smaller figure hung on. Memories flooded back. It hurt too much. *Let go!*

"You think so?" I focused on Delia, trying to shake off the images. The scent remained. Blood, Dirt. Sweet, fresh earth. *Dig.* My own head was throbbing like a kettle drum. "The outbursts, the anger? The sudden fits of temper?"

I turned back to Mrs. Harris. "I like to think that you had one of your spells. That you didn't realize what happened when you 'slapped' him and he started to bleed, that you were just staring into space as he collapsed. But at some point, you came back, didn't you? At some point, you knew."

She didn't answer, and I made my case to Delia. "I don't know how much she was aware of, but I know she had enough sense to cover up the evidence, to clean up and get herself back home. Maybe that was automatic. Years of habit. But letting Lily out of her cage? That took some thought. Maybe she told herself it was a mercy. The poor dog was probably frantic, whimpering and crying to go to her master. And it served Nora well, didn't it? I think she knew it would, that Lily would take the blame. I think she was quite pleased with herself. Everything all tied up. Except, of course, for Lily."

The uniforms came soon after, with Creighton close behind, looking more concerned than I'd expected. After the first cars had taken Nora and Chris away, I asked Creighton to stay. He and Delia followed as I untied Lily and took her out to the garden.

"Dig," I said to Lily, unhooking her lead. "Go to work."

She didn't need any prompting, and within minutes she'd torn up the garden, unearthing the missing garden tools: a spade, a hand-held hoe, and an evil-looking cultivator, sharpened to deal with our tough earth. Creighton would take them in for testing. We all knew what he would find.

But Lily wasn't finished and whined until I released her again. The image of Charles sharp in her mind and mine, she set to digging once more, this time not stopping until she could bring us a shirt, stained dark, and some old khakis, their cuffs still rolled high. I could see sneakers, too, down in the loose earth, but I called her toward me as she went back for them. She'd done her duty. This was evidence, and it was Creighton's job now.

"Good girl," I said, stroking her back. The memories had returned in full now; the pain almost too much to bear.

"We'd found traces," Creighton was saying. "Once we knew it was homicide, we were investigating—"

I tuned him out. Would Creighton have solved the murder? Possibly. Nora was no genius, and the disease was taking its toll. But Lily had put an end to the speculation, and maybe to her own longing as well.

She knew, I could tell as I looked into those eyes. She'd done all she could, but Charles wasn't coming back. I rubbed her ears the way he had. I wasn't the one she wanted, but it was all I could do. "Good girl," I said again. "Good girl."

# Epilogue

Delia refused to press charges. I wasn't so nice, but this was a small town and Chris got two to five, once he agreed to anger management classes. He'd be out in less than a year, if he played it right. A slap on the wrist? Sure—and I was ready to let loose. But when he spoke up at the trial, making a point of saying that Lily had only been acting as a good guard dog, I realized I needed to let it go. He could have made trouble for Lily, still, and she didn't need the hassle. I wasn't going to hold my breath waiting for an invitation to the wedding, though.

Delia took Lily, when Nora Harris was carted away. She might have been willing to take the dog on at first because she'd thought she'd have the drive on her—I'd figured out that Delia had been the one asking Creighton about it—but they'd bonded as women in crisis can. Lily would keep Chris at bay, when he got out, and once I saw the pit bull with the kitten, I knew who would end up ruling that household. It wasn't either of the blondes.

And Creighton? Well, it might not all have been as neat as he'd like, but he saw that there was some kind of justice done. Supervised care for Mrs. Harris: a nice name for psychiatric lockdown. It meant she'd go to a hospital, rather than a prison, but I'd seen the state hospital. She wasn't going to be coddled. Basically, nobody liked the idea of a mother killing her son, and her lawyer made a big deal about her reduced capacity and the paranoia that can accompany dementia. Who knows? Maybe Charles had grabbed her, shaken her out of frustration. Maybe she had yelled for *him* to let her go, even before she struck at him—those wicked metal teeth tearing at his throat. Maybe, for a moment, she didn't know her own son. I didn't know, and I didn't have the heart to grill Lily, even if she could have given me more. Nora Harris was losing her home, her garden, her independence. Everything she had killed Charles for. Creighton was too much of a cop to like it, even if it meant less paperwork. But deep in his heart, he was okay with it. He was an okay guy.

The whole episode had been strange, but as things shook out, it was Floyd who surprised me most. Despite the betrayal, despite the loss, the big cat never stopped yearning for his mistress' brutish ex. Eleanor never did take him back. Her absence was probably supposed to signal some kind of disrespect, but I read it as guilt. She'd lobbed that rock through my window out of jealousy, not having the sense to realize it was Delia all along—and that my face off with Chris at the funeral had been more interrogation than romance. I don't think she thought about Floyd, other than as a possession. To people like her, animals don't register as sentient creatures. So when Chris came calling as a condition of his sentencing, to apologize and offer to make amends, I let nature take its course. Chris had been inside a month by then, and already he sounded different. Like maybe he got it, finally. And Floyd hadn't returned to his neurotic grooming, but he'd been sleeping more than was healthy, even for a house cat. When he heard Chris' voice, he was downstairs in a flash, standing on his hind legs and pushing his smooth black head into Chris' hand, insisting on pets.

"Big boy, there you are." Chris scooped the cat up, his wood slab of a face positively glowing.

"His name is Floyd." I was still cautious.

"*He can call me whatever he wants.*" I didn't need Wallis to translate that one. "*And I'll be waiting for him always.*"

◇◇◇

Such devotion wasn't in my cards, though Wallis and I continue to iron out both our communication issues and our territorial needs. Having a big house helps, and what with one thing and another, I ended up with a bit of a name for myself. Enough to bring in some clients so that when autumn faded, we could afford to heat the old place, at least through March.

It was late October by the time we got everything sorted. Wallis and I were sitting by the fire, watching the flames and dozing.

"You could return Mack's calls, you know." Wallis settled on her pillow. We'd pulled the old sofa up close enough to feel the warmth.

"Yeah, I know." I watched a log collapse and distracted us both by adding another. A complete luxury; in another twenty minutes, I'd have to bank it and crawl into bed. I had three dog-walking clients now, and it was getting late.

Tonight, I enjoyed the flames and let my mind mull over the handsome gambler. I did think about Mack occasionally, much like I thought of Tom and Leo and Stevie. But Mack was different. We'd never had a chance, really. Maybe I was getting more sensible in my old age. Or maybe Wallis was right.

"Gonna be a cold winter." Wallis kept staring at the fire, trying to pretend she hadn't read my thoughts.

"Having a man around is no guarantee of anything."

She shifted, tucking her feet under her. I couldn't tell if she'd ceded that point or not. I reached out to stroke her smooth back, grateful for her company, and found myself thinking about Delia. She was showing now, but I hadn't heard of her hitting up Mack—or anyone else, for that matter—for support. With Nora Harris locked away I didn't know if she had another source of income.

"She could marry Chris Moore when he gets out," Wallis broke in. "She's managed him all those years."

"Oh, please." I wasn't going to forget that afternoon at Nora Harris' place. His rage. The violence.

Wallis yawned and stretched out one white paw, showing her claws in the firelight.

"I get it, Wallis. I've lashed out in anger, in jealousy, before, too. But not like that."

She was silent, and I tried to read her cool green eyes. "What?" I asked. "So now you're saying he's *not* a complete ass?"

"Well, of course not," said Wallis, stretching once more. "He likes cats."

To receive a free catalog of Poisoned Pen Press titles, please contact us in one of the following ways:

Phone: 1-800-421-3976
Facsimile: 1-480-949-1707
Email: info@poisonedpenpress.com
Website: www.poisonedpenpress.com

Poisoned Pen Press
6962 E. First Ave. Ste. 103
Scottsdale, AZ 85251